THE EDGE OF SPACE

THE EDGE OF SPACE

Three Original Novellas
of Science Fiction by

GLENN CHANG
PHYLLIS GOTLIEB
MARK J. McGARRY

Edited and with
an Introduction by

ROBERT SILVERBERG

ELSEVIER/NELSON BOOKS
New York

Introduction copyright © 1979 by Thomas Nelson Inc.
"The King's Dogs," copyright © 1979 by Phyllis Gotlieb.
"In the Blood," copyright © 1979 by Glenn Chang.
"Acts of Love," copyright © 1979 by Mark. J. McGarry.

Library of Congress Cataloging in Publication Data
Main entry under title:
The Edge of space.
    CONTENTS: Gotlieb, P. The king's dogs.—Chang, G.
In the blood.—McGarry, M. J. Acts of love.
    1. Science fiction, American. I. Chang, Glenn.
In the blood. 1979. II. Gotlieb, Phyllis Bloom.
The king's dogs. 1979. III. McGarry, Mark J. Acts
of love. 1979. IV. Silverberg, Robert.
PZ1.E26 [PS648.S3]   813′.0876   79-4406
ISBN 0-525-66625-7

Published in the United States by Elsevier/Nelson Books, a division of Elsevier-Dutton Publishing Company, Inc., New York. Published simultaneously in Don Mills, Ontario, by Thomas Nelson and Sons (Canada) Limited.

Printed in the U.S.A.   First Edition
10 9 8 7 6 5 4 3 2 1

CONTENTS

INTRODUCTION

THE NOVELLA—the story that is shorter than a novel, but longer than a short story—has always been a particularly advantageous form for science fiction. It allows the leisurely development of an idea, a background, a world, the detailed voyage into strangeness that is the essence of the best science fiction; and yet it does not entangle itself in the elaborate structures of plot that a full-length novel demands. Such famous science-fiction stories as Ray Bradbury's "Fahrenheit 451," Wyman Guin's "Beyond Bedlam," Robert A. Heinlein's "Universe," and John W. Campbell's "Who Goes There?" are outstanding examples of what can be acomplished at novella length. In my own writing career I was always fascinated by the possibilities of the novella, with such results as "Hawksbill Station," "Born with the Dead," and "The Feast of St. Dionysus." And, as editor, I have encouraged writers to contribute these long stories to the series of novella anthologies I have produced—*Threads of Time, Chains of the Sea, The Crystal Ship, The Day the Sun Stood Still,* and others.

Here once more is a varied and stimulating group of choice novellas, two of them by writers just at the outset of their careers, the third by a more experienced author. I think they demonstrate anew the flexibility, versatility, and scope of this particularly rewarding kind of story.

—*Robert Silverberg*

THE KING'S DOGS
Phyllis Gotlieb

Canadian-born Phyllis Gotlieb began writing—mainly poetry—at the age of eleven. By the time she was twenty, the poetic inspiration seemed to have left her, and she turned to science fiction in the hope that it would renew her literary powers. Nine years passed before her first published story, "A Grain of Madness," reached print, but since then she has written steadily if not swiftly both as a poet and as a science-fiction writer. Several of her stories—notably the 1972 "Son of the Morning"—deal with the marvelous crimson cats from another world, Khreng and Prandra, and she returns to them here with this elegant fusion of science fiction and the mystery story.

GALACTIC FEDERATION CITY on Sol III stands on tundra under a dome; a solar-electrified, water-recycling, self-supporting civil-service city in a civil-service world. Aliens from hundreds of worlds hop, skim, or lurch in tanks along its huge white-flagstone avenues. On its eastern rim the MedPsych Annex is enclosed in force-fields and white-noise walls. The ESPs within love privacy, and so, even more, do the non-ESPs outside.

For half an hour every dawn and dusk two big red cats pace the hexagonal flags around MedPsych. Inevitably they fall into step, consciously break it, fall in and break. Prandra, the ESP of the two, knows that when Khreng has matched her pace their minds are joined, and neither wishes to share one mind all the time. Distant outworld cousins of the leopard, they are leopard-sized, but their color is incongruously harsh against the white stones, among the green boxtrees in cement tubs. Khreng is bright crimson, Prandra as much darker as if his shadow had rested on her. Both are striped with narrow black chevrons peaking at the crown and falling along the flank to the hip, each stripe centered with a thin white line.

Around his neck Khreng wears a medal, a diplomat's gold star. As the senior representative of Ungruwarkh on Sol III he has been made its ambassador. He knows he has been given the honor because Prandra is the ESP, but he does not care; he is the stronger and the tracker; Prandra does not care for any reason. They do not know completely what ambassadors do: they are aware that neither of them is very diplomatic. Prandra wears the ESP's insigne on Sol III, a steel medallion engraved with a lightning bolt wound by a snake. It is sometimes called the Cracked Caduceus and other names; from her point of view it is a dog tag.

Khreng has caught through Prandra a thought in the mind of some passing lover of literature. "What is that about dogs and kings?"

"It is a piece of what Solthrees call poetry, like the words of singing, written on a tag by a man named Alexander Pope, who gives a dog to a king:

> " 'I am his Highness's dog at Kew;
> Pray tell me, sir, whose dog are you?' "

"Is that directed at us?"

"Evidently."

Her mind is savage and morose; he pushes on: "Why does he think of us as dogs? We are not dogs of a king, nor serve any dog of a king."

"It is how their minds work. They put a tag on a creature they consider animal and call it a dog."

:For God's sake, stop being so damn sensitive. Some idiot

was making an absentminded allusion.: Espinoza, their
own ESP guide and counselor, the centuries-old brain-
in-a-bottle, is wheeling down the hall to have his nu-
trient pump adjusted. His mind fades past the walls of
a white-room.

Prandra snarls, "Cats *are* sensitive and dogs are hypocrites." She hooks a claw in the chain and stops. Responsibility. If she does not work for GalFed, there will
be no cattle or feed-grains for starving Ungrukh.

"That's the price of being Earth-compatible cats,"
says Khreng.

"It is the price of being a bloody damned ESP."

Khreng leaves the walk and wanders about the lawn,
sniffing some fascinating scent.

Whose dog are you, Khreng? Prandra continues
alone. . . . I am alone here. Espinoza has his own affairs. Khreng is bored. She glances at the evening sky
through the dome's roof. She and Khreng prefer dusk
because they do not have to wear tinted contacts to dim
a sun brighter than their own. She begins to trot, chain
jingling. Here, Rover! Here, Rex! Here, Fido! Good
boy! She sneers. The sweat of fear is around her. *The
jaws that bite, the claws that catch.* The literary mind, an
idling engine, intrudes. Shut up, stupid! A leap, jaws
closing on nape, *crunch!* Not here.

The angles of the buildings shift, the sky turns pink,
then red as the plains of Ungruwarkh. Their children,
Tugrik and Emerald, are growing across the dark
emptiness, forgetting Khreng and Prandra. Half
grown now, Emerald mated, pregnant when we reach
home? ESP Emerald chained, brains to be bottled in
the dark globe. Not Emerald! Prandra gallops; no prey
in the scant flesh dangling from bickering alien heads.
Prandra skims the wall: too late to pass the gates, hurl
herself at the dark city. Uncivil servants go to bed early
in the short tundra nights.

Red, red sky, buildings elongated like spears, their

few windows vanished, the sun is down. The spears are
tipped with dying light like blood. . . . An opening
among the spears: she smells blood. A shadow crou-
ches, nipping at greens. Not Khreng. Big fleshy thing,
no mind, only meat. From where? Saliva pools in her
jaw, she is ready to rip meat from bone with her rasp
tongue.

"Khreng?" Gone, white-roomed; she will save his
portion. Drop it at his feet. Here, Khreng the tracker!
Dog. Hyena.

Flesh hot in her nostrils; she goes to ground,
thickens her haunches, tail lashing, up and out her
powered thighs propel, red claws flash, teeth bare—

The shadow-figure turns, rises, is a man, Solthree,
eyes wide, hands raised, pale star palms turned out—
Espinoza!

Screaming:

"Don't—"

"—pull me into your damned bloody dreams,
woman! Hell's blazes!" Khreng's swipe sent her tum-
bling off the bed. "Hyena! Since when am I a hyena
after hunting with you all the years?"

Prandra lay on the floor, tongue hanging out, feet
slippery with sweat. She shook her head, stood and
shook her whole body. She felt drugged.

"Are you sick?" Khreng touched her nose and forehead with his padded hand. "You don't seem feverish."

"I don't know . . . am I here?"

"What are you saying? You are in our room."

She lifted her head and looked at the pale walls, the
great round velvet bed, the rough flagstone slab. She
lay on that, scraped her back and flanks on it. "You
thrash about so much I can't sleep half the time,"
Khreng grumbled, "and when I do you call me
names."

Prandra crouched on the stone. "I never have such

dreams until we come here. It's not in my mind to call you names. That's filthy."

"Whose mind is it in then?" he snorted.

"There are other ESPs here."

"Their thoughts don't come through these walls. What does Espinoza think if he knows you want to eat him?"

"Lummox!" she roared.

He grinned. "Names?"

"Who wants to eat some old brain?" She sniffed. "In my dreams he is not bottled, he is a man as he sees himself. I do not want to eat people. I am satisfied with the meat we get. Something is giving me terrible dreams!"

"We share the same food."

"The kitchens are not white-walled. I know if drugs are put in the food. Something is wrong." She jumped from the stone and began to pace. "Maybe in my mind . . . from being in a strange place . . . with all those strange thoughts. Wearing a tag and being called a dog."

"That is from your dream."

"Not only. Who is not afraid of a creature that is thought of as savage here?" She sprawled on the floor, tail snapping like a whip. "It makes my head hurt . . . maybe we ask for separate rooms . . . if my head is sick you should not be joined to it."

He stared her in the eye, so close that their whiskers melded. "That is not sickness, it is foolishness. If you can handle a Qumedon in a strange place hundreds of years back, you can get along here. On Ungruwarkh you know when a mind is sick and you never say maybe."

"How do I know my own mind?"

"Your sister knows hers, when it is unbalanced; she asks for help too—and you give it. Have you forgotten everything? Ungrukh know. Maybe not other ESPs.

Whatever is bad here comes from somewhere else: we find out." He licked her neck. "If it is a someone, likely it is happier if we separate and become more vulnerable."

"That seems sensible."

"I am glad you think I am capable of sense."

She bit his ear and hopped onto the bed. He followed and they writhed together in their fierce way.

After, they smoothed each other's fur, and Khreng said, "Now maybe you sleep without dreams."

She hissed, "Now I am really awake. I want to go out."

"Better not disturb Espinoza now."

"Later. I want to think first." Before she reached the door he had fallen asleep into a dream of Ungruwarkh and the children. She paused to savor it. . . .

Down the hall padding in silence past guards in green gold-braided uniforms; she had learned to move so that the hateful chain did not ring; her red eyeshine reflected the dimmed ceiling lights. The men on guard thought of jungles. "Here, kitty, kitty," she muttered. Passed Espinoza's door. Not yet.

Don't—

Why Espinoza, whom she loved? Why leaping on fleshy animal? Far back in the time-warp she had killed a pig, stunned and butchered it, like any so-called civilized person. Certainly she had lusted after it, but she had eaten its meat out of a bowl, with Khreng. On Ungruwarkh there were no large food animals; she had caught and roasted the diseased fish, like her compatriots. And why were those low-ESP guards fearful? Big red cats are fearsome, but if they mind their business. . . .

Their business is meat—

Stop.

Something was contaminating their minds.

She trotted, galloped, into the darkness. More guards. ESPs are valuable and cause jealousy. No one else was out. Most went to bed early in the short tundra nights . . . stop. That was in the dream.

She looked up. The buildings stood in their right shapes and proportions, unblooded. The flags had cooled. She smelled the earth the plants were potted in and the worms that coursed it. The sky was paling slightly in the east. She jumped the ornamental fence of the children's playground and rolled in the sand, climbed the bars, slid the chutes, snaked the winding tubes. The patterned coolness of the metal soothed her. She stretched on the sand and watched the fading eastern stars.

Smelled flesh. Her head rose, she growled softly like an engine idling. The Solthree woman, Nema, was watching her, fingers clamped on an arabesque of the fence.

That odd one they considered so beautiful, whose mind was impervious even to the most powerful ESPs. The only Solthree of the kind ever discovered, perhaps the most valuable of her kind. Black eyes, smooth light-brown skin, flowing dark hair, deep red velvet robe. Hands tight on bars, eyes fixed. Seeing what? Glowing coals in the head of red demon? Some transparent mind saw them.

The man Metaxa, tall, heavy, dark-bearded, put a hand on her shoulder. *Get away! Retro me, Satanas!* The literary mind.

Fool! Prandra stared him down, saw her red eyes in his. His arms circled the woman to lead her away. Her hands clamped tighter. He pried them off finger by finger.

Fear.

Not only of savage cats, but of/for—

:*Get out! Get out!*:

It was he who insisted on broadcasting to the universe. "Calm yourself, man. You are creating your own fears."

The woman let herself be drawn back. She moved oddly, bent legs placing one foot before the other with flattened soles.

Prandra leaped, cleared the fence in a red arc that blended with the shadows.

Metaxa, the man of immeasurable wealth, explored alien cultures and collected artifacts. The woman, Nema, like the Qumedon, was a mystery to Prandra, who was not—and might never be—powerful enough to esp her. Metaxa was incomprehensible culturally: he collected facts and objects for their own sake.

Espinoza at end of patience: *Because they're pleasing to look at! You've just been too busy surviving to make or look at things for pleasure. You've done extremely well at tool-making for a people without opposable thumbs, and if you had the kind of climate that snowed you into a hut or holed you into a cave half the year, you'd have been inventing games and artifacts as well.:*

"We have games—"

:Good—:

"But things *are* things."

:—Good!:

"We are only savage and ignorant to you."

:No! Get it straight! You're not savage because you don't kill from ignorance. Your ESP has prevented that. Otherwise you might have become like many primitive tribes. That, and your intelligence, have turned you off the branch that sacrifices to gods. Add the survival crisis that makes you value lives, and you've got an advanced ethical system. Plus complicated tool-making abilities: that gives you a culture. You've still got sore spots because your tribes compete instead of cooperating. You and Khreng have got to change that. All you need now is to understand and enjoy what's pleasing.:

"Why should we gather things we don't need?"

:You don't have to! Just understand those who do!:

"Why?"

:Never mind. Just turn up my oxygen before you go.:

But who could understand Metaxa? The collector of things, of snatches of poems (about dogs and claws) from books, had found a child in the kitchen corner of a slum (community of poor people with few implements, like the village of Kostopol in the time-warp)— and what was he doing there? (*:Going slumming,:* says Espinoza tartly, losing Prandra.) Filthy neglected child who could not move or talk because of behavioral blockage originating in the brain (called autism). Feeding and excreting in silence, broken sometimes by an hour's screaming, and beaten for it.

Metaxa had taken her away and given his life to her, leaving wife, children, mistress (subsidiary mate). Had fed, clothed, tended her, found specialists to teach her to walk, use her hands, signal her needs, though she never spoke. Metaxa had polished her like a jewel. An ESP doctor had discovered her powerful faculty.

And why?

"Hello, Espinoza."

:Go to the window and watch the dawn for me.: Through the dome's struts the sun was rising out of a delicate lavender veil. *:That is beautiful.:*

She grinned. "If you say so."

:One more and one less.: The sun reflected a star from the dark bowl of his own dome. After a moment he said, *:Posthypnotic suggestion.:*

"Ah . . . you *are* first class, Espinoza."

:If I were class-one, maybe I'd know who did it, and why. But there is something going on—you'd have figured it out for yourself in a while.:

"The dreams make me afraid. Fear cramps reason."

:I can't move . . . and I'm tired. That cramps it too. . . :

The room was tiny, the window took one wall. Nothing was there but Espinoza's globe on its stand, the pump humming. Prandra contorted herself to lie down around him. "I am ignorant. Please help."

:You need a class-one.:

Though Espinoza was class-two, she had on his testimony been granted pro-tem second-class ESP status as soon as she arrived. But she and Khreng had come not to be classified but to learn food farming; in Terraform sector the embryos were developing, to be frozen for shipping. She was waiting in Med-Psych because she was an ESP, and she expected to be ratified at GalFed Central on the way back to Ungruwarkh. "The number ones are odd here."

:Everyone is odd here. It's a backwater.:

"You want very much to be here when we are away."

:I always do when I'm away, and vice versa.:

"Espinoza . . . is this ugly thing reaching you?"

:I don't know. . . :

"Wyaerl and the Lyhhrt are odd to me because they're from other worlds. Sheedy is a wasted old man, and the woman doesn't behave like a Solthree."

:Metaxa's the funny one. I'd say he was some kind of fake if I didn't know his mind.:

"But who will help, Espinoza?"

:Nudnik, I'll think about it! Go get some sleep. You've probably had your share of dreams for the night. Leave the door open. All I get to hear is stupid thoughts, but they're better than nothing.:

"I stay with you."

:And break your bones trying to sleep like that? Go on, get out already!:

But there was powerful affection beneath the thought, and in her mind she touched her nose to the cheek of the man-image, long gone, who had lived and walked beneath the sun.

Khreng sighed. "Now I am ready for breakfast, I suppose you want to sleep."

"Yes. Go eat. Now I know how I get the dreams but not who does it, or why."

"So I am right after all."

"Right. Fill your belly and don't say I don't listen to you." She flung herself on the wide bed and dropped into velvet sleep.

Espinoza is dead.
More dreams! She writhed, her claws flashed, her tail whipped.

"Pull in your claws, woman. It is no dream."

Grief . . . Khreng was licking her face, shuddering. A drop of sweat from his nose-tip, his only tear, fell on her eyelid.

She leaped up, electrified. "Espinoza!" she howled. Through the open doorway shivers ran down the halls. *Cracked shell spilling brains and liquids!*

ESPINOZA!

"Be quiet! They take him away." Khreng flung himself on her, pinned her down before she reached the door.

Espinoza. . .?

"You were the last to see him alive."

MedPsych's director, Madame Yamashita, sat on a plain chair in the Committee Room: a small woman in a simple dark blue coverall with the insigne on its breast; her hair was gathered at the back of her neck by a gold-and-enamel clasp. The rest of the committee were faceless to Prandra; she recognized a few vaguely as Earache, Slipped-Disk, and Six-Toes.

She said quietly, "You read me, Madame. I am not shielding." The pillars of her legs quivered, but she would not lie down to stop them.

Yamashita, a stolid and competent class-two, flushed slightly. "This is an inquiry, not a trial, Prandra. I know you are full of grief and anger."

"I regret expressing them so violently."

The director chose to miss the edge. "You discussed with Espinoza your troubled dreams and the possibility that they were induced by some outside agency."

"You know this."

"Please repeat it for our reports."

"Espinoza and I discuss the weather while he ESPS my problem, he says my dreams are perhaps engineered by post-hypnotic suggestion. I reply: If so, can you help? He promises to think about it and tells me to go sleep. I tell him I stay with him, he says no. I leave—and he is killed." Her voice trailed into a rasp.

"There were no witnesses to this conversation."

"What for? It is private business. He asks me to leave the door open when I go."

"When he was found, the door was closed."

"I presume murderers do not leave doors open."

"Why didn't you ask help from someone in authority?"

"I am fearful after having a terrible dream, and I have no friends in authority."

Yamashita clasped and unclasped her hands. 'Don't you consider anyone else here your friend?"

Prandra said patiently, "Madame, I am a stranger and ignorant. I know Khreng is my friend, and Espinoza. I esp no one uninvited because it is not courteous, and perhaps I miss gestures that are offered in friendship."

They faced each other in perfect awareness: Khreng and Prandra had been treated correctly, even generously, but not with friendship. The faint frown-line between the director's brows indicated that she was wondering why; it seemed the wrongness of the atmosphere had spread like a malign growth.

The pale brown hands steepled their fingertips. "Last night you were seen behaving strangely in the children's park."

"That is not strange for Ungrukh. We exercise the way children do here, but not for long, because we tire quickly." Get to the point, woman!

She did. "Espinoza was killed between four and six in the morning. There is no way of identifying the hour more exactly . . . he could have been killed either before or after you went to the park."

Prandra's fur rose. "The guards—"

"Those at the outer doors report you left at four thirty and returned at five fifteen. Metaxa clocked you at five. The guards in quarters don't recall seeing you at all . . . they have probably been tampered with in some way."

Prandra felt caught in the hideous dream. "I am glad you are not accusing me of anything," she hissed.

"Be assured we are not. We are trying to lay down the basis for a full-scale inquiry. It is on record that while you were in the Qumedon time-warp, you used hypnosis to—"

Prandra, claw hooked in chain, was on the point of ripping it from her neck and flinging it across the room. Then she stopped and thought . . . What *can* I do, Espinoza?

Eisenkop! use your head for a change!

She inhaled deeply. Unhooked the claw from the chain and crouched down. Slapped the floor with the whole length of her tail.

Committee jumped.

She slapped the floor again. "Madame, I am ignorant of many things on this world, particularly the numbers of various articles of diplomatic relations among the worlds of Galactic Federation which state that since Khreng and I constitute an embassy, we do not need to answer the kind of questions you ask unless put by an authorized GalFed committee." She stopped for breath. The sentence was sweet in her mouth. "Your inquiry in this area is extra-legal, your committee unconstitutional, and I have the right to ask for advice from the legal department of GalFed. You strike from the record all exchanges following my account of what happens, and—and you leave me alone to be sad for the death of a friend I love." She rose and loped toward the door. Someone jumped to press the button and let her through. Committee was afraid she might claw down the wall.

Khreng was pacing the halls. "What now? Are we in the firepot?"

"Yes. While I am in there I have the feeling that something/somebody is counting on me to jump up and attack them. Is that crazy?"

"Why ask me? If it is true, it is damned strange, and if it is not, it is still damned strange."

"And that is pretty damned helpful."

"What else do you want? If the feeling comes from some particular person you tell me; and if you don't say so you feel it in everyone. It cannot exist by itself in the air." They were passing Espinoza's room with its bored guard, and Prandra shuddered. Khreng stopped. "Air," he said.

"There cannot be any scent left after all this time."

"Everybody and his brother is going in and out all morning so I can't get near, but ventilators are not as bad as wind for carrying scent away and maybe something is left."

"No one's allowed in here," the guard said.

"I don't want in," said Khreng. "Only to smell around, if you allow the expression. If you move down the hall in order not to overload my nose, you may keep your gun aimed at me in case I break any rule or law."

The guard wrinkled his forehead, shrugged, and moved back, gun in the crook of his arm. Khreng inhaled deeply at the base of the door, raised his head, then his body, bracing himself by the forelimbs. "Don't expect much. Khreng the fearless tracker does better on Ungruwarkh."

"Any fool knows that," said Prandra sadly.

"We still must do all we can, woman." Sniff. "Here you are, and Yamashita—I see her this morning—some Lyhhrt, they hardly smell, and—"

"Hurry up!" the guard snapped. "If anybody finds you here, I'll be in trouble."

Khreng calmly lowered his head until his nose was buried in the carpeting. "A scale from Wyaerl, all those guards, very confusing . . . that one, Sheedy, is always pinching—"

The guard snorted. "He tries it with all of them. If he wasn't a blind old fool, he'd get a few punches."

"—that woman, Nema, and . . . myself, of course—" He sneezed. "Carpet fluff, and . . ."

Prandra finished for him. "And what is left of Espinoza."

"Tracked on somebody's shoes—"

"Which are now in some waste disposal."

"For God's sake, are you training to be a hunting dog or something?"

The guard found four savage red cats' eyes fixed on him. He swallowed. "I'm sorry! I didn't mean to insult you!" His fair skin was now hotly flushed. "It just popped into my mind."

"Maybe you ask yourself where it comes from," Khreng said quietly.

"Half the people in this place are visitors of Espinoza," said Prandra.

"All likely with good excuses." Ahead, an apartment door opened and a wisp of vapor escaped from it, followed by Wyaerl. Water and air tanks strapped to his back, he took his walk at high noon.

Wyaerl was not a telepath; he could only have been described as an inside man. He had a sense for the insides of things, and his people were used for surgery, metallurgy, mining, life- and physical sciences. Sky-blue in color, he was shaped like an elongated pancake, two meters long; though his translucence made him look like jelly, he was tough as saddle leather. His rear half was a huge muscular foot that propelled him in the manner of a snail. His front end projected forty or fifty tendrils with specialized uses: light and sound sensors, because he had no eyes or ears; prehensile digits; tools that split into almost invisible ends to explore earth or porous stone.

When he sensed the Ungrukh, he extended his foot to brace himself and raised his front end. His tendrils quivered. Across his half-meter expanse of belly was a slit opening into a pouch that held his generative organs, both male and female, and his feeding and excreting processes. Normally shy, like his species, he rarely invited esping, and breathed through slits in his back; the only way he could speak was to extend his feeding tube, suck air, and expel it in an excruciating squeak.

Khreng and Prandra stopped. The breathing tube came out, sucked air like wind in a chimney. "What is, troubling you," said Wyaerl, "is something, inside something."

"Do you know what that is?" Prandra asked.

"No." Wyaerl withdrew the tube, flopped down with a thud, and pushed off in a cloud of his planet's ammoniac atmosphere.

"That is a very deep thought," Khreng said. "Everything is inside something."

"He goes to a lot of trouble to tell us," said Prandra. "Maybe he helps."

"Maybe something else helps . . ."

They glared at each other. "Say it, big man. You think I am too hard on Yamashita."

"I know she is an arrogant woman who deserves it, but—"

They chorused, "She is also somewhat afraid and un-sure—"

Khreng huffed, "It is your thought in your head. You make her look bad, and among her people that is a great dishonor. She is only trying to do her work properly."

"I'm aware of it. To get us out of the stewpot, I must apologize." She growled, "And you know how good I am at doing that."

"Then have your meal and think it over."

"No. I do it first; otherwise I throw up."

"Damnation, your stomach is iron like your head! Your dinner spoils."

"Ha. It is cold from their food-boxes. You breathe on it and bring it to body heat." She grinned. "Meat tastes much better that way."

But she did not go at once to Yamashita's door; there were words to prepare. She trotted the white hexagons, eyes slitted against the glare of noon because she had not bothered about her contacts. It was hard to concentrate on apologizing (humbling oneself) with her mind still full of grief and fury.

Espinoza had wanted to die. But, as she had once done, he said: *It is always better to be alive today. . . .* He had given her a gesture, his mental shrug, and she had given him the words. *Espinoza!*

Think of Yamashita. . . . She crouched on a patch of warm earth by the playground fence watching the children on the seesaws and slide. A little carousel tinkled faintly. Some of the children belonged to employees, a few were proto-ESPs. One good second-class, possibly higher, a couple of lower unknown quantities. Two or three of them looked delicious. She nestled chin on paws and thought of Yamashita.

"Hey, there's that cat!"

"I can see it, dummy."

Children at the fence, staring.

Madame Yamashita, I come to tell you it is not my intention—

A handful of sand fell on her back.

She opened one eye and met the stares of the children. Mischief. Pull kitty's tail. The skin of her back rippled and shook it off. She was too warm and lazy to move.

—to hurt or embarrass you; I am deeply sorry to offend you. I only try to make clear—

Another fistful of sand.

At her eyes! She dug her head beneath her forearms, stunned by the mind-kaleidoscope of their fury.

"Aah, that's not enough! Get some gravel out of the pots, there!" Children outside the playground encircling her. Stones rained, one at her closed eye with stabbing pain.

On Ungruwarkh she had survived ambushes. She sent feelers to their heads: puppets, bewildered. Some of them enjoyed stoning an animal, some did not care, some hated it: none knew why they had chosen that moment to do it. And there was a kind of shield between them and the adults; no one had noticed.

Prandra had several choices, some disastrous. First she used most of her strength to break the shield; then, well battered, she took the line of least resistance. As the stones rained down she rolled over on her back, exposing her belly with paws in the air, tail limp, eyes closed, neck crooked at an impossible angle, with jaws gaping and tongue hanging slack. She looked like a horridly dead cat.

Guards began shouting, parents screaming, the hail diminished and stopped.

"Prandra!" Arms pulled at her. "Are you all right? Prandra!"

She opened her eyes slowly and straightened her

head. Guards, clerks, one or two Lyhhrt in their curious little gold boxes on wheels. She moistened her mouth with her tongue and rolled over. Parents shaking and yelling at the children, slapping some of them. Good. "I am all right."

"My God, your eye's bleeding, we've got to—"

"Leave it. I attend to it myself." She pulled free and shook herself vigorously, not caring where the dust landed, then headed back toward the residence.

Damned good piece of acting, if I say so.

Her eye hurt badly, she was both exhilarated and furious. She would apologize and go home to Ungruwarkh. Fight and starve. Damned Solthrees, pretending to be civilized. Food and wisdom you get here, says Espinoza. Where are they, you dead fool?

At the residence doorway she sensed a significant presence and looked up. A tall man was leaning there, arms folded, ankles crossed. One of committee. Six-Toes. His name was Kinnear. "I am on my way to apologize to Madame Yamashita," she said. "That must please you."

He said, "That eye's swelling shut. I'll send you a medtech."

"Thank you."

As she passed, he said out of the corner of his mouth, "Quite a good act you put on."

"I say so myself," she purred.

Prandra's rage almost negated the sense of obligation, but she wanted Yamashita to see her in this condition. She knew that was a shameful idea, but she could not control it.

She buzzed Yamashita's door and waited. No answer. The at-home light was on, she buzzed again, paced up and down, tried once more. Nothing.

She esped; a guard came trotting. "What happened to your eye?"

"Never mind. Madame Yamashita does not answer."

"Maybe she's sick. She gets headaches. I'll have somebody call in."

At the end they had to bring techs to remove the door.

Yamashita was sprawled across her bed wrapped in a brocaded kimono. Her hair was loose, the little gold-and-enamel clasp on the floor. Her face was almost beautiful in repose and her hair fine and silky; a thick tress lay across her throat but did not hide the deep claw slashes that spliced her arteries, nor the river of blood that flowed over the bed.

Prandra's belly convulsed, she gasped and choked. She let two guards lead her back to the room where Khreng waited; presently a medtech rolled in to inject her swollen eyelids and bathe her eye with drops to shrink the distended vessels.

She raged. "If I go earlier I save her!"

"Now you are irrational," Khreng snorted. "How does an apology save her life?"

"Don't you see? It is like with Espinoza. How can I prove I do not kill her first and then go out to put on an act with the children? Even Kinnear knows it is an act."

"According to your memory, and it does not fail as long as I know you, Kinnear also knows it is an act of self-defense. You are too hurt and angry to think straight."

"That is true."

"And you tell him you intend to apologize."

"That can seem a misdirection . . . and these claw slashes . . ." She shivered.

"That is not your style," he said dryly. "Any fool knows no serious cat kills like that."

"There is no shortage of fools here."

"Wait and see. One way or another we get out of this . . . take out our ship . . ." He grinned. "At the worst a good bleach and a job in the circus. Here is fresh food. Now eat."

Day and night passed, and morning to the zenith. Prandra slept most of the time. Khreng watched over her, saw the swelling of her eye go down, called the medtech for a shot to calm her tossing; when she quieted and began to murmur the names of their children he lay beside her and slept.

"We go home." She was pacing. Round and round, tail slapping the walls. Her eye was better except for the odd dart of pain.

Khreng sprawled on the bed. "You are making me dizzy. We see what they have to say. There is no choice."

"They likely tell us to get legal advice in a hurry. I use my hurry some other way."

"And that makes the enemy very happy."

"What enemy? There is no substance, scent, thought—track. Nothing to hunt." The door chimed.

"Come in!" Prandra roared. Khreng tsked and pushed the button. Kinnear came in and leaned against the wall in his characteristic pose, arms folded, ankles crossed. He was very tall, with a bland oval face, thinning blond hair; broad shoulders tapered down to a wedge-shaped body. He had the small-pupiled blue eyes that are as good as an ESP shield for hiding thought.

Khreng said, "Excuse me, I don't know your name."

"I'm the one Prandra calls Six-Toes."

"His name is Kinnear." Prandra dropped to the floor, sulking.

"I am polydactylic," Kinnear said. "I had the extras removed from my hands; they weren't pretty. Most Solthree ESPs have some kind of abnormality."

Khreng shifted from the bed to the stone. "Sit."

"In a moment. I haven't apologized for letting Prandra be hurt."

"What's the difference? Espinoza and Yamashita are dead." Prandra blinked. "In committee you are open-minded, so I know you have six toes. I am not, except for evidence, so how do you know I call you that?"

Kinnear coughed. "I have a habit of esping un-invited. I'm head of Security."

"Ah," said Prandra. "And still they are dead. Now I suppose you come to read us our rights."

"In a sense. The autopsy's been done." He smiled grimly. "And here comes Wyaerl now."

Wyaerl appeared with his inchworm step, air tank hissing furiously, food-pipe extruded. "I, hurried." Kinnear extended his hand. Wyaerl bent his top half and with one tentacle dropped something into the open palm. Kinnear nodded. "Iron," said Wyaerl. "Not steel, it broke, with force."

"Look." In Kinnear's hand was a metal fragment shaped into the perfect replica of an Ungrukh claw. "From the wound."

Khreng grunted. "Who makes it?"

"We don't know yet."

"Then you are no further ahead," said Prandra. "It appears someone wishes to place suspicion on us again, or else make it seem as if the Lyhhrt are trying it because they do so much metal work."

Kinnear said, "*Suspicion* on the Lyhhrt? How do you know they aren't guilty?"

"Aah! Lyhhrt? Those little lumps of that stuff—"

"Protoplasm."

"—who make their working shells so fancy in precious metals so others do not look down on them? Do they make a claw in plain iron without all their stars and flowers?"

"But in this case—"

"Find me one. No Lyhhrt here would do that!"

On the surface of his sorrow for Yamashita he was

amused and a little condescending. "Can you esp a Lyhhrt?"

"Of course, but who needs to? You have only to look at them and it is clear as your day."

"You can esp Lyhhrt, ha? Then if it's not you or the Lyhhrt, where would you begin, Prandra?"

"Kinnear, I don't know or care. Khreng and I are leaving. If you believe we are in the clear, we rather starve on Ungruwarkh than stay here another day."

Kinnear flushed with embarrassment. "Um . . . one of your ship's engines has been blown up."

Khreng said, "Blown up . . ."

"A charge, of explosive," Wyaerl piped. Prandra was staring at Kinnear.

"We've put extra guards around your supplies and equipment," he said. "Two weeks of repairs."

"That helps." *Are you sure you don't do that yourself to keep us here, Head Security Man?*

His flush darkened; he said quietly, "I'm glad you didn't say that aloud."

Unrepentant, Pranda said, "No apologies yet. But you make sure *you* stay alive, Kinnear."

He laughed. "Did you know that only a class-one can esp a Lyhhrt?"

"Yes, but who cares?"

"I do. While you're waiting, why don't you take your class-one exam and you can have it ratified at GalFed Central?"

"From what examiners? Old raveled Sheedy, or the Weird Lady?"

He said coolly, "We also have the Lyhhrt, and I'm a good enough class-two to sit on the Board. . . ." He paused. "And . . . if you don't mind another brain-in-a-bottle, Madame Chatterjee is really first class."

"Are all those on your staff?"

"Some of the Lyhhrt are here on their own business, like Wyaerl . . . what about it?"

Prandra considered. "Khreng, if I agree to this, do you tell me I have a swollen head?"

"Do you need to be told?"

Kinnear said, "You don't shield well enough yet, Prandra, and you'll need training. Chatterjee does that, and she can stick a pin in you."

"I worry about stones, not pins." She kept her eyes on Kinnear but was careful not to esp him. "You seem to trust us, Kinnear. Are you immune to psychological poison?"

"No . . . I've had dreams too. But what reason could you have had for killing Espinoza? He was the person you loved most on this world."

"He is tired and longing for death."

"You always knew that about him. You had a thousand chances to kill him and make it look like an accident—"

"After which we are esped and found out—"

"—or even in genuine kindness if you had a simpler morality."

"Savage morality," Khreng growled.

"Yes, our—let us say, enemies, try to make us seem savage and untrustworthy. We are expected to be accused of killing Espinoza and Yamashita—like wild beasts. I am to get insulted and jump on committee, and rip up little children at play. Somebody thinks we have not much control."

"But if they want to get rid of you"—Kinnear scratched his head—"and then blow up your ship . . . ?"

"Nobody tries to kill us yet, Kinnear," said Prandra. "It seems somebody wants us to leave—*but not on our own ship!*"

"Somebody wants you for something. . . ."

"Yes. Isn't that interesting. And no one knows what." She cocked her head. "Yesterday I think you are esp-

ing me from the time I leave Committee until I meet
those playful children. . . ."

"I certainly never expected—"

"I don't mean that. During that time Yamashita is
murdered."

"I know." He licked his lips. "I was fifty meters away
from her and somebody shielded so well I never
caught a hint of it. Same with the ship. And I'm stuck.
I'm short of staff and I have to sit in as head of committee too. . . . God, I wish we had Chatterjee on this,
but she's so damn shy about that bottle she'll hardly
ever come out of her room."

"How long?"

"Nearly two hundred years."

"Very nice for her." Prandra's sigh, like Espinoza's,
was in the shape of a tear.

"If I don't get this cleared up in a hurry, I'll be
kicked out, we may not get our MedPsych division
funded . . . everything happening . . . nobody will
come into this kind of danger, especially with children." He stared at the metal fragment. "I'm going to
trust you. I must, I need help. With my kind of funds I
just don't have that many class-ones to—"

"Play around with," Khreng said, basso profundo.

Prandra having declared she would turn truly savage if she did not get out, the Ungrukh took their walk
at noon. The sun sparkled through the dome, the flag-
stones were hot. After ten silent minutes, Prandra
turned off the path, and Khreng hissed, "Oh, no! Not
the playground! What do you think you are doing,
woman?"

"Something is not good there."

"And you make it better and get beat up again?" He
hooked a claw in her chain.

"Don't stop me, Khreng." Knowing better, he let go.

There was an oppressive air about the playground, and the children went through their games in a lackluster way; in the spirits of some, Prandra sensed a dusting of guilt. "Nine are sorry they hurt me, and four think it is too bad they do not hurt me more. Ha." She grinned. "There is no shortage of bent ones on Sol Three." Since staff was rarely Outworld, all the children were Solthrees.

"See those guards?" Khreng said. "The guns in their hands are not stunners."

"Is it forbidden for a big cat to play with a small child, since yesterday it is the other way around?" She pushed open the gate. Khreng, willy-nilly, followed; the guards shifted their weapons. Prandra paid no attention; she trotted to the silent carousel, pulled the switch, and jumped to the back of a yellow-maned lion. "Come on, Khreng, take a ride with me."

"You are crazy." He found a zebra.

Kinnear's mind broke through her calm. *:For God's sake, Prandra, watch it!:*

:Keep trusting, Kinnear.:

Round and round they went, bodies undulating to the rhythm of the music. Khreng grumbled, "What *do* you think you are doing?"

"Enjoying myself."

The nervous parents at the gate were joined by doctors, clerks on lunch hour with sandwiches and coffeebulbs; a couple of Lyhhrt in wheeled runabouts, two or three more gleaming in engraved workshells with multiple joints and stilt legs. Blind Sheedy with coffee dripping down his zipsuit as usual, one hand on the shoulder of his exasperated eye-guard. And even blank Nema, with Metaxa. "What a marvel," said Prandra. "Maybe we are born for the circus."

"Shut up," Khreng said.

"Tcha! It is you who talk of a circus." She jumped off; Khreng stopped the machine. She rolled in the sand, stood and shook herself; if the air had been less humid, the atmosphere might have matched that of the more habitable places of Ungruwarkh on one of its better days.

But she did not like the guilt on these spirits.

She began trotting in a circle, shoulder to shoulder with Khreng; the children backed away in a larger circle around them. She stopped short before one sullen boy about twelve. "You like dogs better than cats, hah?"

"Yes." ESP-in-training who liked, or thought he liked, to stone animals.

:I don't bite children, baby.: His mouth turned down at the corners, and she laughed. "Dogs lick your face and fetch sticks." She snorted. "Dogs play dead." With a twist she flung herself into her dead-cat position, then sprang up on hind legs. "Cats can play tricks too, and yesterday I play one on you!"

She dropped to fours and circled slowly, abreast with Khreng. The children were small statues of perplexity and suspicion. "I am not badly hurt, so you don't have to feel guilty" —a breath of her mind blew dust from them, and the air lightened,— "but my eye is sore, and next time you think first when you feel like throwing stones—at anyone!" She found a girl of seven or eight, an ESP small for her age, but brash, and young enough to play the games of little children. "You like a cat-back ride?"

The child twisted her fingers and stuck her tongue in her cheek. "Uh-huh."

Prandra's voice deepened. "Do you mean yes?"

"Yes, ma'am."

"Ask your mother."

The child drew a line in the dust with her toe. "She says all right."

Prandra crouched and the child bestrode her. "Not the chain. Hold the hair at the sides of my neck where

it starts getting longer. Khreng gives rides too."
Khreng said nothing, but the stretch of his nostrils
expressed a lot. He accepted a squirming body.

Round and round in tandem spiral. . . . Now, love,
you know how it is on our world Ungruwarkh, with
our children.

Red lava plains, pale sun, a nip in the air; one
tongue of flame from a volcano in the north; Firemaster speaking from one of his many mouths; out of
caves and fissures cats join, running until there is a
tribe, an odd good-humored one, for each cat is ridden
by a cub, thrilled/joyful/half-scared, little claws deep in
the fur prickling the backs they ride on, patches of feverish heat between little body and big one, minds
always open for the marauders over the hills. . . .

"What the hell do they think they're doing? What are
you letting them do?"

The Ungrukh stopped.

"Go on! Go on!" the cubs-children cried.

"In a moment, children."

Metaxa, red-faced, shoving against watchers toward
the gate. Nema, still as a mannequin, hands on the
bars.

"Playing with those animals!" Mextaxa's mouth was a
screaming cave. "Why don't you let them roll in the
snakepit at the zoo?" His face burned with sweat.

Prandra watched, satisfied. She read confusion and
anger in Metaxa, and did not know what to make of
them, but if nothing at all had happened, she would
have been deeply disappointed. Metaxa still yelling,
"Don't you underst——"

Guards to either side grabbed him in mid-word, and
Kinnear stepped up to him deliberately. "Are those
your children, Metaxa?"

Metaxa's mouth clamped shut. He shook loose of the
guards, barreled his way back through the bewildered
onlookers, and dragged Nema from the fence more

roughly than he had done on that evening. She did not even blink.

The little girl yanked at Prandra's fur. "More!" Prandra wrapped her prehensile tail around the thin waist and set her on the ground firmly. "Everyone has a turn."

Finally they lay on their backs with the smallest children crawling over them like ants, rubbing their faces in the soft belly-fur and shrieking with laughter. Prandra plucked them off gently, one by one. "Enough now. Big pussycats get tired fast."

"Can we do it again tomorrow?"

"Yes, tomorrow." The children went back to maps and lessons, and the adults, somewhat bemused, followed. Sheedy was laughing and shaking his head; it had been a circus to him. The Lyhhrt skimmed or stilted away.

"All right, you've defused a lot of fear and hostility, and that exhibition was very pleasing—except for Metaxa," Kinnear said. "Now, Honorables, what were you trying to prove?"

"We are fishing, and there is a pull on the line," said Prandra.

"Also," Khreng said, "now we make ourselves nice kitty-cats, we are pushing. Killer is less apt to try blaming us and more likely to attack us instead of someone else."

"That's a fine improvement," Kinnear said. "Where does it leave me?"

"Blameless. We take care of ourselves."

"But how can Metaxa's blowup be a pull on your line?"

Khreng and his nose knew what to make of that: "Of all who go to Espinoza's door around the time he is killed—Prandra, Wyaerl, Yamashita, Nema, guards and all, there is no trace of Metaxa. Although he keeps himself very clean, there is no one I know who smells stronger—and there is no skin-flake, oil droplet, atom of sweat . . . he is never seen apart from Nema, and she is hardly capable of blowing her own nose without him. Today he is a very frightened and angry man. Isn't that strange?"

:Why do you always speak in the present tense?: Madame Chatterjee asked.

"Yesterday is before my birth and tomorrow is after my death," said Prandra. "That is what Ungrukh feel and how they speak." The blue glasstex globe on its stand, the tiny room, were exactly like Espinoza's. "May we keep the door open? I am tired of whitewalls."

:I understand what you feel—about the present. But I concentrate better with a closed door.:

Prandra sighed, a low rumble. And hallucinate better.

:That too,: said Chatterjee.

The bottled brains—they were called converted, and called themselves bottled—spent much time alone, of necessity; they hallucinated much, because of lack of sensory afference, and learned to control it rigidly, to keep their minds in order. Chatterjee was sufficiently down-to-earth. She had died of mutant cholera at thirty-six, and maintained her self-image at that age: a small, wiry woman with beautiful black eyes and graceful brows; hair beginning to gray.

"I don't mean to offend you," Prandra said.

:You don't, except to make me jealous of your freedom, as every embodied person does.: Image of a wry smile. *:It is not that good a motive for murder. I am not a superb shielder, nor a strong hypnotizer.:*

Prandra, shocked, said, "You are far ahead of me, Madame."

:I intend to stay that way.: She asked abruptly, *:Where is there a white, yellow, and blue ball?:*

"In the seal-pool at the zoo."

:You did not break my shield then.:

Prandra grinned. "No, I remember seeing it when I am there." She added, "Calcutta has many green trees, though there is still much poverty."

:Good. Now you try . . . green . . . ah . . . why do you call your daughter Emerald, which is a green jewel in the English language, when your people are red?:

"Ha. Khreng hears it when he visits GalFed Central, and he likes the sound. Perhaps it is the beginning of an appreciation of Art in us Ungrukh."

Chatterjee permitted herself a smile-thought, and Prandra couched in the narrow space. "Madame, I think we can like each other, if you permit. And I learn as well as I can. But people are being killed, and I must find out why, and what the killer wants of Khreng and me. Can you help?"

Slowly: *:Oh, I am very willing to like you . . . :* and shrinking.

"I understand, Madame. Espinoza also spends over two hundred years in a bottle, and does not care at the end. One day I too howl for death in my bottle and there is nobody to hear. Nobody so kind to smash it, as even I cannot bring myself to do. From the bottle it is dangerous to think of flesh and bone; food, sleep, sex, running in the open air. Even drinking cold water when you are thirsty. Espinoza is lucky. Yamashita is lucky it is too late to save her brain. So you stay in this room, and teach ignorant people like me to do useful work—but you must also have to answer a lot of stupid questions, and you do not come out where the people are alive with their love and hate and anger—and I think that is narrowing and wasteful." She rose beside the door, but could not bring herself to open it, and stood there, head and tail hanging.

:I know.: The mind-touch was light as a peacock's feather. *:You spoke harshly to Yamashita and did not apologize. I have not been aware for so many years without under-*

standing. What you don't understand is that even as an embodied person I was almost as retiring as I am today, and I regret it, but it is too late for me to change very much. I do want to help, not only by teaching you. I will gladly do whatever is necessary, but you can help me to work at my best by bringing me your thoughts and feelings as you brought them to Espinoza. . . . I don't believe—I don't believe you will come to love me as much as you did Espinoza, but I am your friend, yours and Khreng's. Agreed?:

"Yes, Madame," Prandra whispered. "Agreed."

"Wyaerl, Kinnear asks me to help him in his investigations. May I question you?"

"Yes," Wyaerl piped. "You, may, esp." He withdrew his tube and flopped to the carpet like a relieved flapjack.

"Why do you come here?"

:On our world we have colonies of squatters from many places trading in illegal drugs and also farming and processing them from plant matter disturbing our economy ecology and morale which GalFed can't do much about because they don't extradite and because a good number are Solthrees especially some rare impervious types who cannot be esped I came here for help of which little is forthcoming there is no one suitable and we have spent too much credit already so I am going home soon with my disappointment is that enough?:

"It's certainly comprehensive. Can I ask you one more question without insult?"

:Go ahead I know you don't intend to insult my humble self.:

"You go to visit Espinoza some time before or after he is killed—"

:No no without insult I assure you that is not so though there were many times I consulted Espinoza he was most agreeable that was one time I did not you may esp as much as you please.:

"Thank you, I know you are not lying," said Prandra.

"I am sorry for Kinnear," Khreng said.

"Are you sure there is a trace of . . ."

"Old woman, I *know* I find a fresh undried scale with Wyaerl's personal scent and his planet's atmosphere on it. In Espinoza's doorway. If it is a plant it carries the planter's scent. That is it."

Prandra patted his forehead. "You are the authority. I accept."

"Who is there?" asked the speaking-tube.

"Prandra."

The door opened; Metaxa was drawn about the eyes, but the beard hid the rest of his broad high-colored face. He held a glass with a bent tube in it. "What do you want?" His control was brittle.

"I am allowed to ask questions, and you are permitted not to answer.

"Otherwise," he said coolly, "you will esp." He had pushed his sleeves up the arms and unzipped the suit halfway down the chest; gray hair burst from the opening and on his forearms. The hair of his beard was thick and lively brown; she wondered briefly if he colored it, and answered no. It was not himself he decorated with jewels or perfumes; his personal smell was strong, even to her unauthoritative nose.

"No, Metaxa. Sometimes you push your thoughts at me. I don't care for that, because I don't esp without permission, except to defend myself. That is Kinnear's business."

"And you're working for him. . . ." He shrugged. "Come in, read all you like. I'm not hiding anything."

Metaxa and Nema had an apartment of several rooms; the walls were covered with hangings, reliefs, pictures, the floors crammed with furniture and figurines and things Prandra did not recognize, but she did not want to risk knocking them over. She tucked in her tail and crouched near the door.

Nema was sitting in a chair by the window dressed in

one of her beautiful gowns, a blue shimmer. She was twenty-two years old, mature in body and with the face of a sleeping infant. Metaxa sat down beside her and offered the tube to her mouth. She sipped once, blinked, raised a fist and swung with great power. Glass and tube bounced against the wall splashing and fell to the carpet.

Metaxa's face was expressionless as hers. He rubbed his arm, picked up the glass and tube and put them on a table. Prandra's skin prickled.

Nema's hands folded themselves in her lap and Metaxa turned to Prandra. "What do you want?" he asked again.

"Does the lady Nema go anywhere without you, or you without her?"

"No. We're always together, all the time." His forehead was wet; he did not wipe it. "Why?"

"It is the kind of question Kinnear asks. We try to help."

His eyes were shrewd. "I think it's the kind of question an Ungrukh asks. Kinnear would want to know where we were at the time of the murders."

"If Kinnear wishes to know that, he asks."

"He already has . . . Madame." His voice lingered on irony. "I'll tell you and save you trouble. When Espinoza was killed, we were asleep here together, and when Yamashita was killed, we were having lunch here together. Are you satisfied?"

"No, Metaxa. Can you prove you are not drugged or hypnotized either time? That is the kind of question an Ungrukh asks. I am grateful for your cooperation."

"You surprise me. Anything else?"

Before she could answer, Nema stood up and headed for the door as if she were blind to the body in her way. Prandra scrambled to avoid tripping her, and Metaxa jumped to open the door before she crashed into it. Then he took her by the elbow and let her lead him where she would.

Prandra slipped out and watched them down the hall. Nema went blindly in her curious stilted walk. Metaxa glanced back once, but said nothing.

Pray tell me, sir: whose dog are you? Prandra scratched at her neck where the chain rubbed it. All at once her fur stood on end and her legs trembled.

A pinhole had opened involuntarily in Metaxa's mind, exploding volcanic fury: a firestorm of fear, despair, disgust—and hatred for the woman, Nema.

Khreng came round a corner, sniffing, and stopped beside her. "Tune down, or they receive you on Ungruwarkh."

She was shaking. "I can't help it."

"What do you expect from a man with a ring in his nose?"

"I never try to put one in yours," she snarled. "What do you smell here?"

"Metaxa, Prandra, Nema, guards, Lyhhrt."

"Why Lyhhrt? They are not around all day."

"Ask them."

"They don't talk to class-twos."

"Then ask Kinnear."

"They don't talk to me, either," said Kinnear. "I'm a class-two, remember? They think in a way it's impossible to grasp unless you're a very powerful ESP. *You* must have picked up thoughts from them. What were they?"

"Yes, no, and maybe," Prandra said. "And some garble about Cosmic Thought."

"There you are. I had Sheedy question them and they say they weren't anywhere near Espinoza—or Yamashita."

Khreng growled, "Everybody is at Espinoza's door, and nobody is. Maybe my nose is playing tricks."

"No, but somebody is, and I don't pretend to understand." He pleated his hands. "Right now it's Metaxa I'm worried about. He's a walking hornet's nest."

"He's unconscious of it," Prandra said, "or he doesn't stay with her."

"I've never figured why he does. He's very proud, he's what used to be called a self-made man. Worked in a dockyard, at the beginning, earned everything he has, and learned everything he knows, by himself."

"Yes," said Prandra. "The literary mind. And now we work for GalFed, we *are* dogs of the king, hah?"

"Don't put on any stupid act for me. Now that's opened up, he's going to blow—at you or Nema. You saw all the stuff crammed in his place. That's the Art. He's also got weapons collections. I don't have authority to confiscate them, and if I did, he'd find more— and bring in his lawyers too."

"I doubt Nema lets him hurt her."

"Then we'll give *you* some guns."

Khreng guffawed. "Without thumbs, Kinnear? First you spend a month learning to build up the grips so we can hold them, and days teaching us to use them, then we fall all over our feet and shoot our tails off carrying them? Knives are better."

"Carry knives."

"Kinnear, we are good with knives," Prandra said, "but we also play with little children. Even if I am attacked once, we still look pretty odd if we seem to need knives to defend ourselves from them. The kind we use best are in our heads and hands, and we leave it that way."

:*Still your old self, Prandra,*: said Chatterjee. :*You may need weapons.*:

"I am not shy about using a knife if I need one. We still don't know whom to fight. Our ship is ready in ten days and we are not staying longer."

:*When do you want to set the exam, then?*:

"In eight days, if you believe I am ready. Otherwise I take it at Central. I still have a lot to learn."

:You can begin today by picking a lost memory out of my unconscious—within the bounds of good taste.:

"That is not what I have in mind."

:What I have in mind is my stock-in-trade, and you have agreed to learn."

Prandra sighed and shut her eyes so tightly, the bristles above them stood straight up. "The brass table from Benares . . . the one passed down through generations in your family, you plan to give it . . ." Her voice trailed off and she twitched in embarrassment.

:I said unconscious, not suppressed!: Chatterjee's thoughts could sting like arrows.

"I admit I have no tact," Prandra muttered. "Begin again."

:No. I promised it to my daughter, but she refused to see me after I was bottled. Not for many years. She came when she was nearly as old as I. I gave it to her.: Her mind went blank. She asked vaguely, *:What was I saying? . . . Prandra, you are blocking me! Tell me at once!:*

It seemed to Prandra that the pump had speeded up and the glass bubble might burst. "Do you really wish to keep a painful memory?"

:If I avoided painful thoughts, I could not be much of a teacher.:

"The brass table."

:Good. If you hadn't told me, there would have been no exam.:

"Why? Because I block better than you?"

Grim smile-thought. *:Because a pupil shows courtesy—even to a humbled instructor.:*

"I am learning."

:Have you always been able to block?:

"On Ungruwarkh we call it netting, because it is like catching the best fish out of a school of diseased ones—and our fish are terrible. That is why I am here." Prandra grinned. "Madame, there are many things I can do that I don't know the right names for, or can't control properly. I am grateful to learn how to use them."

:Before we are through you, will teach me to block as well as you do. Now tell me the problem.:

"Khreng's sense of smell is not evidence to the law, but it is to me. It tells us everyone is everywhere, and nobody admits to being anywhere. Even Wyaerl, who is as innocent as the morning dew, says he is nowhere near Espinoza on the night of death, and we know he is. Now—"

:Prandra, you tell me.:

"Ah, that is a block . . . but what matter in Wyaerl's head is so dangerous that it must be fished out?"

:Perhaps . . . Wyaerl wondered if he could bring up to Espinoza the possibility you would agree to stop at his world on the way to Ungruwarkh, to help with his trouble. He didn't feel he knew you well enough then to ask you personally, and he was even shy of asking Espinoza—but you seem to have impressed him.:

"I can tell you he is not all that shy when you get to know him, but I find nothing of that in Espinoza. I begin to see past that block: it is not desired for us to become too friendly with anyone here, or leave too early—and our engine is blown up. Ha."

:What else?:

"The Lyhhrt are also among thsoe who are not at Espinoza's door—they say."

:Two of them, Administration and Liaison, I've known well for several years; they work hard and deal honestly. The other three are visitors, and they have never seemed hostile. I don't intrude on their privacy, and they leave me with mine.:

"They seem close to Nema."

:No, they scarcely go near her. She's not really a staff member. More of a showpiece, because her mind is so much like theirs. She cannot communicate very well with anyone.:

"Kinnear considers you much more valuable."

:I am not jealous.:

Prandra laughed. "There's no need to be jealous of that one."

Chatterjee said, :*I am beginning to look forward to that exam. What kind of illusion-form are you planning?*:

Prandra shrugged. "I'm not sure. I'm not a person with many illusions." She raised her hand to the door-button.

:*Prandra . . .* :

She waited.

:*I don't know much—not even where the danger lies—but it is enough to make me afraid. It was probably meant that you be captured and used for some purpose, on the premise that you were savage and ignorant, even though intelligent. Now you are stronger and have learned much more. Perhaps too much. . . .* :

"I know. Now we are on the edge of finding out, I think . . . and we are meant to be killed."

:*I feel responsible.*:

"For what? Our feelings for Espinoza? And our curiosity? No. For helping me out of my ignorance? Kinnear suggests this training and I accept. I am responsible. For Khreng as well."

Two big red cats trotted the grounds in the evening light, followed by two armed guards ordered by Kinnear and mounted on foot-controlled mopeds. "There is nothing like a good run in fresh recycled air and escorted by guards to make one feel alive and carefree," said Prandra.

"As long as they keep behind. I am tired of smelling them."

They passed the zoo's reptile house. "There's a scent for you," Prandra said.

"Better than our fish." Khreng paused by the tiger's cage, where the great beast lay snoring. "Over three hundred kilos, my guess. Khreng times three. I wonder what it is like to be that one." The tiger opened one eye and closed it again. "I think I keep on being Khreng."

Prandra laughed. "A nice toy for children." She stopped at the playground fence.

"No more bloody damned carousel rides!"

"Don't get excited . . . look: over there is where I see Nema and Metaxa the night Espinoza dies. My nose is not yours, but . . . if we close our eyes . . . smell: Nema, Metaxa, fear of/for—what? Her/him/them/it . . ."

Khreng opened his eyes. "It?"

"Yes. Let's go back." She seemed depressed.

Khreng rubbed his back on the stone slab and sat up. "What in Firemaster's name *is* the matter?"

She bit off a loose claw scale. "I believe . . . if we do not come here, Espinoza and Yamashita are still living."

"Maybe. And Ungruwarkh is dead as a stone."

"The tribes fight over what we have to bring them, and many die."

"Not necessarily. If so, they are better to die for hope than from starvation. What else?"

"Why ask?"

"I am with you all these years and I don't know you? When you twist your head twenty degrees clockwise, there is something you are afraid to tell me."

She sniffed.

"Are you afraid I am frightened, or angry?"

She whispered at last, "I am afraid we die."

"That's how you save me?" He stood in a swift angry movement. "Woman, you better tell me pretty damn fast. I am a fine figure of a man on my world if I step down alone from the ship and tell everyone Prandra is dead because I am ignorant!"

"I always know you are vain," she hissed.

"I am vain enough to believe we are equals and can take this risk together as we always do."

"I am afraid others may be killed. That is part of why my head is twenty degrees clockwise . . . everyone

knows everything and nobody admits knowing anything."

"That is a contradiction. You are afraid they may be
killed, and then they are all liars and conspirators."

"I don't mean that. *They* have information they are
unconscious of, and *we* are ignorant. If they become
conscious, they are dead."

"Killer cannot murder all of MedPsych."

"There is no need. (One) when we are not here,
nothing is upset; (two) we arrive and Killer finds some
use for us; (three) Killer finds us too hard to handle
and becomes enraged and frustrated; so he (four) kills
us and returns to (one); leaving what is not conscious,
unconscious."

"(One-a)," said Khreng sarcastically, "only having to
explain two big dead red cats."

"Not if they die by accident or foolish mistake."

"And you have in mind?"

"We lack that carefully hidden information . . .
but—I want to get back to our people, on our ship.
Forget the exam. If we stay under guard until we
leave, we are safe."

He hacked with laughter. "Do we sit safe in that
village long ago and let the Qumedon kill the Rabbi
and his people? Whether the test means anything or
not, you spend the rest of our days hurting your spirit
because you let Espinoza's murderer go free."

"If we move, we risk other lives."

"Whose are you counting?"

"The helpless ones who suspect, like Chatterjee, perhaps Sheedy."

"Why don't we ask them about risks?" He opened
the locker, tossed a knife-harness to Prandra, and
buckled on his own. "This is not the first time I play
the fool for you."

She sighed. "The trouble is, we are not playing *with*
fools."

"What is the use of the game, otherwise?"

Prandra slid Chatterjee's door open a crack.

:Yes, Prandra?:

"Madame, Khreng wants to sleep in front of your door tonight. Do you object?"

:Of course not. In India I was always very fond of cats.: She added with deeper irony, *:Good hunting.:*

"She takes the chance," said Prandra. Khreng crouched at the door, a heraldic beast. He did not intend to sleep.

"I've never seen anything like that before," said the guard.

"Make sure you don't miss anything else." Prandra ambled down the hall. The chain jangled, the scabbard bobbed against her side. She wrenched at the chain until it broke and let it drop. Not only because she hated the Cracked Caduceus: in a fight it might choke her. She stared at the medallion lying on the carpet and remembered the little gold-and-enamel clasp near Yamashita's bed. She went on, pushing her mind against the tangle of occurrence and evidence.

Metaxa goes everywhere with Nema; Nema always carries trace of Lyhhrt. There is something about that shield I break in the playground that smells like Lyhhrt. But—

No Lyhhrt here would do that: says Prandra.

They scarcely go near her, says Chatterjee.

Then what have they created: Nema, Metaxa, Lyhhrt? *Something inside,* says Wyaerl. A structure forms and while it is building, pieces are taken away. Stupid Nema; Metaxa's love/hate/anger; courteous Lyhhrt . . .

One room open and empty: Sheedy, the one she had not questioned—she quickened around a corner and . . . blink, the guards were gone.

Behind another door, silent screaming: *Leave me alone! Help! please don't!*

She stopped cold. Ambush?

She whacked that flimsy door off its mooring with

one shoulder and flattened it with a terrific crack on the tiled floor of a laundry room. Sheedy, gagged with a pillowcase, was being pummeled by four of the guards.

Her breath went out in a burst of mingled relief and disgust. She roared. The attackers had left their guns behind. They jumped, gaped and fled whimpering, clawing at each other to get out. She ripped off the gag. Sheedy coughed and flailed his arms. "What? What ? . . . Prandra?"

"Yes," she drawled. "None other."

He fell to his knees and began to sob. "Prandra . . . I can't see."

She took one of his hands and guided it to her neck. He clutched her around the throat with both arms. "You saved my life!"

"That shoulder is a bit sore, Sheedy. Get up. You are not hurt, only your pride."

He dragged his sleeve across his nose. "I have no pride."

"Find some." She stood on hind legs and hauled him up. "Hold my arm, look through my eyes. I take you to your room."

He whimpered, "You despise me."

"I don't despise you. I need you." Sheedy *was* first class when he wasn't drunk or chasing the boys who hated him. It was his self-hatred she couldn't stand.

"Oh, now I see! I see! Cat's eyes, beautiful strength and graceful . . . everything bright, so strange . . . marvelous, Prandra, oh—"

"And very hard walking hind-legged. Come on, Sheedy. I lend you my eyes another time."

Khreng waited. He did not know what he was waiting for. On Ungruwarkh he knew what was to be hunted, Prandra knew approximately where it was, and he found the way to it. Simplicity itself. Why am I sitting here like a stupid lump of a dog? If I wait long enough I get fleas. He blinked, and the hall began to spin. He blinked again, the hall spun faster. He thrashed against the engulfing dizziness, but his head was being dragged down and down until it thudded to the floor. In the center of a black vortex a tiger's eye flared briefly and died.

Sheedy's room was unlit, but bright enough for Prandra's eyes. Sheedy gulped whiskey, still marveling at seeing through the eyes of a cat. His hand trembled on the bottle's neck, his lip quivered at the glass's edge. "Tremendous, gorgeous, cat's eyes. I should get a cat."

"There is a nice big one in a cage out there. Sheedy, put down the whiskey for a minute, and I don't mean inside your gut. I want to talk."

"Talk away, talk away, long dark nights—hah?— meant for talk, all day I talk, Khagodi, Xirifri, Yefni, every lizard, serpent, thing with gills, talk-talk, nights I get nothing but cats, whiskey talks, says good things to the old gut—"

"Now it's time for Nema, Metaxa, Lyhhrt, Sheedy—"

He belched.

:*Sheedy!* Ah, what a wretch! How she could have grabbed him by the neck and shaken him, broken him, scooped his brain by the roots, picked it for nits and smeared it on the wall!

"That's right," he giggled. "Brains on the wall. Living sculpture. Freeze it and give it to Metaxa." He choked and coughed.

She slumped. He was doing everything possible to shy away from the knowledge that might kill. And she had no right to push further. But.

:*I have no pride.*:

:*Do you not, Sheedy? You let me look?*:

:*Look away, Big Mama, you look. You find it, I'll buy you a drink. You and this flabby old bastard.*:

She startled. Like the bottled ESPs, Sheedy also had

a vivid self-image; but this one stood back and observed. He was a strong, supple young man with ugly contempt for the sagging flesh that imprisoned him; he took unceasing and demonic revenge on it. This was not quite a separated personality of the multiple type—Prandra had met just one in her life—but it was the self that hated Sheedy.

Sheedy babbled on, gruesome nonsense of cats' eyes and mashed brains. Prandra addressed Other: *:Young one, if you are so clever, give me information I need that does not get you into trouble.:*

:I don't care who gets into trouble. Least of all him. Anyone who's stupid enough to let glaucoma blind him without having it treated deserves trouble.:

:If foolishness is a sin, we are all in hell before we start. He sees enough of himself. You are claiming superiority you do not yet show.:

Sullenly, *:What do you want?:*

:Data on Lyhhrt you gather and file for Kinnear. I have his permission.:

:That's a whole world you're talking about.:

:I don't need the whole world. You esp what I want, boil it down. You know how, it's your specialty.:

Faint noise made Khreng raise his head. He thought he might have had some kind of blackout, for he had no sensation of waking. He noticed vaguely that the ceiling lights were out in the hall, then caught the scents, both perfumed and personal, of Nema, and the suggestion of Lyhhrt that always came with her. He padded down the hall, following. She seemed to be moving ahead. If she turned she might see him, but he was the tracker, and silent, so silent he could not have been heard among thorns. Even the guards did not see him because he was so silent, for they did not stir. There was an open door with a blue creature standing in it and waving tendrils furiously, piping, "Don't—"

but that slow one could not catch him. He heard a thump behind, did not turn because what was ahead was so important. What was so important he barely saw, a flicker, a shimmer. And always the scent.

Guards turned to statues by enchantment.

His mind was a dark cone; at its small end a tiny Prandra roared and reached for him. Ridiculous. She knew he was the tracker. . . . Across the lobby through open doors into darkness, past the guard mounted on moped staring at nothing, no swerve toward the infants' park . . . scent always steady and faint moonlight on the shimmer . . .

Pausing at iron gate and snicking of bolt . . . vanishes—

Hot and rank hit him a blow. Green eyeshine lanced his brain.

HA HA HA, says voice from the sky, POOR KHRENG IDIOT KHRENG GOES CRAZY WITH VANITY HE WANTS TO PLAY WITH—

Tiger!

He awoke, shook darkness from his head, skittered back growling.

Tiger on four feet waved its tail gently, stepped softly across the cage, and with one paw pushed open the creaking gate.

And roared. The air split.

Prandra relaxed, began to luxuriate in the flow of information.

—*:not just formless masses of protoplasm, they have complicated nervous systems and muscles of thin fiber. They need food and water to reproduce, but if they're stranded without, they grow skins, shells, scales, whatever they need to wait for good conditions. They reproduce by fission, not often, they're nearly immortal. Before reproducing, a group will fuse to exchange genetic material, hardly any two have the same genes. On Lyhhrr they lie about by thousands with joined* *pseudopods, like the ends of nerve-cells, in marshes and lakes, on hills, under seas, thinking Cosmic Thoughts; don't ask what those are, would have been doing it for millennia more if GalFed hadn't discovered them, shown them how to use the false limbs to build true bodies. They chose metal, I don't know why, probably body chemistry. Once they got separate bodies they became individuals, maybe not such a good idea. They work well enough for GalFed, but it's hard for them to communicate. Superb artistry in those workshells, maybe afraid people won't respect them because they don't look like much. . . .*

:More? The sticky part, private but not classified. Two of them were posted here eight years ago, Administration and Liaison. Liaison had been important at GalFed Central, but got to be a nuisance because he began insisting that workshells were too clumsy for minds with so much power, ought to be controlling animals, insensate life-forms, instead. GalFed hit the roof in whatever they call their Intergalactic S.P.C.A., as well as Human Rights Div. Who knows what'll turn out to be sensate? Sent him out of the way rather than squash him. The shuttle crashed here. Admin was unhurt. Liaison disappeared except for his empty workshell. Theory was he'd crawled somewhere, wounded, then died and dissolved. After a while Admin asked to be allowed to fission to carry out the work of both. That took three years because it's a long way to Lyhhrr. Three years more, and Admin-L'aison asked for more staff and these three showed up. I suspect an investigating committee. That's all.:

:Investigating, after eight years?:

:I said it's a long way. Give the old fart my regards.: Young Sheedy's image collapsed on itself and folded away.

"I've been enjoying our conversation, Prandra," Sheedy said over a hiccup, "but it's time for some serious drinking, and—"

"I am enjoying a conversation with young Sheedy."

"Glad to hear it. He's quite an interesting fellow."

"He has a tough mind. Both of you together make one good man. . . . Sheedy, why not let up on the bottle a little?"

He snickered. "I'm hardly likely to get any *in* the bottle, am I?"

Tiger shrieked.

Sheedy knocked over bottle and glass. "What was that? My God, the power's off, no white-walls!"

Prandra slammed the T-screen's buttons without raising a flicker.

"The door won't open! I'm locked in!"

Prandra pushed the manual release, and dragged open the heavy door. "You can get out. Take my advice and lock yourself in." She bounded down the hall.

KhrengKhrengKhreng? Khreng and Tiger! She found the blue lump, Wyaerl, forced herself to stop. Flattened, great welt across his back. His bottles had been wrenched out; she replaced the tubes in their slits, clumsily, because she was not wearing finger-prostheses for fine-muscle work.

"Badly hurt?" She smelled Metaxa.

:Temporary paralysis, nerves pinched by swelling, and:— his mind was remarkably clear— *:inside something—is at the zoo. . . :*

Not only. She picked up Khreng's thought-track now. Nema and Lyhhrt. Nema plus Lyhhrt.

She broadcast to all quarters. *Chatterjee, give your head! Sheedy, put down your fear and help! Lyhhrt, are you hiding when you know the lost one is an insane killer?* Two of them now, and one in Tiger.

In the darkness and without white-walls, Prandra felt as if she were out in space in a lattice of stars, each star a soul with its flickering intelligence: Kinnear, committee, guards, Chatterjee, Sheedy, Lyhhrt—asleep, hypnotized, fearful, cold as stars seemed from their distances . . . and on the edge of the universe, Khreng facing *Tiger.*

Khreng did not deceive himself. Compared to a tiger he was a runt. He backed up, roaring. Tiger advanced, silent now, jaws open, stub teeth between the fangs a steel gate.

Khreng, crouching, dared not reach for his knife. Tiger's jaws wanted a grip on a limb, tail or throat. He saved his breath, wrapped the long tail around his loins. Claws reached, Khreng snaked under, Tiger reached out again, and raked his side. Most terrible was that part of his self-adored Tiger, gold under the moon and black flame stripes leaping up his flanks. Ungrukh in the volcanic zones had once worshiped a Great Cat until the Prophet of Firemaster had risen in their tribes. Blazing green eyes. O Great Cat!

His pads slipped in driblets of his own blood, his side stung. He was half stunned, could not even smell the beast, an immortal engine, gold and flame rippling. It leaped.

Prandra howled.

Jolted, Khreng ducked beneath the belly. "Away! Get away!"

"There is a Lyhhrt alive in that beast!"

Tiger paused and turned toward her.

"Save yourself, I sacrifice to the Cat for you!"

"Idiot!"

Tiger was bent on killing its challenger, the cat; Lyhhrt Six, on murdering Prandra. Nema, harboring his fission-brother, Lyhhrt Seven, lay in bed, smiling; Metaxa in forced sleep beside her, face twisted in a hideous grin.

The eyes, turned away from the moon, had darkened. Prandra regarded them: she did not worship the spirit of Cat. She had conceived, brought forth in blood, given the teat, cleaned the excretions, and disemboweled the prey; she had burrowed too deep in living matter to respect any ghost. She drew out the knife, wound her tail round its handle and held it against her side. Tiger-Lyhhrt moved forward, gathering speed.

:Wyaerl! Wyaerl!:

Whisper of thought: *Beneath the ribs . . .*

Khreng roared and leaped. Tiger clawed his forehead before he landed, then rose over Prandra, claws out.

:Chatterjee! Sheedy!:

They were trying to rouse the others. There was nothing else they could do.

She slewed, twisting, her teeth caught the skin of the throat, jaws came down slamming the crown of her head as Khreng's knife dashed in and out among the stripes of the flank. The beast turned aside, roaring; Prandra rolled out of reach of the claws, fireworks bursting before her eyes from the pain in her head. Khreng's blade slithered under the loose skin, blunted itself along the steely ribs. A few red lines ran among the stripes. Tiger did not stop. A claw slashed Khreng between the eyes and he retreated.

Prandra backed away, snarling. Lyhhrt wanted her badly, if Tiger did not. She thought briefly of the shelter of the cage; Tiger wheeled and planted itself before the bars: Lyhhrt reasoning.

Three cats made points of a triangle. Khreng whetted his knife on the flags. Prandra's head was pounding; she shook it, flicking droplets of blood from her brow-hairs.

Ah, but Tiger was beautiful. She shook the beauty away with her blood. Lyhhrt hidden among the vitals. She was tiring; Tiger could eat bullets, and his jaws were as wide as the sky.

She pulled Khreng and herself under her shield. Have I learned at all, Chatterjee? It was not safe there, but dark and lonely. She leveled an arrow of thought at Khreng. He tossed her his knife, she clamped her tail round it with the other. One more effort.

She and Khreng charged from two directions,

screaming. Tiger-Lyhhrt, intent on Prandra, was not prepared for the fangs driving into the base of its tail, and reared howling. Prandra took a knife in each hand, an awkward maneuver achieved in desperation, and drove them upward hilt-deep under both sides of the ribcage.

Lyhhrt died in a silent convulsion.

Light flashed, sound burst: Tiger's eye exploded. The head, falling forever, hammered her to the ground.

She dragged herself from under, gasping.

Kinnear was on the steps, cradling his heavy gun with its lights, sights, triggers, tubes, grips. Any number of people had gathered behind him. She had not heard them coming. She did not care that they had come.

Khreng began to howl. He circled the fallen beast, dripping blood, howling prayers to Firemaster, to the Great Cat, to the gods of the equatorial zones of Ungruwarkh where tides ravaged the sands, begging forgiveness, absolution, vowing repentance.

"Khreng!"

He went around and around, raising hideous voice. She forced herself to stand, planted herself before him, cursing. He swiped her aside. She dropped and let him go.

In a few moments the zookeeper, a little stick-limbed black man in pajamas and hastily wound turban, came and shot him with a tranquilizer dart. He made one more round, still howling, and collapsed.

The zookeeper stood scratching in his thick gray beard and looking at the tiger. "He is not badly hurt, your man." He added, almost sorrowfully. "In my native state in India, Tiger is called the dog of the gods, because he does always what they wish."

She raised herself on trembling forelimbs. Kinnear gave his gun to somebody else, crossed the bloodied stones. He bent to pull the knives from the tiger's belly,

wiped their blades on his sleeves and held them out to
Prandra.

With the last of her strength she grabbed and flung
them away into the darkness. "Civilization." She spat.
"Take that thing apart until you find the Lyhhrt."

Khreng woke up in a fearful temper. "Zookeepers!
Tranquilizer darts!" He screeched outrage. "Haven't
they the decency to use a stunner?"

Prandra growled, "Stunner gives you ten days of
headache and we need to lift off."

Both had been crammed with antibiotics; a few hairs
had been shaved off Khreng; the skintex sprayed on
his wounds gave him a couple of sickly pink stripes.
The temper was caused by sheer humiliation that he,
the rational being, had found himself almost groveling
to a foreign god.

"For a groveler you do great fighting, so shut up,"
Prandra said.

The door buzzed and opened. Kinnear was standing
in the doorway with his hands up. "If you feel like
throwing things, I'll leave," he said.

"We're not quite that peevish," said Prandra. "What
I feel like, is a fool. I say Lyhhrt have nothing to do
with the murders, and I am completely mistaken; I
know I must not take risks, and I behave irresponsibly
and risk lives; then I cause the death of an insane person and an innocent beast, and that is horrible."

"I suppose that's the truth from your point of view.
But we did find the Lyhhrt; Wyaerl would be dead if
you hadn't replaced his air and water: now he just has
a big bruise; most of us are grateful that many things
we couldn't grasp before are becoming clear—and
there is one Lyhhrt who is not guilty who would like to
speak to you, if you're willing."

"We're willing," Khreng said. "Don't pay attention to
the old woman's grumbling. Without that shot of yours
we are still fighting Tiger, if not Lyhhrt."

"Listen who is talking," Prandra snorted. "The rational man!"

Kinnear laughed. "I'd better send him in right away."

The Lyhhrt, who appeared in his most magnificent workshell, was one of Admin-L'aison; in near Solthree form, he was wearing all of Lyhhrr's art in precious metals and inset jewels. He was taller than Kinnear, and his shell's head was shaped something like one of the primitive masks on Metaxa's wall. Prandra remembered her conversation with Espinoza, and his pleasure in seeing the morning sun even through her alien eyes. And then the ashy bleakness of the planet where Ungrukh struggled and fought. Primitive.

Admin-L'aison's mind opened to welcome Khreng and herself, and she glimpsed a planet, swirling in marsh and fog, that was even more dispiriting than her own: its crawling lives had been taught by others not only to create their magnificent gleam and brilliance, but painfully to speak to the peoples of the Galaxy. Inside some part of the cold metal was a sluglike being who deeply admired the grace and beauty of the Ungrukh.

:*So much so, unfortunately, that some of us wished to make workshells of you.*:

"We are honored to speak with you, don't blame yourself," Prandra said. "There are so many questions to ask I don't know where to begin."

:*At the beginning,*: said the Lyhhrt; he was very literal-minded. :*Our former Liaison was so powerful, even we could not esp him. He called our shells clumsy and did his best to convince us that others considered them pretentious and ridiculous.*:

"Then he is certainly mad," Prandra said, half blinded by the reflected light of the creature whose people were called the Shining Ones by many weaker ESPs.

:An unfortunate combination of genetic material—particularly since he is a killer. But he is a genius—and in that other respect he is quite right, when we must go about on wheels or walk in such a graceless manner.:

"Like Nema," Prandra whispered.

The Lyhhrt hesitated. *:Yes . . . at first he tried to control animals—wild or domestic insensate beings on several worlds—by telepathy; he found this unsatisfactory; when he decided that he must work from within, he was declared a menace to Lyhhrr and our organization in GalFed and sent with what we felt was a qualified guard to what we believed was a saft post—here. We were horribly mistaken. I-brother are culpable and will of course resign.:*

"I think Kinnear prefers not," said Prandra. "You better stay. I say once already if fools are sinners we're all in hell."

:There . . . were . . . other curious deaths here before you came.:

"I'm not surprised. It is why you ask help. So your rebel gets inside . . ."

"In Nema—we suspected that—and he sent a fission-twin to the tiger, because he admired strength and savagery—:

"And stupidity."

:No. He was aware those others were hardly more satisfactory than metals. He was waiting for someone like you.:

Khreng, reading through Prandra, shivered and tried to suppress the involuntary memory of a case of intestinal flukes for which he had been treated with hearty doses of emetic.

Lyhhrt had little sense of humor and could not smile, but they did their best. *:No, not exactly. We are not—what Solthrees call Protean—not shape-changers: one could not crawl into things, like a worm. Once inside, our man extended pseudoaxons and hooked them into the host spinal cord. To get inside—:* He sprung open a little drawer in his belly and held out a small steel object shaped like a flattened egg. It split, a dozen tiny knives were packed inside. *:We are superb surgeons and dissectors, and* *we leave no scars. This came from our brother in the tiger.:*

"And the false claw is made, I presume, by Nema-Lyhhrt," said Prandra. "It is interesting that the genius who despises metalwork cannot do it very well. And what do you do about Nema?"

:Guard her, and report the case to GalFed Central. We are certain, but Khreng's sense of smell is not evidence against Nema, and you were forced to kill fission-brother to save your lives. . . . Before I-we go it must be said it is good to speak at ease and at length with an Outworlder, as you know we rarely can.:

"Thank you—particularly since I'm still class-two.:

:It is unfortunate that the situation remains essentially the same.:

"I hope not," said Prandra.

"Prandra, it's no use throwing yourself around," said Kinnear. "You and Khreng are going to stay under guard, just like Nema and Metaxa, until you lift off out of here—only, unlike them, you're staying together so you can scratch each other's eyes out."

"In my dreams I tell Espinoza I am too stupid to trap his killer!"

"And what does Espinoza say to you?"

"He tells me he is content and . . . I must remember Yamashita, who is so much worse off, and—and—"

"Espinoza is a wise man even in your dreams," Kinnear said gently.

Prandra was not to be put off. "You tell Metaxa everything?"

"We told him what we suspected."

"And he is angry?"

"Angry enough that we decided to put Nema in a room of her own, with Lyhhrt guarding her—and a nurse to take care of her. If he did try to attack her . . . well, he might find himself putting a gun to his own head."

"I think he is angry at us."

"No, he's angry at having been taken. At first he thought we were accusing him of murder, but we all believe she did the work. He knocked down Wyaerl, we fished that out of his mind, but he was obviously under hypnosis, and no one will charge him. It shocked him enough so that he began to put things together, realize how he'd been chosen to be her guardian, from the start."

"So he goes free. . . ."

"Eventually. We haven't discussed that with him yet. We want him under surveillance, but we don't want all his lawyers. If we can put up a case, he'll be a witness—but he'll go free. It's strange that in spite of everything he knows and feels in one part of his mind, the part she controlled doesn't hate her: it still believes he chose her as a collector's piece. He'll go into a rage, and end in tears."

"She goes free too," Prandra growled.

"The body with the useless brain will go someplace where it'll be taken care of. The criminal—I'm sure the Lyhhrt will keep after that one if it takes thirty years. I gather that any evildoer who disrupts the Cosmic Thought keeps the world at one remove from God—and whatever that is, it's a deadly sin."

"In thirty years I may be a live brain but I am a dead cat." She scratched her nose with the tip of her tongue. "You think Metaxa tries to free her?"

Surprised, Kinnear said, "How can he?"

"You think she can't find a way, with opportunity? And all her power? Especially when *he* is going free? Nema is two: infant and Lyhhrt. We know about her. But Metaxa is three: love, hate, and doubt. We know about him too: he is malleable. Those three parts can be turned off and on; she does not have to be the only one who pulls switches."

Kinnear let out his breath in a long whish. "You've just beaten my head in with the unthinkable."

"It is not forbidden to think about it, surely."

"I will. Believe me, I will."

"Good. You find your cat friends helpful . . . but Kinnear, remember one thing. No harm. I am not just speaking of Khreng and myself. *No harm.* Ungrukh have ideas about sin too."

GalFed's ESP examinations are open to the public in order to dispel the ESP mystique; they are rarely well attended: the exam to a non-ESP is as kriegspiel to a non-chessplayer.

Prandra, at one end of the Committee Room, with Khreng dozing beside her, looked half asleep. She was crouched on the rough flagstone brought in for her by an earth-mover; she did not want to grow too comfortable. She was sulky as always before some difficult task; she would be worse later. Her half-closed eyes skimmed her audience: armed guards, curious clerks, a couple of outworld ESPs she did not remember having met. Wyaerl, a blue rug with a purple welt; Chatterjee, reflecting the window on her dark globe; Sheedy, looking as if the light hurt his eyes. Metaxa was openly yawning; he had been allowed to come because he had not much else to do.

Kinnear, somber and a bit nervous, sat with the rest of the committee, a conglomeration of faces. The Lyhhrt were the surprise, all five in a golden row: they had considered the occasion important enough to come in force, leaving Nema attended by three crack shots in a portable white-wall cage. Prandra was the day's star and could esp as she pleased, but she caught nothing from the Lyhhrt. Committee was backache, triplicate reports, and thank-God-it's-nearly-over, get-rid-of-these-damn-cats-and-back-to-normal.

Yes.

The door closed. The silence lengthened.

"Are we ready?" Kinnear asked.

:Yes.: said Chatterjee. Prandra grunted.

"This is an examination for ESP class-one status of the candidate Prandra, daughter of Tengura of Ungruwarkh, Galactic Catalogue Feldfar five-five-three. Anax Two. Candidate was previously attested class-two by this committee on evidence of Sector-Liaison Diego Espinoza. Examiner: Sita Chatterjee. Begin."

:Forms obligatory,: said Chatterjee. *:Search, collate, shield, lock, block and break.:*

An hour of silence punctuated by aborted snores from Khreng. Metaxa got up and left halfway through, and the guard who followed him seemed grateful.

Prandra was tempted to make slips, out of mischief and impatience. Damned savage trouble-making cats, hah? Respect and affection for Chatterjee stopped her. She picked thought-trains tossed from ESP to ESP, set them in order, flicked them back, sometimes with force just short of headache-making, until Sheedy winced. She took pity and subdued herself. She needed all her control. Set up shields and blocks and withstood battering against them, drove herself against the shields and blocks of others.

Played childish games with adults and wished she were back on Ungruwarkh, where life was simpler.

Metaxa had been allowed to keep his guns and the obsolete projectiles they used; his guards wore metal- and explosives-detectors. There was one half-forgotten weapon hidden and unnoticed behind the wine racks in his refrigerator, a more modern version of the zoo-keeper's tranquilizer gun, made of plastics and tiny enough to be palmed. He had carried it in earlier years through the dark places where he made his deals. It was not lethal, he was no murderer, but it was just as effective as the stunner and far less harmful. Its crystal darts had lain preserved in the cold place where they could not sublimate, and were good for a day of body heat. He did not need a day.

The corridors were almost deserted. He paused at a door. "I want to use the washroom."

"Your own place is up one floor. Can't you wait?"

"No."

The guard shrugged and followed him in. As he was turning to shut the door, Metaxa touched him lightly beneath the ear with the little muzzle and pressed a stud.

"Hey . . ." The man staggered and within three seconds fell. Metaxa came out alone and slipped into the next doorway, an elevator.

The white-wall cage was a collection of wire-mesh panels fastened to a platform with runners, and blocking Nema's door. The men inside were sleepy and hot from crowding. There was no one else in the corridor. Seeing Metaxa alone, one of them, through a yawn, said, "Where's your guard?"

"He had to use the washroom."

They did not react; they could not esp him, and as usual were a bit stupefied from boredom. He stopped before the cage. "Couldn't . . . couldn't you just let me look at her?"

"No, sir. We have orders."

"Just to look, please?" He flattened a hand against the mesh, in appeal. "Please?"

"Mr. Metaxa, I'm warning you, get away from here!" The man grasped his weapon tighter, unwilling to raise it before wealth and power. "You know you're not supposed to be—hey, what are you do—"

Metaxa slid the panel aside, touched him under the jaw, and shoved. He fell against the others so hard they were too crowded to aim their guns, and Metaxa had them. He closed the cage and pushed it aside gently, careful not to trip up the wire that carried the current. Slid Nema's door open. The nurse by the doorway, holstered and armed, was weaving something useful with complicated bobbins and spindles. He put her to sleep before she had time to look up. Seven darts left. He did not think he would need more. The door closed.

"Darling?" Nema in a chair, blank as always, hands folded. Always when he saw her, everything changed. "Didn't you think I'd come for you?" She looked at him.

"Nema!" He came forward, hands reaching for hers. "My skimmer's still on the roof, I've been watching with the telescope and the portway's hardly guarded—"

She sat up suddenly, incisively, pushed his hands away and signed with her own in the language he had taught her: *To the apartment.*

"But, darling, why? I've put out the guards, we can get away now, from here." Once again he tried to take her hands and she pushed them aside.

To the apartment.

He shrugged, helplessly. "You know I always do what you want. But that's so danger——"

She stood, put a hand on his mouth. Grasped him by the wrist and pulled him across the room, to the door.

He was forced to put out one more guard they ran into rounding a corner. A burly one who thrashed and kicked even with the dart in him, and Metaxa had to use another. He began to sweat.

Forms ended. There was a wearied pause. Prandra nestled her chin into her forelimbs, whisked the tip of her tail back and forth, tick-tock.

:Forms-optional,: said Chatterjee. *:Category: illusion.:*

If the other part of the examination had bored her, this one Prandra had been dreading. What was demanded was the creation of an original illusion by mass hypnosis, of a person, place, time, situation, real or imaginary. She was aware that she was not imaginative or original enough to impress an audience of sophisticated ESPs. She came from a long line of realists: she was one of the few people on Ungruwarkh who had never seen the "plains-companion," the hallucinatory cat-companion which often accompanied lonely travelers over the vast barrens, and her own great-grandmother had made a career of convincing the tribes that the phenomenon was psychological rather than supernatural. She had not been helped by researching the examination records of earlier candiates, who had produced marvels. She could extrapolate, reproduce, modify. What could she show here? A sunny day on Ungruwarkh? She had done that for the children, and it was worthy of children. Her experiences in the time-warp? She had given those, in exhaustive detail, to historians and exobiologists. She could bring Sita Chatterjee embodied in her finest sari woven with peacocks on gold, a perfect eye blazing in each tail-feather . . . or Yamashita . . . too painful. Espinoza?

Oh, Espinoza . . .

:Do you want a recess?: Chatterjee asked.

"No . . ."

Khreng raised his tail and let it fall. Prandra swallowed and stood up on fours. "Madame Chatterjee, members of Invigilating Committee and audience . . ."

"What are you doing?" Metaxa, perplexed, stood watching in the kitchen doorway.

Although Nema could not take care of herself instinctively, like normal Solthree humans, she could use her hands to perform other actions—everything, perhaps, a Lyhhrt might do in a workshell. *I am preparing this for you.* She had run a halfliter of water into an ice bucket, found a small metal box, taken out several vials of crystals, shaken them into the water, swirled them to dissolve.

She took the bucket into the living room, in her even

mechanical walk, and set it on a table beside the couch. He followed, a man in a dream. She faced him, slipped the gown from her shoulders till she was bared to the waist. Her mouth formed the shape a primitive sculptor might have created and called a smile.

Metaxa had never felt sexual desire for her, perhaps never had been allowed to. "What is it?" he whispered. Her breasts trembled with pulses. She pulled down his zip and peeled the cloth from one shoulder and arm till he showed a forequarter of gray hair and aging flesh that might have been the record of years in a foreign service. His arm moved as if it were submerged in water. "Don't . . . can't you see the danger? What—" His fingers groped, in slow motion, for the sleeve.

Leave it. She moved back, still with the terrible alien smile. The pale skin below her ribs quivered and rippled. She motioned toward the couch and he sat, slowly. She pushed down his shoulders until he was reclining. Then she took a small metal case from her pocket, opened it, removed a tiny blade and set it lengthwise into his flesh below the seventh rib.

He was too numb now for shock or horror. He stared at it, watched a drop of blood gather and run down his skin.

She picked up the bucket and held it at her waist; in her own abdomen an opening appeared, a few centimeters long, a drop of blood gathered and ran, a tiny blade pushed out, slowly, came clear, fell into the folds of her dress. A tentacle emerged, a pseudopod, like the tongue-tip from a mouth; inside the skin something writhed struggling among layers of muscle.

Metaxa did not know how long it took. In the time he knew it was an eternity until the creature freed itself and slid into the basin: a Lyhhrt, half normal size. A newborn, newly divided Lyhhrt-brother enveloped in the crinkled transparent membrane of fission.

"Dearest, I know . . . I understand. . . ." There seemed to be a thickness in his speech. "You're making sure . . . . we'll be together . . . always . . . wherever I go. . . ." He could not tell whether he was babbling wildly or muttering to himself. Inside his head a person struggled and screamed.

And the Lyhhrt was not ugly, better-looking than an octopus or starfish. It was translucent pink, the size of a hand, and looked more like a flower; its five true limbs were rounded at the ends like petals, and on its back there was a star pattern of deep red spots. Underneath was a tiny pulsing heart, and just below the surface veins, nerves and muscles extended. It was a brain with limbs, a fearful intelligence. It lay placidly in the water, absorbing nutrients into its birth membrane, welling and gathering strength. Nema's wound closed, a little blood crusted on its lower lip.

"Always together," Metaxa babbled. "A part of you in me . . ."

The Lyhhrt grew, absorbed half the liquid, reached three quarters of the way toward adulthood. . . . Nema knelt beside the couch and offered the bowl, like a priestess. Offered Metaxa to the bowl. The Lyhhrt stirred; its envelope was smooth, the skin beneath would grow to match. It extended the tip of one limb into a thin tentacle and hooked it over the edge of the bucket on its way toward the blade embedded in Metaxa's flesh.

Metaxa shuddered, pulling on his strength. Sat up cautiously, not to disturb the knife, drew on saliva and swallowed before he got words out:

"Did you really think you could?"

". . . although I believe I qualify as a class-one ESP," Prandra said, "I have no ability to produce the illusions you expect in these examinations. I create only what I see or know. I am also affected by what happens here. I cannot show you imaginary rainbows or fireworks when people are murdered and I want justice. Therefore I set myself the humbler task I consider most useful, of—can you show yourself, please, Kinnear?"

Heads turned. Kinnear stood up, hands knotted white. His image wavered, rippled, reformed . . . darkened. Blond hair and blue eyes turned brown; his face grew ruddy, beard lengthened and thickened. And he was Metaxa.

"Thank you for your help, Metaxa. Members of the audience, for my illusion I set myself the task of convincing you from the time you come into this room that Metaxa is Kinnear and Kinnear is Metaxa." She added dryly, "Convincing the murderer is, of course, the work of the Lyhhrt."

Still-life: the man on the couch, Nema, the bowl with its reaching Lyhhrt.

The man's outline wavered, his face and hair paled, his beard dissolved . . . and he said much more sharply, "Administration-my-brother, do you witness?" He looked straight into Nema's eyes, wondering if Killer could see through those blank dark disks, and what he saw.

:Yes, Kinnear. I witness and will so testify.: Over Kinnear's shoulder spidery metal limbs unfolded themselves and hooked, pulling up the small steel workshell of Lyhhrr's official Administrator, who had accomplished two marvels of his own: speaking to Kinnear for the first time, after lying crowded and uncomfortable against hot flesh for two hours.

"Thank God," said Kinnear; his face and chest were running with cold sweat. But the gun was in his hand; while Admin scuttled to drop the lid of a cloisonné vase over the bucket, he shot three darts into Nema's neck.

Admin grabbed the bucket as Nema jumped up in a

convulsive whirl, gave a single shriek, and crumpled.

Kinnear addressed that T-screen. "All right, Comm-Unit, cut the video and ring committee. And Admin—will you get this goddamn knife out of me before I split open?

A Lyhhrt could not laugh. But it tried. *:Take it out yourself, Kinnear. It is barely cutting your skin.:*

In the Committee Room the T-screen buzzer sounded, and everyone jumped.

The door slammed open. Metaxa rushed into his apartment and stopped short. "You said she wouldn't be hurt!"

"She wasn't hurt," said Kinnear, and sighed. "No harm. She got three darts—a tranquilizer for her, and two to paralyze the Lyhhrt, they won't have any effect on her. We made up four of them."

Metaxa fell to his knees beside Nema. She lay curled up, her breath came in whimpers. Her gown was tangled about her waist; he pulled the bodice up over her back and breast, the skirt over the plastic covering of her diaper. The look on his face was something to turn away from.

Kinnear, drained, raised his eyes to the red shape in the doorway. It was Khreng, planted square, the whack of his tail keeping all comers at bay.

"Where's Prandra? What's happened?"

"Nothing," Khreng said. "She is gone back to quarters to sleep, what do you think? She leaves a message: Tell Kinnear he is a brave man."

"Brave? Anything and everything could have gone wrong. I was half crazy with fear."

"That has nothing to do with bravery! I think," Khreng considered for two seconds, "you are maybe even as brave as I am."

Ambling back to quarters, Khreng paused at the

open door of the deserted examination room, where a
blaze of reflected light caught his eye. One chair was
still taken by an empty workshell, brought by the four
Lyhhrt to sit in while its usual inhabitant was occupied
elsewhere.

:Well, Prandra, are you satisfied with your status?: Chatterjee asked.

"It is good to be class-one," Prandra said quietly. "It
remains to be seen whether I become first class."

*:Yamashita would also have been your friend one day,
if . . .:*

"I know. Now I know we have friends here, and we
can say good-bye to Espinoza, through you."

A committee had formed in the lobby of Administra-
tion-Quarters: Kinnear, Sheedy, two Lyhhrt, and Chatterjee. Wyaerl, bubbling quietly, was there too because
he was leaving for his world with Khreng and Prandra.

Khreng wrestled the chain of the gold star over his
head, untangling it from ears and whiskers. "Kinnear,
I thank you for the use of this beautiful artifact, but a
gold star does not make me a big man on Ungruwarkh."

"I'll want to know how you're getting on," Kinnear
said. He seemed to be trying to find something else to
say, and failing.

:We will get on beautifully!: Wyaerl's mission had suc-
ceeded and he was filled with happiness. *:Although you
may find it somewhat boring on my poor world—:*

"Good!"

*:—where we hunt the eggs of the plaak or lie about at the
edge of the waters and sleep—:*

"That's exactly what we like to do," said Prandra.

*:—and occasionally the drug-runners have a fight and kill
each other, but otherwise—:*

"Your world is the marvel of creation!" Khreng
rumbled. "It is on the way home to ours."

IN THE BLOOD
Glenn Chang

Glenn Chang, born and raised in Hawaii, took his bachelor's and master's degrees in chemistry at Northwestern University, "with dreams," he says, "of becoming a famous scientist." He had dreams also of being a writer—he sold his first story in 1969, when he was eighteen, and sold another to Terry Carr's Universe *series in 1973—but, he reports, "somehow school kept getting in the way." From 1973 to 1976 he did graduate work in chemistry, but then decided to take a year off from school to concentrate on writing. This suspenseful and intense novella is the first product of that year; Chang has since written a novel and has several other projects under way, so he may never see the inside of a classroom again. He lives currently in Eugene, Oregon.*

SOME THINGS never change. Rivers still run downhill to the sea, salmon come upstream to spawn and die, the scents of spruce, pine, and fir still pervade the crispness of the mountain air. When I got the cable from Jock that the old man was dead, I wanted to retreat back up into the woods, above the stink of the metalloy and electronic-component plants, and never come out. It was Jock who convinced me otherwise, appealing to my sometimes-inflated sense of self-worth. A dirty trick, but one that always worked, and he knew it.

That first night we camped near the foot of the Middle Sister, near a pretty rockbed stream in a sudden clearing of the trees. We were up near the timberline, and from our vantage point we could look down over the expanse of green forest to the barely discernible Willamette Valley and its smoky haze, beyond it to the shadows of the coastal mountain range, to either side and behind us at the icy peaks of the Cascades. While Jock pitched camp I walked upstream and found a small pool, where I caught four fair-sized trout and several exhausted salmon—females heavy with eggs, males gaunt-formed, all already too hook-jawed for good eating anyway. Those I threw back. The rainbows I kept.

Jock had a fire going by the time I returned. We stuffed the fish with wild herbs, onions, some asparagus; I made some coffee and we grilled the fish and ate. It was all delicious. By the time we emptied the second pot of coffee, the cool mountain air had a distinct bite to it, and the setting sunlight cast our shadows behind us against the granite outcropping, long and hulking.

"Still pretty up here," Jock said. He played idly with his empty cup, bouncing it against the stump of his left wrist, his bald head glistening with the reddish-pink hue of the sunset. You'd never know we'd been cloned from the same host—I still have all my hair left, still manage to keep in fair shape living up here in the Northwest mountains—but then Jock had been the first, a dull dozen years before me, his life programmed a lot more rigorously by the old man. And I'd never been a high-energy-physics experimentalist either—nor suffered the shielding-breakdown exposure that had kept Jock shuffling in and out of hospitals the past three years and the surgeons busy removing progressively malignant sections off his left arm the past half decade.

"I guess that's because we're above everything, right?" I nodded in answer. "I thought so," he continued. "Now I see why you stay here. If you're lucky, it'll be like this a long time."

"Wishful thinking," I remarked. "They're fighting tooth and nail right now down there in the Salem legislature over whether the heavy industries will be able to expand out of the Valley. Luckily there's opposition from both the environmentalists *and* the timber industrialists keeping them at bay so far."

"Huh. Strange bedfellows."

"I know. Who knows what'll become of it." I shrugged and looked at Jock. "Maybe I'll join you in Alaska in a few years."

"If I'm alive then." He said it matter-of-factly, like you or I would mention the possibility of rain in the afternoon, but it made me wince.

"Jock, how much hope is there? I mean, did they give you any idea?" Tactless, I know, but when in doubt, forge ahead. "Are they going to be able to take care of you up there?"

"Oho, do I detect regional chauvinism?" Jock laughed, a good-natured, healthy-sounding laugh. "Don't worry, Sparks. They really are civilized. The one boon the Great Pipeline Folly brought was a hefty measure of modernization, even though the Pipeline itself is only wreckage now. I'd be as well cared for there as if I were next door to Cal-Sector Medical. In the settled parts of the state, anyway. Ooops, sorry. Sovereign Territory." He shook his head as if marveling. "Still different country up there. Hard to believe it exists now, but that's why I'm going there."

"To see if it's real."

He nodded. "And easier to get to than, say, Siberia, or the Mongolian steppes. Even my government clearance won't get me past sealed borders." He dropped his cup accidentally, caught it on his stump and twirled it. Involuntarily I winced again. "Think about it. Fifty years ago they were worried about missile strikes and invasions from the Eastern Hemisphere, a whole new world war. Now the Asian borders are closed, no one knows what happened after that first big blowup between the Russians and the Chinese, what's going on today. Here on this side of the world we're on our own." He picked the cup off his wrist and set it carefully next to the glowing fire. "Crazy? Improbable? No more so than the secession of the Islands, the Northwest, the craziness down in the Low Forty-Six—" He stopped abruptly.

"Take it easy, Jock."

"Relax." His voice was suddenly calm. "I'm all right. No tumors in the brain yet. Just thinking out loud." He turned and looked at me intently. "You wondering yet why I decided to come up here with you?"

I played dumb. "What do you mean?"

"Come on. Fifteen years in SanSan, no more than a couple of letters between us, no calls at all. We were hardly close, Sparks. Especially after the blowout you had with the old man that made you leave."

"I never had anything against you, Jock," I said. "It was him. All the way."

"Um." Jock looked away again, over the dark green and the smoky scar of the Valley. "And now?"

"Now?" I thought for a few moments. "Now I can understand why he did what he did. For someone in his position and his temperament, it was the natural thing to do." I fell silent.

"Go on."

I turned and looked at Jock. "I can understand, but I still can't sympathize. He *made* us, expecting us to fulfill all his dreams, be what he wanted—little pieces of himself putting his personal stamp on the world. It doesn't work that way. We all need our own room, no matter what our origin, womb or test tube. You finessed your way out of it, Jock. I couldn't. I'm not that subtle." I stopped again.

"But how do you *feel* about him?" Jock asked.

I hesitated, then: "I loved him," I said. "Despite everything. Even though we nearly killed each other.

Don't ask me to figure it out—haven't been able to, not even now. Somehow—" I fumbled for words. "I needed him in this world, even at a distance, to measure myself against. If love can be that kind of need, then that's it."

"How far does it go, Sparks?"

"How far?" I wasn't sure what he meant. "I mean, he's gone. That's the loss, but we go on, the rest of us, right? We all have our own time soon enough."

"That's the trouble. It wasn't his time yet."

"What are you talking about?"

"It might not have been a natural death. Someone might have planned it."

I felt a melodramatic chill then. "Be right back," I said, went over and got the blankets, brought them back and wrapped one about myself while Jock did the same. It only helped a little.

"Now," I said. "Tell me."

Jock adjusted his spectacles and took a deep breath, exhaled, and began. "SolarCorp was the old man's baby, even after you left and he moved it to the Southwest Sector. He survived the Union Breakup because he held all the energy patents solely; all the rights, too. SolarCorp and Southwest patted each other's back, became synonymous, and thereby became the Americas' most stable state. Naturally he had no shortage of enemies—you know how he was—but he held them off with his typical maze of deals and manipulations. But he had to go sometime. So he made preparations. Supposedly a Grand Design—promises to the other Board members, settlements for the young turks in the company, a whole hierarchy of stock redistributions that would keep them all checked and balanced against each other. And he had the fix in with the company legates and the State regulatory commissions. He was a practical as well as a laboratory genius.

"Trouble is, no one can find this schema he set up.

There was supposedly a copy deposited at the State Hall of Courts, another in his company vaults, a third in his private one. They began a systematic search of his papers twelve hours after his cremation: no will, no final instructions, no results at all. At the moment its only existence is in rumor; the courts pushed through an injunction against litigation of the company for ninety days, but that'll be over in a couple of weeks. Then the barracudas move in. Good-bye SolarCorp, energy supply, stability, Western bastion against the Eastern strongholds."

"That bad."

"They're awful hungry." Jock shook his head. "Someone wants that power, bad enough to hurry up the old man's death and damn the consequences."

"How do you know he was done in?"

"I don't. But remember this: he was a fitness addict, took a lot of long hikes into the desert. And he wasn't that old. His last physical showed he was in extraordinarily good shape."

"Cause of death?"

Jock's mouth grimaced ironically. "Myocardial infarction. Heart attack. Justify *that.*

"Listen. They found him three days' hike out of Lacklund, Arizona. No signs of distress, not even dehydration. His canteen was a quarter full, most of his food intact. No poisons evident, and believe me, they looked. Nothing out of the ordinary in the autopsy."

"But if they couldn't find anything wrong, how can you say—"

"I can't, not without proof. But it was a pretty quick autopsy. Funeral and cremation within the week. A heart attack doesn't ring true, not with him. It had to be something else. The question is what? And who? But—" Jock hesitated, his voice uncertain. "I can't look into it myself. I don't have enough . . ." His voice trailed off.

Time? Energy? I didn't want to hear what he wanted to say. "So in essence," I said quickly, "you want me to look into it."

He flashed me a look of relief and apprehension. "I'm hoping you'll want to go down," he said. "For your sake as well as his. You may not realize how intimately SolarCorp's fortunes are tied to Southwest's. That state is the big buffer against the East. If it takes the fall, Cal and Northwest won't be too far behind."

"There's that," I admitted. I looked upward. Against the dark-violet ceiling of sky swiftly becoming black, the stars began to show themselves.

"So now to save myself—and my little haven—I'm to get back into that world again," I said. "Why me? And just how am I going to accomplish this?"

"You'll find a way. Some things you never forget." Jock's smile faded, and he looked at me seriously. "Maybe the personal stake will give you that extra edge."

"Or an extra blinder."

He shrugged. "Maybe. But for what it's worth—" He leaned slightly closer. "Anna's down there, too."

"Anna?" I felt a knot tighten in my belly and my body tense around it. "She's back? How long? What's she doing?"

"She showed up suddenly three years ago in the old man's office. He put her in Environmental Quality. She's head research analyst now."

"How tidy," I said, trying to relax. "How neat. We all come back together in the end."

"She was always the most like him. Even considering her walkout." Jock paused. "I don't know what she stands to gain from this, if anything. She just might get lost in the shuffle."

"I'll keep her in mind when I look," I said, then belatedly realized what I'd said. The commitment was made. The look on Jock's face showed he knew it too.

"All right." I sighed and wrapped the blanket tighter. "So be it." I leaned back and studied the sprinkle of stars overhead. "So tell me more about your new home in Alaska."

Man is a social animal. They've used that as justification for the creation of cities since the invention of pen and ink. A century ago a man named Mumford showed how they were all talking through their hats, that the cities' unchecked growth was only a manifestation of the machine-myth, and if we didn't get out of that mind-set, we'd all eventually take the fall. Well, of course, not enough people listened, and the man-made wasteland east of the Mississippi sewage line bears mute evidence to his prophecies. The Midland Strip in the center of the continent that the refugees swarmed into is a no-man's-land of roving bands and warlords, a domestic DMZ (who remembers *that* term?). There are border skirmishes with Canada and the Southwest Sector constantly. In the Northwest we're rather shielded from the full force of it, but we have a devilish-enough time holding to this uneasy truce with the California Territory. (The latter seems destined next to suffer Mumford's Syndrome, rest his weary bones. He'd regret not at all being absent from the event. I'm sure.)

As soon as the shuttle touched ground at Phoenix, I saw that the Southwest Sector was having similar problems—not as bad as present-day Cal's, but uneasily reminiscent of it twenty years ago. Picture the San-Fernan-SanDiego complex, a hundreds-kilometer-diameter metalloy/plasteel behemoth, transplanted from the seashore to this unrelenting arid plain under a hot, cloudless sky; that's a mind-bending initial impression. The view from the glassine-topped monorail as you ride to the Sector inspection station brings you closer: here there's no excuse of the polluting overheads being trapped in a valley by the laws of atmosphere dynamics. The killing cover is *there,* an unbroken blanket over Southwest, augmented by the drifting clouds from the Midlands and the East, placed with deliberate care by a myopic urban animal pathologically crawling toward suffocation. Add the signs of decay about the city's edge—idle rail lines askew, the mucker hovels and cardless-citizen habitats in the abandoned conapts, here and there the detritus and waste of their life—and the urban dream becomes a seedy, septic nightmare.

Most of the passengers were State citizens, commuters from local shuttles; I seemed the only out-of-Stater in my car. All about me they displayed the urban symptoms I'd forgotten: lowered brows, hunched shoulders, taut expressions, heads bowed under the pressure of city life. Soon I began feeling that uneasy tension, too.

We coasted in and slowed down among the canyons of the city proper. Fifteen minutes later we came into the enclosed station, a bustling whirligig of rushing people, arriving and departing rails, bright lights, a busy hum of noise that infused the place with false energy.

Most of the passengers passed through the gates with no trouble. As an out-of-Stater I was given the business.

"Stop there, please." The inspector was a big, unsmiling man, with a block-shaped head and granite-surface features. He glanced at the scan of my passport and spoke with quiet authority. "State your name, origin, destination, duration of stay."

Most of what he asked was on the passport, but I restrained myself. "Granville Thurston Lee," I said shortly. "McKenzie Pass Collective, Oregon, Northwest Sector. Phoenix, Leetown, Lacklund. Duration unknown."

I saw the inspector's eyes look to the scan again and

read my name more carefully. He turned back to me, his expression one of appraisal and mild hostility.

"What is the purpose of your visit, Mr. Lee?"

"Business and pleasure. Seeing to my father's estate. Relaxing a bit at Lacklund."

"Your occupation?"

"None."

He didn't like that one. The veil came off his expression and his face became stonier.

"We frown on vagrants in this state, Mr. Lee. There are enough antisocial elements on the outside. We don't need them here."

Then you should weed them out, starting with you, I thought. Aloud I said, "I've stated my business. That should be sufficient. I won't be a burden on your state."

"That's easy to say, Mr. Lee. However, we must see visible means of support for any transients or immigrants."

I reached into my briefcase, pulled out my ace in the hole, and placed it in the scanner. "This should be sufficient," I said.

He looked again at the scanner and his eyes widened.

"That's an unlimited travel visa," I said. "Nonrenewable, nontransferable, coded to my genotype, granting me full immunity. The Southwest Sector still honors the Union Accord, does it not? After all, it's written in your charter."

The inspector stammered slightly. "I've never—"

"No, you've probably never seen one. There are only eight of these around. The Lee family has four. Your scanners are automatically coded to make genotype ID upon presentation of this." I placed my right palm down on the auxiliary screen of the scanner. Thirty seconds later the screen glowed green about my hand.

"*Voilà.* I pass." I took my hand away. "Would you like to check my credit rating with the State bank?"

The inspector's face seemed to sag, then froze as he brought himself under control. "That won't be necessary," he said stiffly. "You may proceed."

"Thank you so much." I nodded curtly and moved past the detectors.

"Thank you, *Mr. Lee.*"

The tone of his voice made me glance back, and what I saw made me pause. The mask had slipped again, and the inspector regarded me for an instant with pure, utter hatred.

I turned around again and strode with somewhat forced briskness into the cavernous kiosk beyond and toward public transportation.

It could not have been for me alone. Some irritation, perhaps, but not the depth of feeling I'd just seen. The only other thing was my name.

In other words, Andrew Tsing-Hao Lee, corporate and planning and scientific genius, creator of Solar-Corp, savior of Southwest Sector and in essence of the best that remained of the old United States of America, was not universally loved as befitted such a person here in his own territory, if the reaction of my friend the inspector was typical.

Which led to two immediate ramifications: if he had been murdered, the hypothetical number of suspects was most likely much higher. And there would be a proportionately higher number of ways it could have been done.

Despite this, on some weird level I welcomed the intrigue. So things were different from what I'd been led to believe. Well, if nothing else, I'd find out why.

In 1992 the crisis of crises we'd been living in for several decades came to a head. Runaway inflation and unchecked Keynesian practice brought Western Europe to economic collapse. Rabid nationalism did the same to the African continent. With the United States practicing a strict hands-off policy, the newly rich Asian and Arab countries picked up the foreign-aid baton, but quickly found it a much harder task to save the world than to regard it as a customer. The crunch in hydrocarbons, minerals, and agricultural feedstocks, coupled with another drought cycle, threw the world's order out of kilter, beyond the help of even the South American magnates. Nations began to withdraw into themselves, trying to patch up their tattered homes. Then in the fall of that year the Russo-Chinese War began.

In the musical chairs of diplomacy the Chinese had maneuvered themselves into favorable position with the world, and the Russians had become odd bear out. Within two months they found themselves trapped in a two-front war, their worst fears confirmed. That was when the borders shut down—the Russians to hide their losses, the Chinese because now they didn't need anyone else to help them take care of their old enemy. Half of the world was a closed arena.

As if taking a cue, the big breakup on the domestic front began: the Hawaiian and Caribbean Islands seceded in 1998, Alaska at the millennium, the Northwest a year later. It was like a thread unraveling the whole fabric; our world-views shrank down to the boundaries of our various Sectors.

Out of the confusion rose Andrew Lee (Anglicized upon his childhood immigration from Li). Before the War he'd been a research associate at Cal Institute in organometallics, then biophysics; when government funds dried up he saw the writing on the wall and sold his talents to the top international chemical firm. He didn't languish in his tenure there; the Lee filter-mask and the cyborg-eye are only two of his accomplishments (sole patent-holder, too; how he got the firm to agree to that is a mystery). Sometime in that period he began dabbling in the private wing of the laboratories, and thus Jock was born. The old man was nothing if not versatile.

This being in flagrant violation of company policy and the long-standing International Human-Genetic Tampering Ban, the company was pressured into letting him go. That was the first incentive. With his patent dividends he put up the front money for his own company, SolarCorp, originally a concern based on house-by-house power supplies run on sunlight, made possible by innovative application of his earlier organo-metallic work. Profits and growth came steadily; when the War broke out he was in the middle of negotiations with the government to underwrite his ambitious plan for orbiting solar-power satellites. The plummeting market queered that plan, and the government backed away. That was the second incentive. He pulled in SolarCorp's overseas tentacles and established his domestic power base in the Sunbelt. Here the unrelenting sun fed and nurtured SolarCorp, keeping its domain intact while everything else about it slowly degenerated.

For him it was a fitting personal revenge. For those around him it should have been occasion for gratitude. Why wasn't it?

"Perhaps you don't realize the extent of the power your father had here, Mr. Lee." Stavros P. Kostakis said the word "father" without a pause. "Essentially he made Southwest what it is today. Leetown is the hub about which this State revolves. Andrew Lee's word was law here, and pretty well incontrovertible by any means. Human psychology being what it is, people naturally resent such an overriding presence in their lives, no matter how benevolent it may seem. After all, feudalism is dead; at least, we like to think so. To encounter it in any form is not a pleasant experience for most people."

"That may be true, Mr. Kostakis. Somehow, though, I get the feeling that's not the whole story."

Kostakis gave an elegant shrug and reached for the gold cigarette case on the desk. He opened it, proffered the joints inside toward me, which I refused—Kona Nonpareils, which you can't get anymore—took one himself and lit up. I fidgeted in the calfskin-upholstered chair on the other side of the oak desk from him while he took several tokes. He was a slender, narrow-faced man, seemingly frail and sitting-room soft until one saw his appraising eyes and calculated movements. The Phoenix SolarCorp director was totally in command here in his plush office, a perfect little homeostatic world at far remove from the city's choking squalor.

"The question of its being the whole story is rather moot," he said at last. "Affairs such as this are always more complex than we like. The real question is what you're looking for here. I cannot imagine someone like you coming out of the defile of the Northwest merely to pay tardy respects."

"You're being very direct," I said.

"I find it the best policy." Kostakis smiled faintly. "People tell me they find it a refreshing change of pace."

"Then I'll reply in kind," I said. "Circumstances lead me to believe Andrew Lee's death was not a natural one."

"Ah." Kostakis sat back in his chair and regarded me levelly. "And you have taken it upon yourself to investigate." He reached for the joint resting in the ashtray, took a last puff, pinched it out, then looked at me again. "Am I to take it, then, that you're doing this out of a sense of filial duty?" He steepled his hands in front of him. His gaze didn't waver.

"In part," I said. "As you say, things are always complex."

"I'm glad to hear that, at least. I wouldn't have trusted an unqualified yes." He placed both hands on the table and leaned slightly forward. "On the other hand, *your* presence is a bit of a surprise. We expected the older one."

"The older one?" I stiffened in indignation. "What are you, a clandestine psychoanalyst? You think you can categorize us so easily?"

"Please. No misunderstandings." He held up a hand. "Andrew Lee has been the cornerstone of Southwest for a long time. He left a considerable legacy, almost a crucial one, the administration of which is certain to be extremely complicated. Anyone bound to be involved in it has been thoroughly investigated as a precaution. Considering the deceased Mr. Lee's position, and the potential of what he left, any possible heir would be a fool to pass up this opportunity—or else exceedingly satisfied with his own station, for some unfathomable reason." He smiled faintly. "That's why we expected the other male heir and not you."

"Well, you have me now." I was not mollified. "For better or worse."

"Yes, I realize that." His smile gave way to a reflective expression. "I'm aware of your situation—your past—and perhaps of several of your motives. But you do present a problem."

"Oh?"

Kostakis nodded. "We have our own suspicions regarding Andrew Lee's demise."

"I see," I said after several seconds. "You're investigating, too."

"Or trying to." His mouth twisted in irritation. "Cleaning one's own house is difficult. Especially when—I'll be frank, Mr. Lee." He leaned back again. "Phoenix and Leetown have always been in contention.

My position is as insecure as anyone else's in the company now. In several Board meetings portions of Andrew Lee's plans were outlined. In them I was well provided for. The minutes of these meetings are now missing. Thus there are no records at all, of any kind, of his plans." The smile returned. "You see: motives again."

"And now you're afraid I'll get in the way? Queer your own investigation?"

"You *are* an unknown factor," he said. "Theodore Lee was predictable. The other heir, Anna, made it convenient for us by being on the premises. Our sources made it clear that you were not at all interested in the welfare of the family business." He spread his hands. "Yet here you are. What exactly are you planning to do?"

"I'm not unversed in the arts of investigation."

"I'm aware of that. I'm also aware your last duties as professional ombudsman were completed twenty years ago. The world was much different then. There are factors to take into consideration here in Southwest."

"You mean the game might be too rough for me."

"It might be too rough for all of us. Someone is planning to make him or herself the master of the biggest game in town, to use a vulgar phrase, and is willing to risk chaos to get there. Against such a person, or persons, a sense of duty might not be enough."

"Then you'll help me when I need it, won't you?" I asked.

Kostakis regarded me steadily for several seconds. He blinked once and sighed, then folded his hands together in front of him

"So be it," he said, his voice resigned. "I can't very well deport you, not with your diplomatic visa. I sincerely hope you don't make things too messy here."

"Don't worry. I deplore loose ends as much as you do."

"Good." He looked suddenly grim and hard. "Let's hope we don't get in each other's way."

"Granted." I leaned forward. "Now. I need some information."

Beyond the Phoenix complex the Southwest desert asserted itself with abrupt emphasis: burnt-ocher expanses, the occasional patch of darker reddish-brown iron-rich soil, or the rarer green-and-brown of scrub brush, steadfastly soaking up the sun's heat. From my vantage point high above in the shuttle, I couldn't see anything of the Lee converters supposedly blanketing the State beyond the tiny glints off the reflecting met-alloy pinpoints. Once we passed over a lonely concrete dome, isolated in a shallow canyon. I asked the passenger next to me what it was. "Old breeder reactor," he said. "Abandoned." That was all I got out of him the whole trip.

The meeting with Kostakis had been heartening. Despite his overly fastidious nature, I felt I had at least one ally here. (No, Anna didn't count. Not yet.) I had a hunch for an out-of-Stater here it was a necessity.

We dropped into approach to Leetown after two hours' flight time. If Phoenix was the urban nightmare, Leetown was the Machine carried to its ultimate absurdity. Huge, glittering, antiseptic, it sat in the middle of nowhere, incongruous as a unicorn in a garden or a sofa in a jungle. By the time the shuttle settled into its resting pod and we disembarked, I had a one-word description for the city: Automaton. Everything was taken care of by servos, robots, waldoes, and holos; I didn't see a single human being outside of the other shuttle passengers until I reached the rail terminal. Even then it was little solace; not a word was proffered, not a look past a cursory inspection was directed toward me as the bullet-shaped rail hurled itself silently on its magnetic-induction track toward Lee-town Central. Nor was it different in the elevator-cars bearing me upward in the arcology to the executive levels of SolarCorp. The Machine had conquered. I actually found the experience of battling through the batteries of flak-catchers to get to the Board members a relief.

That feeling quickly died. The six members of the Executive Board of SolarCorp obviously lived in an orchestration of suspicion, backbiting, conniving, petty jealousies, and not a little fear. Nelson Carrera was a short, corpulent, fat-jowled man who made insinuations about his fellow Board members, but quailed at the prospect of coming forth and naming names. Celeste LaFollette didn't bother: she remained cool and Sphinxlike behind her chiseled-ivory face and green eyes, neatly sidestepping my questions with ease. Malcolm J. Reuters, in contrast, was quite vocal—a red-faced, blustering buffoon who made specific accusations and did name the culprits, but threatened to throw me out of his office when I suggested that he wasn't doing much to remedy the situation.

Those were the only ones I was able to contact the first day. That was enough. Yet something disturbed me, something underlying all their sham and evasiveness, and I felt a need to air it out with Kostakis.

"That's a disturbing possibility, yes. We had considered that in light of the—ah—lack of cooperation we've had from them." Kostakis' ascetic face on the vidphone screen showed his concern.

"But if our hypothetical mystery man has gotten to them, what incentive would he use?" I asked. "These people are rather venal, and culpable as hell, but with what they have at stake I hardly think they can be bought off."

"True," Kostakis said reflectively. "Unless the price is something they value more than their futures with SolarCorp."

"What—" I began, then stopped. "Oh." Kostakis nodded in affirmation.

"Well," I said slowly, "the next question, I guess, is who. One of them?" I thought. "They all have motives. But would any of them be willing to play for mortal stakes?" I looked at Kostakis speculatively. "Someone outside that inner circle?"

Kostakis narrowed his eyes slightly. "I don't—" Then he got the point. The face became severe and uncompromising.

"All right, all right," I said quickly. "But you realize I have to consider all possibilities."

"True. But I do not have to like it." His expression didn't change. "Phoenix and Leetown have always been in vigorous contention and at far remove from each other in policies and business attitudes."

"You mean ethics?"

He shrugged off the gibe. "Andrew Lee was a hard-driving man—even, at times, a tyrant—but he was eminently fair. He was contemptuous of those who were mere sycophants."

"Okay, I apologize." I paused. "Describe your investigation so far to me."

The security organization in Phoenix had conducted interviews with the Board members, run through the logs on the monitors perpetually keeping them and Andrew Lee under surveillance wherever they were in the State, and thoroughly investigated whoever came in contact with them. In Phoenix and Leetown it was fairly easy: electronic surveillance was *de rigeur* literally everywhere in those two urban complexes. At Lacklund there was none, at the old man's insistence—yet all incoming and outgoing traffic was carefully checked.

All this, though, had turned up nothing unusual or out of the ordinary—not even the activities of the Board members after the old man's death and up to this point.

I sat a moment and thought after Kostakis told me this. "I'm wondering," I said. "Electronic records can be doctored. Given the right equipment, enough time . . ."

"Expensive. And a lot of trouble. Communication lines in Southwest have a modulated 'watchdog' beam. The codes and frequencies are classified top security. There are different sets for surveillance monitors."

"But once our friend got these codes, he could go back and fix everything, could he not?"

"Conceivable. Except he would have to know what he was looking for. Trying to get them by random sampling . . ." He shrugged.

"Which most likely means an inside job," I said.

He nodded.

"Back to square one," I sighed, and sat back in the molded-plasteel chair before the vidphone and looked around at my room. Typical Leetown decor: hypermodern-motif furniture, looking like the inside of a shuttle cockpit; curved viewing-wall which I kept opaqued (the only thing outside were the other metalloy silos of this hotel complex); doors to the other rooms irised shut, the comfort-robos resting in their niches in the walls beside them.

I turned back to the vidphone. "All right," I said. "I'd like a list of those people he saw, records of all calls and meetings—transcripts, if possible—maybe a complete log of his activities. Say, beginning two weeks previous to his—" I faltered slightly. "To the end."

Kostakis smiled faintly. "You are somewhat retracing our steps, you know."

I shrugged. "Maybe something was missed. Besides, there's an unknown factor involved this time, isn't there?"

"True," he conceded. "You may have an advantage." He seemed to ponder something. "Unless our friend is keeping busy with his toys."

I looked at him for a moment. "You mean he may be on to me already."

"Once one is able to tamper with the communications lines at will—" His eyebrows lifted slightly in emphasis.

"Well, I'll take that chance."

"So be it." He glanced to the side. "I can send your information over the fax-wire. Better take it in printout rather than storage."

"All right," I said.

"You're staying at Olympus Tower?"

"Right. Thirty-one-oh-one." I paused. "A lovely room."

He smiled again. "Too bad. Sixty floors higher you would have an impressive view of the desert at sunset. And the arcology outskirts, of course."

"I'm green with envy."

The smile grew wider, then his face became serious. "Good hunting, Mr. Lee," he said, nodded curtly, then faded away to the gray blankness of the dead screen.

"Thanks," I told it, and killed the line on my end. I stared about at the interior of my burnished-metalloy-and-molded-plasteel suite. "You and me," I said, then sat back and waited.

Ten minutes later the soft *ping* from the fax-wire console warned of incoming information. I got up and punched "Printout" on the keyboard. Another thirty seconds, then the console chattered angrily; the printout sheets slid out and accumulated into a neat pile in the collector.

I gathered them up, settled as best I could in what passed for the room's lounge-chair, and began going through them.

Kostakis had provided the old man's daily schedules for the denoted two-week period, along with the logs and transcripts I'd requested. It soon became apparent that keeping track of him had been a hectic and exasperating task. His appointment schedule showed him to be a busy man, his surveillance transcripts made him look even busier. And somehow in that period he still found the time every fourth day, like clockwork, to journey to Lacklund for a day or day-and-a-half outing into the desert, with one secretary, one security guard—and Anna.

Anna, Anna. What was it—had he been grooming her as his successor? How close had they become before the end? Was the reconciliation complete? ("The most like the old man," Jock had said. Was he right?)

I put the printouts aside, got up and walked the perimeter of the room, several times. I was suddenly restless, couldn't stay inside room 3101 anymore. Quickly I changed, got a light coat, palmed the room circuits to low, and stepped out into the hall, coding the door to my genotype as it irised closed.

It must have been dinnertime: I passed people on the pedwalks and rode with them on the induction elevators, all dressed in evening wear. Very few of them looked like out-of-staters; the majority wore the muted colors and conservative cut of tunic and pantaloons favored by those in SolarCorp's employ. Even the foreign expatriates—a few Pakistanis, some Nigerians speaking their foreign language in low tones, here and there an obvious Slavic refugee—sported the emblem of The Company on his or her tunic. A business town through and through.

Presently I spotted the chronometers inlaid in the walls, high up, and saw my estimation of the time was right. I wasn't hungry myself. Not for food. I kept walking, on some purposeful search.

Thirty-one floors down, ground zero was a busy thoroughfare, though the shops and robo-vendors were still. People were on their way in, out, up, down. I dropped two more floors, then five, then ten; the halls became dingier, some lighting cases broken and vandalized and rubbish was heaped in corners. People of poorer status were here: their looks more furtive, clothing more worn, appearances unkempt. A faint smell of something like decay came to me; here and there I saw several people hunched in shadowy corners, on the nod, occasionally some shoving or yelling matches in the corridors I had to walk around. On Minus Nineteenth I began to feel the thrum of the arcology's steam generators through the metalloy floor, getting stronger as I descended further. On Minus Twenty-Fifth a one-armed beggar in an oversized tunic barred my passage. "Hey, good-looking. Want thrill, twenty cc's, prime? No cuts." He held up a sealed ampule with the pale-green liquid in it, shook it so the contents sloshed. I shook my head. "Don't trust it? Come on. The real thing, from outside, snuck in past the detectors. Good scope, bo, no lie." He grabbed my arm suddenly, the ampule magically palmed and hidden somewhere. "What's the scam? Saving this meat for hawks?" I pushed him away; he fell back and laughed raucously. I moved toward him and he melted into the shadows and was gone, leaving only his laughter and obscenities.

Suddenly I felt oppressed, unable to breathe. I walked as fast as I could to the nearest induction-elevator and rode it in express-mode up past ground zero, above Plus Thirty-One, my ears feeling the changing pressure faster than the elevator's manostats could compensate. I watched the numbers flicker on the CRT indicator—47, 58, 63, 79—then take longer to change as the car slowed. Finally it stopped at 104; the doors opened and I stepped out.

The floor was clear plasteel. I was on a giant balcony, unlit from above, but illuminated from below by the myriad pilot-lights of the maintenance systems for the lower arcology units. Looking to each side I could see no details, only small clusters of colored lights: the shingles of professionals.

"Stop a minute, friend. You look tired." The

woman's voice was sympathetic, her face partly obscured as she leaned against the partition. I could see
enough to tell she was attractive and had gray eyes.

"I am," I said, and leaned against the partition next
to her. Ahead and behind me the lights stretched like
old-time streetlamps; I could hear muffled murmurs,
a sudden moan, now and then an outburst of laughter.

"Pretty big service station," I remarked. "Not much
privacy, though."

She shrugged. "Something wrong with the fields tonight. You don't hear anything inside."

"Funny."

"Um. I can't explain it." I saw her smile. "I can give
you the hard-sell, the come-on, the tease—or just the
straight list of goods. Take your pick."

"Don't know yet. Just exploring."

"Ah. New in town?" I nodded in answer. "Where
from?"

"Out of state. Northwest Sector."

"Really." Her eyes widened in interest. "A friend of
mine moved there. Never wrote or called, the trollop.
They have service stations in Northwest?"

"In the Valley. I don't get in the Valley much." I
glanced around, then back to her. "I just took a walk
below ground zero. Down to Twenty-Five. Nice."

She shook her head. "You don't want to go down
there. Nothing good below. Only bad characters, bad
acts."

"How did something like that come up in Leetown?"

She sighed. "In this great city of ours, you can get
anything you want if you try hard enough. Even
mucked up." She spread her hands. "Laws of the city.
It's inevitable."

"Yes," I said. "Mumford's Syndrome."

"Mumford, uh-huh." She nodded. "He said it well."

"You know his work?"

"Some. I'm a book-*amateur*." She gave the word a

French accent. Then, with a sudden smile: "In others, though, I'm a pretty good pro."

"Ah." I looked at her, felt myself relax. "The price proportionate with the level?"

"Afraid so. We're the highest station in Leetown, except for the penthouse guild, but they're a special class. You do get your credits' worth, though."

"We'll see about that," I said. "What's your name?"

"Celeste. And yours?"

"Just call me Sparks." I touched her face with my fingers. "Celeste. I just met a Celeste." I looked more closely. "The eyes are wrong, though."

She laughed and stepped back into her space. "Great," she said. "Tell me what else is wrong about me." She stopped and beckoned me inside.

I glanced around at the lights, upward at the opaque ceiling. "Tomorrow," I said softly. Then I went in.

SolarCorp, Environmental Quality, was a subordinate department of R & D. It was housed in its own wing in the latter's complex, their supposedly crusading staff protected by a formidable staff of secretaries.

"Anna Lee is not available at the moment. Perhaps if you called back in an hour." A Ms. Hodkinson gave me that in smooth delivery—very trim, very black, very alert.

"Could you tell me where she is?" I asked.

Hodkinson looked slightly offended. "Who is calling, please?"

"Oh, no one special. Only her brother. Granville Lee."

Hodkinson blinked and her mouth twitched a bit, but otherwise she maintained admirable control. "She's in scenario," she said slowly. "It's a closed session."

"I understand," I said. "An hour, you say?"

"Most likely." She glanced at the chronometer. "They're half-day sessions."

"Fine. I'll wait." I walked over and took a seat against

the far wall. This was the fourth office I'd come to since the front door. An improvement, though: large potted cacti and an impressive specimen of the unkillable dieffenbachia were in the corners, several tasteful airbrush desert scenes were on the walls.

Hodkinson gave me several sharp looks as she shuffled things about on her desk. I nodded and smiled whenever our eyes met.

One hour and ten minutes later, the door behind Hodkinson opened and people began filing out, still talking, some laughing as if at a joke. In the middle of the bunch I recognized Anna. I stood and took several steps toward them.

She was talking to someone, and as she finished saying her piece her eyes drifted in my direction. They widened, blinked several times, and an expression more like shock than surprise came over her face. It lasted only a fraction of a second; then she was smiling and striding toward me.

"Sparks! How've you been?" We hugged briefly and stepped back.

"Fine, Anna," I said. "And you?"

"Great. Well, as best as can be expected," she amended, with a little shrug. "What with the confusion in the company these days." Her eyes regarded me with a calculating look.

"Yes," I said. "I know what happened."

She nodded. "That's why you're down?" I returned her nod. "Paying last respects, or . . ."

"Listen," I said. "Got some free time?"

"Sure. We're breaking for lunch." She went back to several others who hadn't drifted off yet, spent a few seconds in low-voiced conversation, then came back to me.

"Come on. Let's go. My treat," she said, laying her hand on my arm.

"All right," I said. "Talked me into it."

"I came back about two and a half years ago. Got out of Caracas just before the oil-field explosions and they declared martial law." She stopped and attacked the shrimp salad for a few seconds. "Luckily Dad was in a forgive-and-forget mood when I showed up. Plus he knew I was good at what I did—just like him." She grinned. "So here I am, top of the heap in EQ."

"No cries of nepotism?" I asked.

She shook her head. "Uh-uh. I had to work for it."

Desert life seemed to agree with her. The frailness and insecurity had given way to a sun-baked hardness, an energetic durability. The old man had experimented a lot more in her case than ours—altering that last pair of chromosomes is the trickiest part—but the essence of Andrew Lee was there in her. The animated way she talked and moved, that wide-shouldered lanky body, the eyes always watching you, judging, measuring—she was the old man's, all right.

"So what kind of work does EQ have to do in a solar-powered society?" I asked.

"A lot. We're geared a lot higher than Northwest. After a certain point, environmental concerns become significant no matter what your power source. In our case it's the fundamental limit on amorphous-silicon-cell efficiency that dictates life here. Our power needs are very high; that means a lot of cells for every purpose. The process is cheap, but the scale-up in manufacture brings in all the old problems: land use and conservation, stack and effluent waste, water and hydrogen consumption, and so on." She nodded once. "We keep busy."

"Being watchdogs, you mean?"

"No, we make ourselves known earlier than that. We get in on the planning stage." She paused. "It's a bit tricky. Southwest still isn't quite the steady-state no-growth society Dad envisioned, probably won't ever be. Maybe people don't work that way. Consequently we still have to reconcile whatever growth we do experience with whatever there is out there."

"Out there?"

"The non-city dwellers. The Indian tribes and communities still around. The loners out on the desert, in the mountains—" Her face took on a determined look. "It can be done. We can coexist with little trouble if we work at it."

I studied her for a moment. "That's a change from your original hard-line stand," I said.

"It's the synthesis stage of the dialectic," she said, and grinned again. "I do my best to set an example. Like Dad. We were actually pretty close before—" Her face sobered. "Up till the end."

"Another surprise," I said lightly.

"Everybody changes. We have to." Her eyes looked away.

"I know," I said. "Sorry. Excuse me."

She looked back. "That's okay," she said. "How would you know? It's been so long."

"It has," I agreed. Then: "You're still beautiful," I said, and immediately wished I hadn't.

For an instant the new-Anna veneer slipped, and there she was again, vulnerable and vaguely afraid, the one I'd known and yet not known in that dead past. Only an instant—then the new Anna reasserted herself, and once more we were two just-met people getting to know each other.

"Well. Enough of that." She forced a smile, leaned back in her seat and folded her hands in her lap. "I've been dominating this conversation, Sparks. Tell me about yourself. And Jock."

"Not much to say," I said. "Life in Northwest is pretty stable." I told her about Jock's trip, daily life in the cooperative, the ills of Valley life, my impressions of Phoenix and Leetown.

Eventually I got to the purpose of my visit.

"It was unexpected," she agreed. Her mouth set in concentration. "Dad was pretty fit—more so than I was that day."

"You stayed in Lacklund?" I asked.

"Until I felt better. I don't know what caused my dizziness—probably dehydration and exhaustion. I'd just come back from a field trip upstate the day before. I was back in Leetown when I got the news." She gave me that frank look again. "I guess I was the last one to see him alive."

"That we know of, anyway," I said. "What do you think?"

"About the cause?" Her brow furrowed. "I don't know. The autopsy couldn't find anything. Yet somehow heart failure just doesn't scan." Her mouth twisted in irritation. "It was a pretty cursory autopsy, though."

"That and the cremation came by unanimous Board vote?"

She nodded. "He certainly owed his soul to the company store."

"If you were close as you say you were," I said, "you must be the only one." I told her of the Board members I'd talked to. "The other three are probably of the same ilk. Not much help for me. You have any ideas if one of them might be a likely suspect?"

She shook her head slowly. "They all had it in for Dad. They and a lot of others." She looked at me directly. "We're cursed with a wealth of suspects." Her look became one of curiosity. "You're really set on finding out, aren't you?"

I made a slight shrug and didn't say anything.

She nodded as if my non-answer explained everything. "Of course," she said. "It all comes around in the end, doesn't it?" She *tsk*-ed softly.

"This master plan of his," I said. "Did he mention anything about it to you?"

"A little. He kept talking about what would happen

when he was gone, who would take over, what direction the company and Southwest would take—ah, no. What *should* happen, what they *should* do." She gestured. "You know what he was like."

"Anything about you in particular?"

She hesitated. "I think he was leading up to making me the one to take over, but he didn't quite say it. I don't know why. I couldn't be that type of boss. Maybe his familial sense of duty finally got in the way of his logic, though it's hard to believe."

"Maybe not so hard," I said. She shrugged at that. "But you never saw anything in writing, in storage?"

"Nothing." She shook her head.

"Would they keep you on if the company went public?"

"Depends who has the final say." She grimaced. "There are a lot of people aiming for the top who don't like the name Lee."

"Including your esteemed Board members," I said. "Which I still can't understand. They're in perfect position to take over the reins. But nobody is. Business goes on as usual and no action's being taken. As if someone's telling them not to move."

"I don't know about things higher up. Our department practically runs itself. We don't run into the administrators too often outside of the yearly reviews."

"It doesn't sound right," I went on. "They're the ones who stand to lose the most by inaction. Is there someone behind them? Cowing them? Forcing them to stay their hand?"

She shook her head. "I don't know," she said again.

"Well," I said irritably, "we have to start somewhere." I stabbed at the remainder of my sandwich in silence for a couple of minutes.

"Maybe we shouldn't worry about it," Anna said at last. "I mean, he's gone. SolarCorp is too big to be dependent on just one man; he held the reins mostly by inertia anyway. It's outgrown him. Maybe this shake-up will do the company *and* the state a lot of good."

I put my knife and fork down carefully. "You really think so?" I asked.

"I'm saying it's possible. There would be new faces, new blood, a change. Where would the Board lead SolarCorp and Southwest? Stodgy, conservative, rigid thinkers, supporters of the status quo. They've been licking Dad's boots for twenty years. There's not an original thought in their heads."

"There are other considerations," I said. "I mean—"

"I know. You are what you are." She smiled faintly. "I'll do what I can to help."

"Thanks," I said. "As long as I don't take you away from your work . . ."

"Of course." She glanced at her watch. "Speaking of which, it's time to go back. How time flies, hey?"

She signaled and the robot-waiter wheeled over, the payslot already extended. Tally and log of the debit was over fifteen seconds after she slipped her card into it. We got up and took the leisure-pedwalk outside— that is, into the clear-plasteel-domed concourse leading back to R&D and EQ.

"Look," she said, pointing. To our left, beyond the edge of the arcology, a purple-tinged mesa stood on the horizon, looking close enough to touch. I squinted and could perceive tiny bright points of light glinting off metal surfaces in the sun.

"A joint Indian community we helped set up," Anna said. "Pimas and Kickapoos. The Kickapoos are more amenable and open to change; they maintain the collectors, the generators, all the survival systems. The Pimas grow the crops, teach the rituals—sort of care-takers of the old way of life."

"Is that common?"

"Not much. Not as much as we'd like the old and new getting along." That determined look was back. "But there's always hope."

We rode the pedwalk in silence after that. At the entrance to the EQ pod I stopped her.

"Think about it," I said. "Anything that might help—who he might have talked to, something he might have mentioned. Some kind of clue."

"All right," she said, nodding. "I'll think hard." Her face had a serious expression, and she looked at me with close scrutiny for several seconds. "I'll see you soon."

"Okay," I said, reached out and touched her face reassuringly, turned and stepped onto the outgoing pedwalk.

Things began happening that night. I'd spent the afternoon trying to chase down the other Board members and had gone one for three: James T. Kirkland was an overweight, overweening, overeducated fop, a black emigré from Cambridge in the wake of the British food-riots of 2009 who'd obviously ridden the coattails of the then-recent Equality Act into his present position, and of the same general cut as Nelson Carrera. Hazel Swansea was unreachable; Philippa Grenoble was out of town. I was rather glumly studying the logs of their movements in the two weeks prior to the old man's death when the ceiling-lights dimmed, brightened back to normal, dimmed and brightened again.

I put down the logs and waited. Somehow it struck me as a kind of signal. Thirty seconds later the fax-wire sounded its soft alarm: a message. I got up and, as a precaution, took it in printout again.

The message was brief. "May have information pertinent to your purpose. Ye Olde Apothecarie, Level Three South, tomorrow 0900. Hazel Swansea."

So there it was, like an act of Providence. I sat and pondered what she had to tell me. Then the vidphone rang.

"There has been an interesting development." Stavros Kostakis was as phlegmatic as ever. "A technician at Leetown R & D has come forth and offered to explain to us how one might bypass the 'watchdog' circuits. You might want to come along."

"Oh? What made him come forth?"

"Personal disgruntlement, I suspect. He dabbles with electronic scenarios on the computers there during his nightshift—technically a violation of regulations—"

"Well, don't hold it against him yet."

Kostakis shrugged. "In any event, he seems to have stumbled onto the semi-random sequence that unlocks the codes, purely by chance. It struck him as an interesting pattern, so he used it as the basis set for one of the stimulation-games he devised to while away the hours." He lifted his eyebrows for emphasis. "About three months ago he tried to call up the subroutine for his game and found it gone—as if someone had come along and wiped it."

"How did he know to come to you?"

"As yet it's only indirectly related to our case. There is a standing order to report all irregularities to the investigative arm of SolarCorp, the central bureau of which is under jurisdiction of my office. Our young friend's reluctance to come forward is obviously explained by his necessarily having to admit his own minor culpability."

"Three months," I said, thinking aloud. "The time's about right. Does he think there's a connection?"

"Who knows? Andrew Lee's death is still a *cause célèbre*. In any event, we are interviewing him in Leetown at oh-nine-thirty tomorrow."

"I have an appointment of my own," I said, and told him of Hazel Swansea's message.

A thoughtful expression came over his face. "That's interesting," he said. "Hazel Swansea was remarkably closemouthed during our initial inquiries. If her opening up now—" The sound crackled, cut off abruptly, and the picture on the screen flickered, became indistinct. "—revelation," Kostakis said.

"What? I can't hear you, Kostakis." I fiddled with the knobs. "Something's wrong with this phone."

I saw a suddenly alert Kostakis mouthing something at me, then the image was fuzzy and run through with lines. None of my efforts did any good. Several seconds later the picture abruptly shrank to a bright dot in the center of the screen, then faded away to nothing.

At the same time I noticed the lights dimming again. This time they didn't get brighter; slowly the room darkened, then was pitch-black.

I felt my way around furniture to the viewing-wall and found the dial alongside its edge. I turned it to full transparency. Nothing happened. The power had been cut off.

Well, that wasn't too bad. I'd been temporarily lost in an underground cave once, and this artificial one at least had known perimeters. I stood still and listened to the silence for a while before I realized what I was not hearing: the near-subliminal muted thrum of the ventilators.

That was bad news. The way these rooms were constructed, that meant all the conduits were shut off; the room was hermetically sealed. I fumbled my way to the bathroom and checked the drains in the sink, bathtub and toilet with running water; in a short while they filled, indicating even these were blocked.

With no power, the doors would not iris open. I was sealed in like meat in a can. In this situation suffocation would only be a matter of time.

I found my way back into the main room and pressed my face against the cool smoothness of the viewing-wall. By squinting I could see through it, very faintly, the lights of the other towers. Nothing in here, I knew, could smash through this plasteel; a conscientious building industry had developed it to withstand any force a human could muster. All in all it was a very neat trap.

I stood plastered against the viewing-wall, trying to keep my breath calm and shallow, when suddenly I heard a loud pop, like the opening of a pressurized container; then it subsided to a low hiss. With sudden elation I took a deep breath: had the air come back on? Did this mean the power would return, too?

Somehow I didn't think so. A warning signal rang in my mind; if someone had gone to all this trouble to shut me in, why would that someone all of a sudden relent?

I moved toward the walls, trying to remember where the ventilating ducts were, stubbing my toes and banging knees against things more than once. High up on the walls, just barely within reach, was the rim of one duct. I dragged a chair over, stepped up on it, and measured the duct's contours with my fingers. The hiss was more audible this close up; I thought I could feel some movement in the air with my fingers, but I couldn't be sure. I brought my face up against it and felt the draft lightly play on my lips; something was coming into the room, all right.

I took another breath, rather tentatively this time. There was no detectable odor. I breathed again, several times. Very curious. What possible motive would this person have for turning the air back on? (By this time there was no doubt this was not an accident.) If he or she wanted me to suffocate in the first place—or could that really be the reason? But what else? I shook my head; the movement caused a dull ache. I was thinking foggily, trying to devise motives, but somehow they wouldn't come to me. I was on the verge of finally formulating one when I slipped and fell off the chair, crashing onto the floor in a limp heap.

I lay unmoving for what seemed like minutes, then it

finally came to me. Something else—not air; gas, odorless, lethal. What? I tried to get up and found it impossible; my limbs wouldn't function properly. Moving my head was only slightly less difficult. It lolled back helplessly, thudding into the floor, and I felt a vague pain from the impact. It seemed to be a giant balloon, kilometers across, floating incredibly far away from the rest of my body on the thin thread of my neck. Drowsily I contemplated what would happen if the thread broke and the balloon floated away, but I could not quite imagine it.

Something told me not to breathe, but it seemed silly. "Why?" I tried to ask myself, but my mouth wouldn't form the word. Through the fog I was dimly aware of my heartbeat: an irregular, arrhythmic thudding of a sped-up drum, *boom da boom da-da boom da*. I couldn't see anything. Why couldn't I see anything? Wouldn't anyone tell me? Was anyone there? Somewhere in front of my eyes I saw an indistinct roseate circle in the darkness. I watched it glow, become cherry-red. Roses, I thought. Springtime. Then it became a soft yellow, getting brighter. Rhododendrons. From yellow to white, and I blinked and squinted against the melting hurtful light. Lilies of the valley. Death. I heard dull booms, louder than my heart, like metal striking metal in an old-time forge.

Suddenly the darkness was gone, and light, safe strong light, was shining in from the hallway onto me. I saw figures like shadow-play silhouettes moving around, toward me. Things fumbled at me, slipped under my arms and helped me to my feet. Hands, I thought. They're giving me hands. Then they were propelling me outside, toward that strong light; someone said, "You'll be all right. Breathe deep, get some air," and I answered, "Air. Yes, I haven't had any for a while," and I gulped it in in great breaths that hit me like ice-cold water does a thirsty man.

"Carbon monoxide. High purity, reagent-grade. That's why you didn't smell anything." Kostakis' face was rather grim and tight-lipped on the screen. "Simple, old-fashioned—and quite clever. Once it combines with the oxygen in you and goes to carbon dioxide, what trace is there of it? Simple suffocation would have been the verdict, once our friend flushed out your room afterward."

"Please," I said. "Let's not be overly morbid. My head is killing me." I leaned back in my chair and tried to ease the throbbing in my temple by rubbing it with my fingertips. It didn't work.

"Be that as it may, it appears we haven't overestimated this adversary." His look didn't change.

"I know," I said. "Thanks for your call." I glanced about at the security guards standing around in the station-house. "I guess I should be grateful for your suspicious character."

Kostakis gestured gracefully. "We do have an interest in keeping you alive, Mr. Lee. To avoid adverse publicity if nothing else."

"Well, thanks," I said. "Anyway, what now? Did you check—?"

"Yes. Or rather, the crews there did." Kostakis inclined his head slightly. "Perhaps you should ask Security Chief DeBray."

I turned toward him. DeBray was a lean, tough-faced man with gray-flecked wiry hair and a coolly efficient manner. He stepped forward a few precise steps and said, "We discovered the ventilating ducts shunted off into the backup-system line. This was isolated from the rest of the hotel's system and connected to an old air duct, abandoned when the Olympus Tower was built, leading to a warehouse down on Minus Two. A jury-rigged connection was made to two cylinders of reagent-grade carbon monoxide, one of which was pressurized to several thousand kilograms per square centimeter, in series." He blinked once, as if in emphasis. "The other was nearly empty."

"No surprise. I suppose you're trying to trace these tanks now."

"As best we can. The ID tags had been pried off. We can do it through the serial numbers on the canisters, but it will take longer: we'll have to go through the manufacturers and distributors, then check their customers' inventory."

"Shouldn't it be relatively easy? How much use does anyone have for that much carbon monoxide?"

"Actually a lot, even these days. Atmosphere research, laboratory use, quite a few industrial processes like exotic heavy-metal-catalyst production. We can do it; it just won't be easy."

I turned back toward Kostakis' image. "Well," I said, "at least we're getting some response, eh?"

"Yes," he said. "Let's hope it doesn't become too lively—or successful. Your presence has proved quite auspicious here in Southwest so far, Mr. Lee." His eyes had that calculating look again. "I'm wondering what other interesting events it will give rise to."

I nodded, but couldn't answer. I was wondering the same thing.

Level Three was one of the small independent business districts—rather a misnomer, since practically everything here could be ultimately traced back to the same source, SolarCorp. The South quadrant was a quiet mall built in what they'd probably thought was the style of the old European commercial thoroughfares. Tucked behind a fountain and flanked by two kinetic sculptures made of thousands of pieces of real glass, Ye Olde Apothecarie stood at the end of a short shrub-lined path like a scene out of an absurd picturebook, awkward and garish in its baroque decor.

Not many people were about. As I passed between

the art-constructs they flashed and tinkled softly in the induced breeze. I ran my hand over the door—real oak, I noticed—reached for the brass knocker, changed my mind and reached for the doorknob. It didn't turn; instead I felt a slight vibration in the door, then it swung easily inward at a gentle push. Electronic lock: obviously antiquarianism wasn't carried to extremes even on Three.

Inside was a sudden shadowy coolness. My eyes adjusted to the darkness and I saw a clutter of bric-a-brac which at first glance might be termed quaint: dusty laboratory flasks, antique retorts and distillation columns, a large ceramic mortar-and-pestle, pewter mugs and measuring cups, ranged along cupboards and counter tops. There were displays of conveniences dispensed by such past establishments—cosmetic powders, various bottles labeled "elixirs," prophylactics and birth-control devices—and against one wall was ranged a set of drawers such as one might have found in the old-time Chinese herbalist's shop (even down to authentic characters on the labels; I'll give them that). Behind the main counter were rows of bottles and boxes labeled with various pharmaceutical names; on closer inspection I saw they were also for display only. I wasn't sure if this was an actual dispensary or a museum.

Which led to the next question: where was the proprietor—and, for that matter, where was Hazel Swansea?

My watched showed it was 0935. I felt surprisingly alert, considering what little sleep I'd had. Perhaps it was the adrenaline induced by apprehension: I had the nasty feeling something was a little bit wrong about this. Surely she wouldn't be late for an assignation she'd made.

To the side of the front counter was a door. I approached it and rested my hand lightly on the doorknob. A lock similar to the one on the front door un-latched; resting on the balls of my feet, and with not a little tension, I pushed the door open.

Contrary to my expectations, the back room was well lit and spacious. That was the only contrary thing. Quickly I amended my opinion from a little bit wrong to very bad: I had found Hazel Swansea.

She sat in a chair, almost directly below the phosphorescent spotlight, hunched down in it with her limbs sprawled out. The formal, old-style tweed tunic and pantaloons she wore were scrunched up by her position. She would have appeared to be an attractive middle-aged woman, were it not for the death-rictus on her face: an expression of extreme agony.

I pushed the door all the way against the inside wall, stepped inside quickly and looked around. No one else was there. The room looked to be a storage compartment for the pharmaceuticals (so one more question was answered, anyway). I went to her and checked her body; rigor mortis had not yet set in. Her death had been recent—and excruciating, I thought, looking at her face again.

Another door led to a small room that was obviously the delivery room with small induction-elevators and belts. Beyond was the opening to outside, another part of the south mall, a few people walking and riding pedwalks about on their business, unaware of this death in their midst. I went back in, found the vidphone, and began punching out the code for Security.

"You have an uncanny ability to draw undue incidents to yourself, Mr. Lee. I don't know if Southwest can survive your presence." Kostakis' expression was one of rather perplexed severity.

"What can I do?" I said. "I can't help it, I don't go looking for it. Trouble follows me." I paused. "Quote, unquote."

"Pardon?"

"Never mind." I waved my feeble joke away. "You know, we should have realized . . ."

"Yes, I know." His mouth twisted slightly. "Regrettable. We should have placed her under surveillance as soon as we heard of last night's occurrence. A mistake."

"Was that really her shop?"

"Yes. She was rather—eccentric—"

" 'Dotty,' I think is the word."

"Whatever your preference. Usually her daughters run the establishment; harmless curios are what they normally sell. How they obtained poisonous alkaloids . . ." He shook his head. "Those are controlled substances."

"Well, she was a Board member. Easier for them to cover their tracks. What was it again—brucine?"

He nodded. "Dissolved the powder in tea and probably forced her to drink it."

"Like Socrates and the hemlock," I remarked. "A very bitter cup indeed." I paused and thought. "But no traces of it, or of any other questionable substances, were found in the shop, right? Only in that teacup. As if somebody brought it in himself, made her take it, then took it with him when he left."

Kostakis looked dubious. "Sounds rather elaborate."

"Maybe symbolic—or a bit unbalanced. I don't know. And I keep wondering what it was she had to tell me. Was it important enough to warrant her death?"

Kostakis said nothing.

"Oh, hell," I said a bit wearily. "How'd your interview go?"

"Rather well. Our young friend in R & D did indeed have the correct codes. And once one knows those, it would be a relatively uncomplicated affair to devise ways to bypass the checks on the lines."

"So that much is confirmed. Any leads who might have snatched the information?"

"Yes. Too many. Whoever has programming experience and has kept a watchful eye on our friend. We are checking his movements also, but he doesn't appear to be a likely suspect. Clever, but rather unmotivated."

"Which is exactly the problem," I said. "No one has a clear-cut motive." I looked at his image on the vidphone screen thoughtfully. "The other Board members?"

"They are quite upset about this. If it is one of them, that person is a masterful actor."

"Well, no harm keeping up the surveillance. What about Philippa Grenoble?"

"She is due back in Leetown day after tomorrow. You may interview her then."

"Any personal impressions?"

The image gave me that famous Kostakis shrug. "The same likelihood as the others. I doubt she will be very revealing on first meeting."

"We'll see," I said.

"You wouldn't be inclined to leave Southwest quietly and let us handle this alone, would you?"

"Not now," I said. "Whoever it is made it personal last night." I made some closing pleasantries and signed off. Then I sat back and thought.

There was a pattern in this, somehow, though it was muddled. The carbon monoxide, the brucine in the apothecary—someone was dispensing death in a rather sophisticated way. But a death was still a death, no matter how elegant—and when doled out by human agency, it was still called murder.

And through it all the image of the old man, succumbing in the desert with ample food and water, nagged at me with all its contradictions.

"Maybe there's only one way," I told Anna. "Go to Lacklund, retrace the old man's steps. Whoever it is might find it a golden opportunity to make history repeat itself."

"That sounds too extreme to me," she said, her face worried. "You'd just be inviting danger."

"Exactly. But what else is there? Security hasn't turned up much, and it seems I'm the vector for all this recent violence. No use causing any more unnecessary deaths here."

"And yours is necessary?"

"Well, I didn't mean it that way," I said.

We were walking though the analytical labs in EQ, beyond all those stalwart secretaries, Anna giving me a guided tour. Surrounding us on all those benches were the chromatographs, gel-electrophoresis platforms, combustion modules, mass spectrometers, and other esoteric equipment; against the far walls were the more massive pieces of instrumentation: magnetic-resonance spectrometers, isotope detectors, other things I didn't recognize.

"I have some private lab space in here," Anna said, and we walked through a passageway into a smaller cubicle with four lab benches, looking as cluttered as the big room outside.

"Keep yourself busy, do you?" I said casually.

"A bit." She walked to the small desk at the end of one of the benches and shuffled some papers and notebooks about.

I touched a few bottles and flasks gingerly, tried to remember the names of the pieces of glassware and equipment. "What's this?" I said, lifting a canister from the floor. "Cute footrest. Deuterium oxide, hey?"

"Oh, that." She glanced at it distractedly. "We use it for densimetry. For checking geological samples—mix a set of water standards, get the density of the sample in each one, plot the data. More accurate that way."

"Use a lot of it, then." She nodded. "Must be expensive."

"Not too bad. Cheaper now than when nuclear energy was the going fad. Of course, since the heavy-water reactors were discontinued along with everything else, we use much less—mostly for research. You should see how much the fusion people over in what used to be New Mexico use."

"It all comes back to me," I said, "though very slowly. You've got the chemistry knack. I'm afraid the old man lost the codons for it when he made me."

"You can joke about it?" she said sharply.

Her tone surprised me. "We can't exactly do anything about it, can we?" I said.

"More's the pity," she replied. She folded her arms about herself and looked away.

"Hey, look," I said. I moved closer to her. "We are what we are. We have to live with it. What are you going to do—change the genotype in every cell of your body? Maybe it was an error in judgment on his part, but who says we have to follow in his exact footsteps? We haven't really done so anyway, have we?"

"Our lives aren't over yet."

"Besides, we surely aren't the only ones. I can't believe everyone obeyed the Tampering Ban."

"But we were the first ones. The marked ones." She looked at me, her face tense and taut-lipped. "You can say he couldn't help it—that he did what he did because of his character, to prove to all those who discriminated against him that he was worthy of their respect—but that's no excuse for not considering the consequences for us."

"Do you hate him for that?" I asked.

"Hate him?" She looked suddenly uncertain and shook her head as if in doubt. "If I hated him, I'd have to hate myself. And Jock. And you."

"A long time ago I thought you did."

"Maybe I did," she said slowly.

"And what about now?"

"I should ask you that question. Who tried to kill him first?" Her look was defiant. I did not answer.

Suddenly a lost expression came over her face. "Oh,

Sparks," she said. "Why are we going over this again? I wish it would stop, all of it."

"Easy," I said, and then I opened my arms and held her. She stiffened momentarily, then relaxed.

"Maybe the only way," she murmured, "is when we're all dead and gone."

"That'll come soon enough," I said. "Let's not hurry it up."

After a while—I don't know how long—she looked up at me. "You are going to Lacklund?"

"Yes. Tomorrow."

"I'll go with you. I have leave coming up."

"You don't have to—" I began, then stopped. Perhaps she did, after all. "All right," I said. "Safety in numbers."

"It's pretty barren out there. Not many conveniences. That's the way he wanted it." She paused. "Maybe we should ask Security, just in case—"

"No. We'll leave them behind. It would scare him off."

"That's too big a risk. You can't—"

"There's no other way. We'll never see him otherwise. And that's the whole point of this, isn't it?"

Kostakis, of course, disapproved of the whole idea.

"You must have this secret urge for death," he said. "I thought the day of the lone hero had passed on two centuries ago."

"Come on, Kostakis. It's only logical—"

"There's logic and there's reason, Mr. Lee. It appears to me you're noticeably lacking in the latter."

Eventually we compromised: Security would accompany us as far as Lacklund. From there I'd trek out on the old man's trail—well, Anna and I—for a week. If we weren't back by then, they'd come after us in full force.

"One more thing. You'll be physically alone, but I

want you to stay in touch with your transmitters. Report in once a day, at an appointed hour, so we'll know you're all right." Kostakis paused. "To be frank, I have little hope for this scheme of yours. However, it doesn't hurt to take all possible precautions."

"And I thought you didn't care," I said, and made *tsk-tsk* sounds. Kostakis looked slightly affronted.

"Promise me, though," I went on, "you won't send any overhead shuttles to buzz us, okay?"

"I promise, Mr. Lee," he said with a touch of resignation. "If you're intent on foolhardiness I shan't stand in your way."

When all arrangements had been made, I stopped off at EQ about 1800 hours, the end of Anna's shift. I arrived in that last inner office to discover she wasn't in.

"She left a message." The secretary Hodkinson handed me the printout.

It read: "Had to make an emergency supply pickup. Will be working tonight. No need to call. Will meet you in Lacklund tomorrow, early afternoon, Okay? Anna."

Okay, all right. Maybe it was better this way. "Thanks," I told Hodkinson, and left.

Back in my new, high-security room, I considered the possibility of setting out from Lacklund without waiting for Anna. So far our mysterious stranger had designated myself as the target; Hazel Swansea had picked an unfortunate time to come clean. (And Kostakis had assured me it wouldn't happen with that technician.) I still wasn't sure I wanted to involve Anna in what was fast proving a danger zone about myself, especially in light of her turmoiled feelings about our situation. A preoccupation like that upon one's mind could prove fatal if an encounter indeed did occur. The prospect of such undue hazards to others bothered me.

What also bothered me was our adversary's intent to

do me in or even keep me from finding out too much. I hadn't got anywhere before things started happening—yet in three months of investigation, with the facilities of SolarCorp behind him, Kostakis had come up with no more than I had. Why?

Was it someone with an intense, overpowering hatred for Andrew Lee—so much so that it extended to his relatives? Yet Anna had not encountered any difficulties. On the other hand, she had also maintained a low profile; I'd come barging into Southwest with all the grace of a falling tree. Whoever it was might just be acting defensively, with pre-emptive strikes (to use a quaint, obsolete expression).

Perhaps, perhaps. Yet too much was missing. I worried about it overlong, with little results. Finally I fell asleep in the early morning hours.

Lacklund reminded me of the smaller towns in the eastern sections of Northwest, though in drier terrain. There was a modicum of conveniences—a shuttle landing area, vidphone and fax-wire communications lines, some module-type plasteel-and-metalloy buildings—but for the most part the town, if it could be called a town, was that archetypal border outpost of the West. Not even SolarCorp could change this: in the outskirts and fringes of an enclave there would always be those living this way, primitive, unchanging, caught by their temperament in a calm eddy of time. I could imagine the old man walking this flattened dirt runway toward the town's few buildings, as the Security men Morello and Hightower and I were doing now, and something coming into his mind as he surveyed beyond them the splash of colors like a pastel painting in horizon and sky, making him nod and say to himself yes, yes indeed.

It was barely 1000 hours, but we were already beginning to simmer in the heat. Gravel suddenly crunched under our boots as we came to the terminal walkway, then the smooth-worn boards thudded to our arrhythmic steps as we stepped up and then inside the building.

"I'll call in and check in with the Chief," Morello said. He was a large, beefy man just barely running to fat, with a young, florid face. "Johnny here—" He thumbed at the other guard, Hightower. "He can tell you more about this area than I can. He grew up around here."

Morello clumped away into the inner office. Johnny Hightower and I walked through the tiny vestibule and out the door fronting what I assumed was Lacklund's main street. There were two buildings on the terminal's left, three on its right; across the way five more ranged against my gaze. Only two or three people, desert-hardened types, were about, giving us the briefest of uncurious glances. That was it for Lacklund; beyond it was sand, scrub brush, desert, sky.

We sat on the steps, just barely in the shade of the overhand from the roof, and waited.

"Do you come back here often?" I asked.

"Not too much." Hightower shrugged and looked across the street. He was tall and rangy, with big hands, dark-brown skin, straight black hair, prominent high cheekbones and nose. His eyes were a startling pale blue in his dark face. I guessed he was somewhat more than half Indian. "I was assigned to Mr. Lee when he came here maybe twice. Usually I'm too busy in the city."

"You from Lacklund?"

"No. Thirty kilometers east." He inclined his head slightly. "My tribe is there. Zuñi. I'm three quarters Zuñi myself." He said it matter-of-factly.

"Was there any local hostility or resentment against Andrew Lee? Or SolarCorp?"

He turned and looked at me. "No more than usual against strangers or newcomers—those who don't appreciate life being tied so closely to the land." He paused, then went on: "If you're wondering whether any foul play may have originated among them—possible, but not likely. Mr. Lee was somewhat—difficult at times. But he was a lot more perceptive than most city folk who ever come out here. Unless he was somehow bothering some of the more radical or criminal elements here, no one would have given him much trouble."

"Was he liked, or respected, or—?"

"He was tolerated." Another shrug. "As for respect—well, he was the big head of SolarCorp, wasn't he?"

"And what about SolarCorp?" I asked.

He looked away again. "You'll find a lot of people out there tilling their ground, burning wood and cattle-dung fires, sleeping under nothing but wool blankets in winter. But you'll find just as many who won't go anywhere without a portable Lee converter. Some people change, some don't. It's their choice."

I didn't answer for a while. Presently I said, "I'd like an idea of what he usually did whenever he came out here."

"You should talk to Old Peter, then. He was the supplier and outfitter Mr. Lee always went to. His place is right down there."

Old Peter was just that—a grizzled, hardy fellow of about seventy, the living picture of the old prospector type. But his eyes were bright and alert, and his stare frank and direct when he talked.

"Old Lee, he was a singular man, all right. No nonsense, knew just what he wanted. Always had an itinerary picked out, a timetable he followed to a tee."

"How big were the groups he went with?"

"Not very. Not too many city folk could keep up with him. Young Johnny here a couple times—" He grinned at Hightower. "The young daughter a lot, especially recently. Now she did all right.

"But he tried to keep it as small as possible. Two, three others at the most. A lot of times by himself, which I figure gave the boys who escorted him here conniptions. He got to know the area right well.

"Look here." He pulled out a survey map of the area, crisscrossed with the wavy red lines of the routes he had traveled. "That last time he went southeast— desert land, pretty dry for about thirty-five kilometers, then there's a small ravine with a creek. Some abandoned copper mines from a couple centuries ago along the way. That's where they found him: right outside one of 'em. They say he looked like he'd been poisoned, but they never could find what it was, did they?" I shook my head, and Old Peter acknowledged with a quick nod. "Real strange. Healthy as a horse, too, I could see that. I never did believe it was a heart attack. I don't know who'd have it in for him, though. I mean, he was a pretty salty fellow, but he sure didn't seem like someone you'd have a big enough hate for to knock off."

"He wasn't, was he?" I thought for a second. "Anna—the daughter. She didn't go with him then."

"Nope. Picked up her stuff here, then took two steps and fainted dead away. Looked like she'd been up for a week. The old man stayed with her half a day to make sure she was okay, then set off. She spent the night, then flew back to the city. Came right back here when we sent word of—what happened. Pretty broke up about it at the time. They looked like they were close folks."

"Who found him?"

"Some boys from here, out scrounging for old wood for a house they were building. Called it in, and Security was out there in a flash. Couldn't have been more than a day after he'd died."

"And these boys?"

His mouth set with slight irritation. "They're good

fellows. And Security checked them out real thorough, too. If you're looking at them you're barking up the wrong tree."

"All right," I said, and we bade good-bye and walked away.

The wrong tree? Well, so far they were all that way. Which one was the right one?

My reason for this excursion seemed flimsier the more I thought about it—but I decided to go ahead anyway. Perhaps some opportunity for relaxation, if nothing else: being out here seemed, at the moment, infinitely more desirable than going back into the rabbit-warren of Leetown.

I also decided to go ahead without waiting for Anna. It was an almost impulsive decision, prompted by vague feelings involving relationships between us, the old man and myself, the old man and Anna, the future relationships. . . . Or perhaps I just didn't want to think about it more deeply.

Johnny Hightower and I set out on the old man's last route in late afternoon. We could probably get in ten kilometers at a leisurely pace before dark. He talked me into letting him accompany me about halfway, then he'd camp and wait for my return. It sounded like a reasonable compromise, so I relented.

It was relatively flat country at the outset. The last half-hour we walked toward a gorgeous sunset, red and gold and orange hues outlining the gentle hilly horizon like black filigree. We made camp in a shallow arroyo, atop a dry riverbed Hightower assured me hadn't seen water in twenty years.

He expertly struck a fire, and in the shadows and swiftly fading light the flames flickered and cast their inconstant orange glow over our features.

"We won't need this tonight." He held up the knapsack containing the Lee converter. "Summer nights aren't too bad out here; our blankets should be enough. If it were November I'd have left it hanging outside so the superconductors on the monolayer tent would charge up, and we'd have kept warm all night."

"I see you have little misgivings about our heritage from SolarCorp," I observed.

I saw him shrug again. "It got me my job, out of the desert, into a pretty nice position. The only bad thing about it is Leetown. Some things about Phoenix, too." He reached forward and stirred our sizzling dinner about in the pan. "That doesn't mean I forget where I came from. Even nowadays there are those who won't let you forget. Even your father met those, I'll bet." His face turned toward me.

"That's true," I said. "We all run into it from time to time."

He nodded and turned back to the cooking. "That's what I see. Your father, being what he was, rising to the top of the pile, the very top. It shows it can be done. We aim for the future, but we remember the past. We keep both." He picked up the pan. "Food's ready."

Our meal was quick and generally silent. We got to the dregs of the coffeepot before our conversation resumed.

"What exactly is it you're aiming for?" I asked.

"Don't know for sure just yet," he answered. "Some aspect of law enforcement—not what you might think. There are still a lot of failings in the system, especially when the city police are dealing with those outside. A lack of understanding—which leads to a lack of caring, then to no help at all. It would be nice to change that."

"Police work has always had that problem," I said.

"You know about that, don't you?" I said nothing, and Hightower made a brief amused sound. "I was there when the Chief checked out your record. Must have been pretty rough down in SanSan territory at the turn of the century."

"Let's say it was disorganized," I said. "The breakdown was around the corner and everyone was making arrangements to save their own skins. And whatever else they could cop." I shrugged. "As it turned out, all it did was delay things another twenty or thirty years. It's exactly the same way now as it was then."

"But you must have been a popular target," he remarked.

"A moving target," I said. "And believe me, I learned to move pretty fast."

We laughed together at that good-naturedly. "I'll make some more," he said, and bent to pick up the coffeepot.

I felt rather than saw the laser beams pulse past my cheek. The rifles are inefficient—a lot of waste heat is generated—and the skin of my face felt a sudden stinging hotness. The coffeepot clattered as it fell onto the wood and embers; sparks and glowing chips erupted upward, and in the sudden light I saw Hightower's severed right hand clenched about the pot's handle.

I looked up at him. He was holding out his arm, still bent as if to pick up the pot, and the stump of his wrist was dark brown and somewhat shiny, cauterized by the beam so there was no bleeding. His face held an expression of utter astonishment. In the next few seconds I felt the hot flashes whisk past my face several times before I ducked, threw myself to the side and rolled over. I caught glimpses of Hightower, his head snapping back and his body twisting and jerking suddenly—do coherent light-beams have enough momentum to make a body do that?—before I was scooping dirt frantically into the fire, and then we were in darkness.

I lay there for perhaps a minute, holding my breath, my eyes slowly becoming adjusted to night vision. I listened and looked around carefully. No sounds came; no more laser flashes showed. I moved as quietly as possible in the general direction of Hightower, feeling utterly naked all the while, like a fly on a white wall.

The first thing I encountered was his handless arm. I felt along his body; there were several holes in his torso, a pair in his left shoulder, another in the middle of his cheeks. There was little blood on him. I felt for his pulse in his neck and his arm. The throbbing was weak, irregular. I felt trapped and helpless; all I could do was straighten him out and make him more comfortable. I went for his pulse again. A short while later I felt it speed up dramatically then abruptly slow. Then it was gone.

I lay there unmoving, unthinking. The only image in my mind was this: Hightower, young, big, strong, now quickly dead. Somehow in the darkness I could see him lying still and supine beneath my hands. Another image slowly crept across the first: a second body draped over his, crumpled and cold: mine.

Then I was moving, crawling away from the camp up the incline of the arroyo toward the top, as swiftly and silently as I dared.

Few stars were out, and no moon. I reached the top, turned and looked down; there was only featureless black below me. Again I listened and watched.

For a time, nothing. Then I heard faint sounds, like wordless far-off cries. As I listened, they became someone's halloos; with them came steps, the sound of boots on loose rock. I lay still, anticipating the flash of the unseen lase rifle again, and wondered who this soon-to-be unfortunate was. Then I suddenly recognized the voice: Anna's.

Shock at her presence gave way to anger at her stupidity. I crawled toward the sound of her progress; presently I saw a lamp, its tiny glow swinging gently in the night. I moved toward her more quickly, now making some noise myself in my urgency to reach her before a lase rifle discharge did.

Rocks scrabbled under my feet as I neared her. The lamp stopped swinging. I saw her dim form in its light, peering in my direction, just before I grabbed her with one arm and the lamp with my free hand.

She gave a startled gasp just before I covered her mouth. "Get down," I said urgently in her ear. "Now. It's me." I found the switch on the lamp and turned it off, then forced her down to the ground. She didn't resist— probably out of surprise—and we sprawled prone against each other.

"What's the matter?" she whispered. "What's going on?"

I told her what happened, and I felt her body tense.

"My God. It could have been you." Her hand reached for me, fumbled up and touched my face.

"It may be anyway," I said. "And you. How'd you get here?"

She'd finally got away, she said, about 1600 and came to Lacklund with a groundcar. They'd told her where we'd gone, and she had driven out, stopped some distance behind our position, and walked up in hope of finding our camp.

"Not very smart," I observed.

"I thought I'd find you by your campfire," she said a little defiantly. "Who else would camp this close to town?"

"All right, that's not our worry now. What is is our murderous friend out there. He may want to finish this job tonight. If he has infrared equipment—" I stopped, then: "Where's the car?"

"Back there about, oh, half a kilometer."

"Does it have Night-Vision accessories?"

"I think so. You're thinking of making a run for it?"

"We've got to get away from here. If not tonight, what will happen when it gets light?" I rose to a crouch and eased her up next to me. "Let's go. Quiet now."

We found the car after what seemed an incredibly long and jittery interval, with the help of some luck in the dark. I climbed into the driver's seat and helped

Anna into the other. Running my hands over the dash, I tried to remember what was where.

I felt Anna bend forward and reach into some compartment; then she handed me something soft and pliable. "Here's the mask," she said. "Watch the leads."

I slipped the mask over my head and fitted the visor to my eyes. The controls were at the temples; when I turned them on, the representation of the dash appeared in the lower field of my vision, the 180-degree sonar map of the terrain in front of me in the upper.

"All right," I muttered. "Let's start moving."

I felt for the pressurizing switch, turned it on, and imagined the steam building up in the chamber. After a reasonable interval I disengaged the clutch, tapped the accelerator, and we began moving forward slowly. I grabbed the steering wheel, stepped harder, and we sped up.

"Which direction?" Anna asked.

"Out. Farther out on the same trail." The car was silent, but the ground and gravel crunched under the tires, and I urged us on faster. "We'll play this out to the end."

Anna said nothing further. I continued to drive on. At one point I became aware of the transmitter on my belt, the possibility of calling in our situation.

But that would mean Kostakis sending more men out here, and the possibility of our friend's being scared off. I dismissed the thought quickly, as I'd essentially done already by my action. This one, I thought, was mine.

Near midnight by Anna's watch the sonar-map showed the contour of what seemed to be an old mine entrance. Despite our zigzag route, the directional finder showed we'd stayed fairly close to true, and probably no farther than the end of the old man's trail in straightaway distance. Perhaps this *was* the end of his trail; be that as it may, I decided to stop here. We were probably relatively safe—for a while, at least.

I stopped the car about ten meters from the entrance. My own unaided night-vision showed the mine entrance as a darker blocky shadow in the nocturnal sky. We climbed out, Anna with her equipment, and walked toward it.

"Do you have the lamp?" I asked. She nodded. "Let's have a look, then."

The immediate interior was dry, the rock walls smooth. We hunched down in the darkness, sharing the one blanket we had between us, staring at the rectangle of the night showing through the entrance. Suddenly I felt very tired and slouched against Anna. As if sensing my exhaustion, she moved closer to support me.

"Why don't you rest?" she said. "You've been through a terrible night."

"We both should. We couldn't do anything about this tonight anyway."

"And what could we do about it in the morning?" she said softly.

"You mean, what plans do I have?" I sighed. "I don't know."

"You think—that was the one, wasn't it?"

"There's no doubt in my mind. Although he's being a bit crude this time. Out of character."

She ignored my sarcasm. "Maybe we should call for help."

I shook my head. "Not just yet."

"Oh." She was silent for a moment. Then she moved her hand up, placed it on the back of my neck and began rubbing. It felt good, and I slowly relaxed.

She leaned closer and I slipped an arm around her. We sat there a long while, not speaking, the only movement her massaging hands.

Then: "I'm getting tired," she said softly. "Would it be safe to turn in?"

"May as well." I moved away, adjusted the blanket closer and tighter about us. "If he comes, he comes. If not—"

"Tomorrow," she said, her voice almost a sigh, and slid down under the blanket into a bunched heap. "Figure it out then."

I nodded, didn't say anything, and made myself more comfortable. I stared at the framed night before us and finally fell asleep.

We spent a large part of the day waiting and trying to decide what to do. Our murderer didn't show—or at least make his presence known. As a consequence the hard-edged purpose I'd felt became a bit vague, and made me not a little restless. Waiting games like this I didn't need.

However, something was sure to happen, I felt. Consequently I didn't let on anything was amiss on that first call to Kostakis.

"You left the guard to wait for you?" he asked.

"Yes," I lied. "We'll meet him on the way back."

"We?" I told him Anna had shown up and where we were. "That's slightly ahead of your timetable, isn't it?" he continued.

"Yes, well," I said, and made some excuse.

"Oh, by the way. We did trace those carbon-monoxide containers. Our suspicions of an—inside job" —his voice became suddenly dry on that phrase— "seem to be proving sadly correct. They have been traced to Research and Development in Leetown."

"Um. Nothing more detailed?"

"No. They have a general warehouse and everyone signs out what they need. These containers were removed without authorization—"

"Stolen," I said.

"Yes. Stolen," he said a bit stiffly. "Other than that we know nothing.

"Oh, yes. Philippa Grenoble has arrived in Leetown, so whenever you wish . . ."

"We'll see this through first," I said, and signed off. I could hardly tell him now our culprit was out here somewhere, stalking us. (Unless it was some hired gun—but I doubted it. I had an intuition this person liked the personal touch.)

I returned to the mine. Anna was at the car, wiping off her hands.

"Spilled some water," she said apologetically. She lifted up the canteen, indicating it, then threw her knapsack into the back of the car. "What did you tell Kostakis?"

"Not much," I said, and recounted our conversation. She looked thoughtful as we walked to our small camp-fire area, carrying our dinner equipment.

The rest of the evening was uneventful. If our friend was out there, he or she was certainly biding his or her time. Psychological warfare? Or just the toying *modus operandi* of some psychopath? Whatever it was, it wasn't conducive to easing our minds, and after a bare minimum of conversation we turned in early.

I lay in the blanket next to Anna, watching the sunset's colors fade to gray and then, more swiftly, toward black. Somehow I was restless. Beside me Anna was already asleep, breathing easily, resting on my arm. I watched her, thinking, remembering; then I carefully slid my arm out and away and slipped out of the blanket. She moaned softly, but did not waken. I dressed and stepped out into the cool night.

More stars and a thin sliver of a moon gave a bit more light than the night before. I walked gingerly over the pebbly area to the shadowy outlines of the car. I leaned against it and gazed out at the dark, thinking distracted thoughts.

Things had come full circle. Here we were again, the Lee clan, battling for survival as we had in those last

confused days in the California Territory before the
old government fell to the warlords, who were conquered in turn later on. Yet this time it was against out-
siders, not among ourselves. The internal conflicts—
well, perhaps they had been resolved. Heaven knows I'd
come a long way since that day in the old man's office
when the blowout came and we nearly killed each
other. Even Anna, whose differences with him were
worse than mine, had reached reconciliation, if what
she'd told me was true. Jock had been the only stable
one, neatly removing himself from the arena of con-
flict and finding security in the autonomous Institute
city-state.

Separate, isolated, flung across the world, we'd
thought ourselves to remain so until the end. Yet Jock
had come north to find me, Anna had returned, and
now we were here. Time healing all wounds? Not so
much healing, perhaps, as a replay. Or not exactly a
replay: more a restaging, a second run-through to see
if we could do it right.

Yet in the place of that internal complication we had
another. If it was not resolved, our lives would be
unraveled again, this time with finality, as swiftly as it
took to spot the blink of a shot from the killer's rifle.

Well, what of it? Wouldn't it be easier that way?
Anna's words came back to me: "Maybe the only way is
when we're all dead and gone." Maybe SolarCorp and
the Southwest Sector would be better off with no more
Lees around.

Foolish questions, foolish answers. A waste of time. I
straightened and let my arms fall into the back compartment of the car, knocking Anna's knapsack onto its
side. The top was loosely tied; something metallic
slipped partway out and thunked against the inner
door.

I pulled it out and looked at it. It was a canister,
about two liters' capacity, and vaguely familiar in shape.
I turned it in my hands, trying to remember where I'd

seen it before. There was no label or markings, outside of some serial numbers. Some commercial container?

Then it came to me: in Anna's office. The "footstool" by her desk. This was the same shape, albeit smaller.

But that had had a label. What was it? Suddenly I remembered: D_2O, heavy water.

Something vaguely disturbing came to my mind. Why would she bring this out here? For a canteen? I shook it, but there was only a very small amount sloshing about inside.

Then I remembered she had a canteen, even shown it to me. I reached into her pack and found it. I also found another one, just like the first.

Would she bring two canteens? One for me? But how would she know I'd need one?

Another image came: wiping her hands that were wet, spilled some water she'd said. Spilled it drinking? Transferring?

Then the last image, of the old man dead in the desert, his canteen still holding ample water, no visible mark on him. The vague feeling of disturbance became an alarm bell.

I checked the canteens again. Both were identical. How could they be told apart? Unless there was something to check the contents . . . I dug into the pack again and came up with a compact little instrument with a plethora of dials and a vidscreen; I had no idea what it was.

With sudden resolve I walked quickly behind several large boulders and got out the transmitter.

"What's wrong? What's the emergency?" Kostakis was, for him, clearly disturbed.

"I can't tell you now," I said. "Trust me." I glance back once at the mine. "Just connect me with someone at the—the analytical services at Environmental Quality. Any competent technician would do."

Kostakis grumbled a bit, but he did it. The man I talked to had a bored, youngish voice—graveyard shifts are slow everywhere, I suppose—which showed some interest when I asked my questions.

"Sure," he said. "They make portable mass-spectral and elemental analyzers like vidphones these days. You can hold it in your hand."

I described what I held in my hand to him, and he answered, "Yes, that's it all right," then told me how to use it.

"Okay," I said. "Now one more question."

A few minutes later, I stood with the activated analyzer in my hand, waiting for the results. Slowly they appeared on a tiny screen: first sample, then the second. What I feared had been confirmed.

I pocketed the analyzer and went slowly back to the mine. Inside Anna was still asleep. I slipped out of my clothes and under the blanket, but was unable to sleep for what seemed an interminably long time.

Sometime in the night I felt Anna sit up, and it seemed I could feel her eyes looking at me, studying me. I kept my breathing as regular as possible, pretending I was asleep. After a while she lay back down again, and I listened to her breathing become shallow and regular.

I didn't drop off until until nearly dawn. Even then it was a fitful rest, plagued as I was with what I knew.

The sun was bright when I awoke. I was roused by the sudden absence from my side. Quickly I felt for my clothes; they were still there. However, the transmitter which I usually hung on my belt was gone.

I sat up and saw a fully clothed Anna bending down by the car. She seemed to be doing something underneath it. I got my clothes, quietly dressed, and stood just inside the mine entrance.

She stood up and reached into the car for her knapsack. I saw she had the rest of her gear stacked on the ground. I felt in my pocket; the analyzer was still there.

Her knapsack was open, and she was rummaging

through it. The two canteens hung over the side of the car. I stepped out and walked toward her.

"Pretty handy tools, these," I said as I came close, holding the analyzer in one hand. "Wish I'd had them when I was going to school. Maybe I'd have become as good a chemist as you."

She'd spun around at my first words, and now she stared at the analyzer and back up at me. Her expression was quizzical, but I thought it also looked slightly guarded.

"Amazing capabilities, too," I went on. "They can tell the difference between isotopes with such a tiny instrument. I'd never thought it possible."

"Did you find that, Sparks?" she said. Her voice was calm. "I must have dropped it."

"Really," I said. I bent down and looked quickly under the car. Something was disconnected, and water dripped downward. I fiddled with it and made the connection again.

"That can be dangerous," I said, straightening. "No water in the tank, no steam in the compressor, no car. Someone could get stuck out here." I stepped closer to her. "What are you doing, Anna?"

She didn't answer. Her face set, and she looked away.

I held up the analyzer again. "Are you doing the same thing that you did to the old man?"

Slowly she began, "I don't know what you mean—"

"But I do. I learned how to work this just last night. That's how I found out how neat an instrument it is. Used samples from those." I pointed at the canteens. "Very interesting. One is full of good old water. The other has ninety-eight point eight percent deuterium oxide."

Her mouth seemed to set even harder.

"Funny, hydrogen and deuterium," I said. "Easiest isotopes to tell apart in a dynamic sense. The old deuterium primary isotope effect: we all learn that in chemistry, don't we? If you substitute deuterium for hydrogen in a chemical reaction whose rate is determined by a hydrogen transfer, that rate slows down to about one half to one seventh of what it was before. Not much, except in vital processes—like in the human body, where water is everywhere and used in so many reactions.

"Is that how you thought of it? The old man, out here under the hot sun, several days from any town or oasis. He gets thirsty, so he takes a big swig out of the canteen. All that D_2O enters his system; a lot gets washed out, but not enough. A fraction of his metabolic processes suddenly slow down. He feels a bit strange. Maybe some more water. The processes slow down further. Maybe he starts to panic and tries to drink more. Total system shock: his body can't take it, and it fails him.

"And of course, no one can find it in the autopsy. There's nothing in the water; it *is* the water."

I lowered my arm and stared at her for a long time. "It's been you all the time, Anna," I said. "The old man, Hazel Swansea, Johnny Hightower. And me." I hesitated. "Why?"

Her head turned back to me suddenly. "You know what you are. What we all are. And you still have to ask why." The face was still a set mask, but her eyes had a wild, lost expression. "After what he'd done—how can you forgive him? How can anyone?"

"Who says I have forgiven him?" I replied. "I know what he was. Is that justification for killing him?"

"You knew the answer once. You almost showed the rest of us."

"I should have realized," I said. "In your laboratory, when we talked—how you felt about him still."

"And you don't." Her voice was bitter.

"Not anymore," I said vehemently. "You accept it, but you don't have to stay with it. You grow, you change. Anything else—"

"Is what? Unbalanced? Unstable? Crazy?" she retorted. "This was the only thing to do. Seeing him there, day after day, and you knowing you'll be that way in twenty, thirty years—even if you are of different gender—" Her voice and wide-eyed stare mocked me. "That makes no difference. It makes it worse."

"So you did this to rid yourself of him? And all the rest, too. The missing future plans for SolarCorp, the cover-up—"

"This world doesn't need any more of Andrew Lee or his creations." Her voice was barely under control.

"And that extends to me, too," I said. She didn't answer, only glared at me. "Never mind. I can guess the answer." I pushed her out of the way and climbed into the car.

"Don't tell me you would have done differently," she said. "The only difference is who would have got to him first. You know that."

"Maybe I do," I said. "Or maybe not. I do know this: I don't feel about you the way you apparently feel about me."

"Don't you?" she asked. "Does that mean you'll be merciful? Won't turn me in? Besides, this is rather flimsy evidence, isn't it?" She reached for the canteens.

"Don't come any nearer," I said sharply. The tone of my voice made her pull back quickly.

"I came down here to find out something," I said. "What I did find sickens me. Not because I see it in Southwest, or what the old man's actions have wrought, or even in you. It's because it's in me.

"I can't turn you in. They wouldn't know what to do with you. I don't either." I started up the car.

"Is this revenge, then? Or just plain hate?" Her voice quavered with tension, fear, rage. "Or some perverse justice?"

"Maybe justice is the closest. The same chance the old man had." I grabbed a canteen, lobbed it at her, and it chunked into the loose dirt at her feet. "You should have marked the canteens so you knew which was which. I did." I began to pull away. "It's only three days to Lacklund. And you have lots of water."

"You're no different," she screamed, but I didn't answer. I gunned the accelerator, and her screams became wordless cries, growing ever fainter.

The sun was hot, and I was broiling. I'd sweated out all I could after several hours; I didn't drink anything from the canteen because I didn't know what was in it. I wondered feverishly if Anna would guess I'd been lying. Besides, I was neither hungry nor thirsty—only interested in getting away, getting back.

In the late afternoon the car coasted to a stop. Too much water had drained out of the tank. I poured what I could into it from the canteen, drove slowly so less steam would escape, and found myself near the arroyo where Johnny Hightower and I had camped that first night before that reserve was gone, too.

I got out and walked to its edge. Several Indians were there, dressed in modern-day clothing, except for one very old man, who wore calfskin pants, moccasins, a poncho, and a headband about his flowing white hair. The others were carrying a man-sized burden on their shoulders up the arroyo, and gave me frank stares as they passed.

The old man stood at the top, watching them. His face was impassive, with deep lines that made it look like carved wood. When the others reached the top and got their burden onto a car I hadn't noticed before, the old man turned to me, but still didn't speak. I recognized the dish of a Lee converter on his back.

"Is that Johnny Hightower?" I asked.

He regarded me for a time, then nodded. "Yes," he said. "Two days dead. Coyotes found him."

"There are still coyotes out here?"

"They will always be here. Them, the buzzards, the crow, this land. Long after we and those cities are gone." He raised an arm slowly toward the horizon.

I said, "If you need someone to take him back to the city—"

"We'll take him home. He belongs with us. That's his proper place."

I didn't protest further. "Who are you?" I asked.

He said, "I am Four Winds Drifting. Johnny Hightower was my grandson." He turned to the others, then back to me. "Are you going to the city?"

They dropped me off at Lacklund, and I checked in at the shuttle terminal. The next one back to Leetown was in three hours. I sat in the terminal quietly, fending off Security's questions (that is, Morello's), saying I would tell all in the city.

We boarded the shuttle and rode in silence through the starry night to the lighted city. "Go on," I told Morello. "I'll meet you at Security headquarters. I have to go home and do something first." Reluctantly he agreed.

I went to my hotel room, sat down and dictated a long report, detailing what had really happened in the death of Andrew Lee and giving an edited account of events up to this day. I fed the tape into the typing-servo and made two copies, one for Chief DeBray and one for Stavros Kostakis. I called the travel service downstairs and made arrangements to leave Southwest, then packed and checked out.

On the way to the shuttleport I mailed the two reports. The trip from Leetown to the California border took forty-five minutes. I changed, sped through security with my visa, and barely caught the night flight into Northwest territory. An hour later I was on the induction-rail going up the McKenzie River, on my way home.

There was an ending of sorts after the tumultuous aftermath of my flight, in several parts. The SolarCorp breakup deadline came and went, and of course it was nowhere near as cataclysmic as some people had foreseen. Especially since all the erstwhile Board members were vigorously booted out of office (even the elusive Philippa Grenoble, who, I was assured, was no less deserving) and there arose a new, publicly elected Board, with Stavros P. Kostakis as President, no less—the result of a canny publicity campaign, so I'm told. Southwest would change, go through growing pains, but it would probably muddle through.

I received a personal cable from Kostakis eventually. It told me that Anna Lee's body had been found where I had left her. She had died of dehydration—a possible suicide, since her canteen had been full. (Of *light* water, Kostakis emphasized.) The cable ended, "P.S. All is forgiven."

The last part involved another cable. This one I received from Ketchikan, Sovereign Territory of Alaska.

It read: "Am sorry to report the demise of Theodore Peter Lee on the night of 22 October 2025. Cause of death lymphatic cancer. James W. Snowfox, M.D."

So it came to pass that I was the last one left. And soon enough—probably too soon—my time will come too. When that happens, the dream of Andrew Tsing-Hao Lee—eternal life through his scions sprung full-blown from his cells, and through the children of his mind—will vanish as if it had never appeared on the earth.

Is that what we were—mere extensions of Andrew Lee's *persona?* I know what Jock would have done: dismissed it as an improper question. But is that what he'd really have thought, deep down inside? For I remember how I had been in younger days, and what Anna was like in those last encounters. How had he avoided that stage which we latter two found dictated so much of our lives?

Luck, perhaps. Or perhaps the old man's hand had been surer on the first try, preserving the genes coding for stability and levelheadedness in that blastula he would call Jock, somehow mangling them in my case, tearing them to shreds in Anna's.

Maybe it was the converse. Maybe the flaw was already there in the old man—in the blood, locked in the nuclei of his cells—and his earlier effort was a personal plan for self-improvement. Yet as age came upon him, his desires became those of preservation instead. Pick one or the other. Does it matter?

Maybe not. But there were things in the old man, Anna, and myself that I could see were common. Things not there in Jock, no matter how closely I looked at him. Andrew Lee had not been gentle in his rise to the top. Anna had done what she'd done to him with full justification in her mind. And I, may whatever gods there are help me, had left her there in the desert.

Are there codons for insanity? For psychopathy? Is there a genotype that forces its bearer inexorably forward on the path to tragedy? Is there a chance we may ever know or learn?

I doubt it would be soon before we learn. The universal antipathy to Tampering is still strong; to the world, the tragedy of the Lees will only be more fuel on the fire. Once I am gone, there will no doubt be a collective sigh of relief. The last reminder will be gone.

As for the other questions, knowing the answers would not help me, not now. Too much of life has passed. Too little of it remains to try redeeming what has gone before. If luck will have it, I shall spend my remaining time here among the foaming gorges, the spruce and evergreens; by the seaward-flowing water to watch its inhabitants struggle uphill, cast about their seed and then expire in their seasonal rhythms. Perhaps that is what I will remember in the end, and not this. Perhaps.

ACTS OF LOVE
Mark J. McGarry

Not all science-fiction writers begin their careers early. Robert A. Heinlein was past thirty before he began to publish, and so was Frank Herbert. But a quick start is a common event: Isaac Asimov, Ray Bradbury, Frederik Pohl, James Blish, Robert Silverberg, and a lot of others were published authors before they were twenty-one. Add to that list now the name of Mark J. McGarry, born in 1958, currently a college student in upstate New York. Like many avid young science-fictionists, including the editor of this volume, he spent his high-school years trying to write for professional publication, and made his first sale immediately after graduation. Here, now, is his second published story—a far-ranging and expansive novella of space exploration and the inner growth of a complex human being, written with skill and assurance belying its author's tender years. Watch him in the years to come.

May 2054
Omaha and *Manchester*

THERE IS A HEMISPHERICAL SECTION three kilometers in diameter and depth that is gone from the earth, taken from the northwest corner of a place that was once called Omaha. The crater has largely been filled with magma that flowed up through the rent crust from below, and the area radiates heat that can be felt across the Missouri River, and a glow that can be seen from beyond the horizon. Scattered about the rim of the crater are buildings flattened and all fallen inward, accusing fingers pointing to the center. What animals there are—men among them—forage for food amidst the ruins.

First demolition, then pillage; nowhere is there metal. Not here, or in dozens of other cities that have fallen is there any quantity of titanium or structural steel or molybdenum or aluminum. Any buildings that have survived the initial nuclear strike and its consequences have been toppled by the survivors of the holocaust. The skeletons have been stripped from the towers, ships and trains have been swallowed whole, in the frantic search for steel.

Some distance from the edge of the crater, on the very outskirts of the city, a woman pats flat the dirt over her youngster's grave with calloused palms. The grave is far from the shattered office building where she now lives. She knows from the signs at her man's burial site that creatures will be attracted by the perfume of the freshly dead, and she hasn't the strength to beat them off again.

It happened not very long ago. She remembers quite well the unexpected sirens echoing in the gleaming streets, warning whose meanings no one had remembered. Then lightnings had appeared, arcing across the sky, and dark clouds following, then new suns had blossomed in the air high overhead. Somehow she had survived. Spider-limbed cranes had descended on the ruins some months later, and she had hidden from them. The machines had picked and felled and picked further, harvesting the city of its buildings. Then they had gone and had not come back, though she still glanced upward at any sudden sound, expecting them again.

In geosynchronous orbit 36,000 kilometers above the flaming shuttle-field at Dallas, Wing 23 makes its preparations to depart. Having burned the final bridge behind, the last shuttle rises and matches orbits with the *Manchester* on hydrazine bursts.

The *Manchester* is typical of her six wing-mates and of her one hundred sixty sister ships. She is steel on steel, twenty-seven hundred meters in length, one fifth that through her greatest cross-section. The greater cylinder of her main hull, once sun-gleaming, is now scarred and dulled by micrometeoroid impacts, and is interrupted by weapons blisters and airlocks. The main engines and exhaust channels lie aft; forward is the five-hundred-meter-wide hydrogen collector, gaping like the maw of some celestial anemone. Dozens of electromagnetic vanes, each several kilometers long, radiate outward from the edge of the collector like tentacles.

Tucked within the hull are thousands of square meters of decks given over to facilities for the maintenance and operation of the starship, and for supply stores and crew quarters. These are located closer to the longitudinal axis; surrounding them are cavernous lofts brimming with grains and embryos and ten thousand other items: heavy machinery and electronics goods, library tapes and hand weapons, clothing and prefabricated dwellings.

The outer hull is composed of five layers of thin steel plate, cemented over with rock boosted from Earth's moon. The ship's water-supply tanks are sandwiched by the hull plate. This arrangement may absorb radiation from a near miss, or muffle the impact of a slight hull-strike and leave the ship in fighting trim.

The shuttle has docked, and airlocks seal with thick, plastic lips. Pressures equalize, lock doors open in both lander and mother ship. Of the thirty men and women who exit the shuttle, all but one make their way reluctantly, uncertainly—for most have never been aboard before—to their designated places. Colin Murdoch nods to the shuttle's pilot and engineer as they seal their craft behind them and depart.

Murdoch, at twenty-four, will be *Manchester*'s youngest officer. He is of slightly below average height, but is heavy-set. His muscles are hinted at by the rust-colored uniform which he wears loosely. His blond hair is shaped close to his head and reaches to his stiff collar. His eyes are sharp and blue, like jagged, broken glass.

Murdoch pauses in *Manchester*'s expansive receiving area and looks to the raised lettering alongside the inner pressure door. He has seen the words before. He carries a thick book, bound in black leather, and the words are printed on its first page.

Therefore I decided to leave the country,
Therefore I have come as one charged with
    a special duty,
Because I have been given my arrows and shields,
For waging war is my duty,
And on my expeditions I shall see all the lands;
I shall wait for the people and meet them
In all four quarters and I shall give them
Foods to eat and drinks to quench their thirst,
For here I shall unite all the different peoples!

The words, from Aztec legend, are the pledge Colin Murdoch has given the commandant of the Rescue Expedition—as well as those of the god Tetzauhteotl to his high priest Huizilopochtli. Emblazoned over the words is the symbol of the Rescue Expedition: a white star superimposed over a black ring so as nearly to hide it altogether. Here, where no one can see him, Murdoch voices the words to himself. Then he leaves the lock, towing the Rescue Manual on its short golden chain, and his personal duffel. Soon he passes the group of emergency recruits that rode up with him; he makes his way along padded and subtly curved corridors and his hands feel the smooth nylon line against his palms as he pulls himself along. A descent-shaft takes him deep into *Manchester*'s bowels. His quarters are only a short distance along the corridor from the shaft. Murdoch secures his luggage in his rooms, then leaves. A few meters away there is a door, dead black in sharp contrast to the pleasing cream color of the corridor and the vibrant pastels of the other doors. There is a thumb lock set in the center of the door like a staring glass eye, and stenciled above it are the words WEAPONS ROOM.

The thumb lock allows him to enter. The door seals itself behind him.

Presently, *Manchester* and her sisters stir to life and grow warmer. Miniature prominences flare from their sterns as the ships depart from their orbital tracks. They move inward toward Sol, where they will make a single collection run and then, glutted for a time with hydrogen, will proceed to the stars. In command centers and observation decks, all cameras mounted forward transmit a polarized picture of the sun while those abaft are cool, dark, and blind.

October 2045
Omaha

The class was surrounded by symbols of puissance: there a scale model of an asteroid-ship, there a hovering silver beachball that represented an Outstepper, and there, on the table before them, a precisely scaled miniature of the Portal Authority Building, awesome even at such a size.

Citizen Oikawa pointed to the vast ground floor of the building that was taken up by a single room. "The Portal is located here," he said. "It has a diameter of roughly thirty meters, and it's kept that size at all times by something we call the containment apparatus. Like the Portal itself, it was given us by the Outsteppers."

"No container," said Roddy Biggam, "and blooey!"

"The Portal," said Oikawa, smiling indulgently, "would expand almost instantly—and of course, anything entering it would be transported, as now. But remember, its own power cables would be among the first items transported, and the Portal would then fade, almost as it expanded.

"Nothing happens, then?" asked Roddy, with a certain measure of disappointment.

"Oh, there would be a substantial crater," Oikawa assured him, "and the sudden drop in air pressure when the Portal disappeared, leaving nothing behind it, would be catastrophic." Roddy looked inordinately pleased. "Now, who knows when we received the Portal?"

"Two years ago," said Tilda Marquette. "Harold Mawson brought it back."

"Right," said Oikawa. "And when he brought it back, it wasn't more than this big." He held his hands about a meter apart. "Why do you think he kept it that small?"

"So it would fit in his spaceship," said Tilda.

"Because the power consumption of the Portal increases in geometric proportion to its surface area," said Colly Murdoch. "Any larger, and the ship's generators couldn't have taken the load. As it is, he almost didn't get back."

"Yes," said their guide, "you're both exactly right. Harold Mawson very nearly was lost. But he did return home, and that's why he's a hero today. Now let's go down to the debarkation slip and see the Portal." The fifteen children followed Oikawa into a descent-shaft.

The class emerged into an airy, vaulted chamber half a kilometer square and one hundred meters high. The walls were the pale gray of naked structural stress-crete; strips of cold-light panels ran around the walls, casting no shadows. The simple black ring that was the symbol of the Portal Authority, ten meters high, dominated the wall directly opposite the descent-shaft. To the right were corrugated metal doors rolled open; sunlight struck in. Tracks with flatbed cars on them ran from outside, across the stresscrete floor, and into a large black, nonreflective dome—the Portal—at the opposite end of the building. Bulkheads, girders, and huge pieces of machinery were set about the Portal, partially hiding it. Two lines of rail-cars moved forward, then disappeared into the side of the dome. There was no ripple on its surface, no obscuring haze, no shimmer or dramatic hail of sparks—the cars, loaded with whatever cargo was scheduled for export today, vanished with no more fanfare.

"Where are they going?" asked one of the children.

"The Portal is attuned to a central receiving station orbiting Wolf 359, a star about eight light-years from Earth. All Portals open onto that station, the Outstepper Forward, and from there these cars will be routed to their destination-worlds. We have an office at the station to keep track of things and make sure everything is properly routed. The Outsteppers tell us they have Portals set up on over three hundred planets, not all of which are inhabited."

"Can we go to any world we want?" asked Tilda.

"No. For trade, there must be an agreement between both our world and the one we wish to trade with. For colonization, we must pay a fee at intervals, and it is a steep one—which is why we have colonized so few worlds." Oikawa shrugged. "But who can judge the worth of an entire planet?"

"Why do we have to pay them at all?" asked Colly Murdoch harshly. "I saw on the screen this morning that we just gave the Outsteppers half the paintings in the Louvre."

"It's a business agreement, Citizen, as any other," Oikawa replied. "In exchange for our use of the Portal we have to give the Outsteppers so much, by prearranged contract. For this fee we may trade ideas and

goods with another world, or colonize. It is the same
for all the races doing business with the Outsteppers."

"Why can't we build our own Portal, then?" asked
Colly defiantly, "or take this one?"

Oikawa frowned. "It wouldn't be fair to take it—
though a better argument for you might be that we do
not know how to build a Portal, and certainly we could
not duplicate the incredibly complex system that con-
nects this Portal to others. Maybe someday, though."
He smiled at the boy's frown. "You ask a lot of questions," Oikawa said. "That's good. Maybe you'll be up
there" —he pointed to the overseer's deck depending
from the roof— "running the whole show, when you're
older."

Murdoch shook his head. "No. The Force doesn't
have to pay the Outsteppers."

Most of his class laughed, and even Oikawa could
not wholly suppress a smile. "We've been told it's
nearly a forty years' journey by light-speed ship to the
world where those cars will eventually arrive—and
forty years more to return. Citizen, your friends would
be old men and women when you come back home."

Colly said something, but he had turned away and
Oikawa did not hear.

"What did you say?"

"And you'd be dead!" Colly returned to the descent-
shaft, not quite running.

"He does things like that all the time, Citizen Oikawa," said Tilda apologetically. Across the floor, a car
loaded with sculpture rolled smoothly, soundlessly into
infinity.

July 2058
Manchester, **Deep Space**

In every cabin, every corridor, above, below and between decks, the hum of the central engine-core pene-
trates. It varies in pitch and intensity with the vagaries

of the hydrogen currents of space, but it never quite retreats from the threshold of audibility. It is all-pervading, constant, annoying except after long months of acclimatization, and often even then.

But it does not penetrate here. Here are heard only the gentlest of sighs from the circulation vents set in the low ceiling. The keyboards themselves are silent, as are the computerized monitors, as is Colin Murdoch as he paces across rubberized flooring, glancing at each dial face and graph. He makes small, precise checks with a blue marker next to items on his checklist.

The instrumentation lies in a horseshoe-shaped battery in the center of the weapons room; the open end faces the single door. Around it, forming a ring broken only by the door, are the control systems and manual overrides for the weapons banks that are scattered over the ship. Sienna-colored housings have white legends stenciled across their canted surfaces, advising that the directors and control-computers for missiles, lasers, three-ton solid iron projectiles, plagues, and a compilation of like forces all lie waiting here.

Colin walks the circle, glancing up and down each silent face before moving on to the next. The instruments have already told him that all lies battle-ready, but Colin studies each housing as if it may tell him something more.

But they do not; and, having completed his rounds, Colin pauses at the door to throw his checklist into the destruct-bin and to clip his marker to the wall. This done, he opens the door manually with a lever set along its edge. He turns in the hall outside to make sure the black door has closed behind him. It will open only for him.

Recreation deck six is nearly empty. It is a shelf of steel and plastic that juts out from *Manchester*'s hull. It is twenty-five meters wide and eighteen deep, and two decks thick, and it can be retracted if necessary. The lower level is a gaming area, the upper the observation deck. Clear supraplastic forms three walls and the flattened dome of the ceiling. It reflects none of the chamber's soft illumination; it is as if this part of *Manchester* were open to space.

Murdoch stops for a moment a few meters outside the descent-shaft door. From this vantage at the rear of the deck he can see two women nestled together several meters to his right, partially hidden from him by synthetic palms. An engineer (her name, Burdick, comes slowly to him) reclines on the turf an equal distance to his left. The ship is under drive, and Murdoch feels his full weight upon him as he moves to a couch an equal distance from the people to either side of him. The tension of the day slowly leaves his muscles.

Through the transparent ceiling he can see the dark hull of *Manchester* poised as if to topple on him. Beyond it are the stars set in dopplered rainbow wheels, with the hydrogen scoop as their center. The rim of the scoop glows with ionized hydrogen, as do the strands of the electromagnetic vanes that stretch away until they are lost to sight. Lightning flickers all along their lengths, and brief sheets of current sometimes arc from one to another in a pale ballet.

Now standing behind him and to his left, watching the stars but also him is Theresa Burdick. Her pulse is loud in her ears, and she is embarrassed by it and chastizes herself.

"How long before we reach the Forward?," she asks, coming over to his couch.

"A little over a year. It's almost time for turn-over and deceleration." His tones are polite—but impatient. He would prefer she leave him alone.

"You won't be able to see the Forward then," she says. "Not from here."

He smiles mechanically. "I can't see it now. It's gone into the ultraviolet."

Of course. The dopplering effect. "Yes," she says, "I'd forgotten."

He nods, politely.

"Where is it that you usually take your dinner?"

"Mess Eight, at twenty-four hundred hours."

"Midwatch?"

He nods, then says: "There are fewer people; I can finish faster. Then I sleep until oh-six-hundred, when I make my first duty tour. Why?"

"I thought perhaps we could have dinner together sometime, but my watch doesn't end until oh-four-hundred."

"I'd be sleeping at that time."

"Yes. I know." He looks at her for a moment more, and she says as he starts to turn away, "Perhaps another time, when the shifts have been changed." This will happen in less than a month.

"Perhaps." And he does turn away.

She waits a measured time, then moves away from him, but forward also, so that she remains within his field of vision. She sits on the turf, legs stretched before her, hands planted to either side of her and behind. Five minutes pass. Time enough.

"The stars are beautiful, aren't they?"

His gaze does not waver from them. "Yes."

She says nothing, he says no more, and presently she leaves—he is not quite sure when.

Murdoch's gaze pierces the coronal haze of ionized hydrogen that wreathes the collection-maw. He perceives the dim red star that lies at the end of this journey. The encounter slips easily from his memory, as the skies and *Manchester* again take him. These endless ship days are empty, but his memories of other days are whole and clear, and not at all left behind him as *Manchester* accelerates into the infinite midnight.

September 2050
Fishguard

The bus whined down an old asphalt road, packed two cadets beyond capacity. Its aged motors could no longer handle the load effectively, and it rode low on its air cushion. Murdoch gripped the edge of his seat as the vehicle listed heavily to one side, then recovered itself.

"Coming up on the right," said the driver. The rust-clad cadets on that side of the bus looked out through streaked windows; most of those on the left went into the aisle to get a glimpse. Murdoch did not move from his place by the left, rearmost window. Through road-film he could see the outlying buildings of Fishguard disappear behind him. Fields of wild grasses supplanted those of late-blooming flowers. Small, pleasant trees were set a distance back from the road, and low hills rose beyond to hide the Welsh interior from Murdoch's eyes.

The bus suddenly lurched to the right and dipped down a steep grade. It leveled off, then stopped; the engine cut and the bus dropped with a disconcerting thump. The doors fore and aft squealed open. "All out."

Murdoch stood in the doorway, blinking in the unpolarized sunlight, then stepped down into dust still unsettled. He walked until he was clear of the crowding around the bus's luggage compartments. He looked around. The lot surface was unprepared dirt, baked dry by the summer sun, though still damp in those places where last night's shower had collected. Ten meters from the road was a two-story stucco house, glaring white in the sunlight of late morning. The house was not wide, but it stretched far back; a plastic roof was the only outward concession to modern times: the structure seemed to have been built over a century ago. Beyond it were tangled shrubs and briers, and farther back was a small stand or grove of trees. He caught the faint tang of the ocean even here, several kilometers from the coast.

"Got a Murdoch here?" From the driver's tone, it was not the first time the question had been asked.

"Here," said Murdoch.

"Come get your bags."

Inside, the original construction of the building had been refurbished and largely replaced with contemporary furnishings. Diffuse light came from ceiling and wall panels. The room the cadets stood in held them all easily; it measured the width of the house and, as best Murdoch could determine, went to two thirds its depth. Long tables and benches occupied the rear half of the room. To the left, stairs of wood led upward into a darker loft.

There was a relative silence, in contrast to the gabbling of their approach and debarkation, broken once by the sound of the bus leaving, and intermittently by the muffled sound of a dropped duffel bag or the whisper of an unanswered question. True silence came with the appearance of a man at the head of the stairs.

He was huge. Two meters tall, or nearly so, and all of one hundred twenty-five kilograms in weight, all of it appearing quite solid. His Force uniform stretched tight over slabbed muscles; it was immaculate, sharp-creased, and his pants-legs were tucked into black calf boots that shone. Gold flickered at his right shoulder: a full captain. He walked down the stairs, stopping two steps above the level of the floor, and looked out over the newcomers.

Portelance was the cadets' group leader. He strode briskly forward, nodded to the captain, then turned on his heel to face his charges. "Rank for inspection," he ordered, in a voice a little too loud for the close confines of the room. The cadets fell into three rows. Portelance about-faced and saluted the captain. "Cadet Group Fifty-two," he said, "Atlantic Union, United States, West Coast, reporting for training as ordered, Captain."

"Your group received, Corporal. Join your people." Portelance fell in at the end of the first row, to stand in front of Murdoch.

The captain stepped to the floor. "This is Center Two," he said. "We are two kilometers south-southwest of the town of Fishguard, where I understand you spent the evening, as per your travel orders. There will be no leaves to the town, nor anywhere else, until your period of training here has been completed. You have been told this already.

"There are two ways to complete this training course. One is to follow the directions I give you, and accomplish the tasks and exercises I assign you as they are given, with no lagging or grandstanding. In this manner you will leave here four months from today, no longer as cadets.

"The other manner is one I do not prescribe. If you cannot successfully complete this training, you will be reassigned elsewhere in a secretarial or supportive capacity for the remainder of your term of service, at which time you will be discharged without pension or benefits. If you are injured or called away and by your own decision leave, the same. An honorable discharge, but with no provision for reenlistment. Some of you—and I will not tell you the predicted percentages—will successfully complete this stage and advance to further technical training. Some of you will probably be expelled today, or on the final day, or on any day between." No one stirred; they were stone.

"I am your instructor. Other staff here include one medical assistant and one cook, both civilian, both from Fishguard. My name is Captain Hadden. You may address me, without leave, by that name. In a few minutes you will go upstairs to your quarters, three cadets to a room. Are there any questions?" There were none.

"Your first exercise, then. You, third row, fifth rank. Stand forward and state your name." A girl stepped between the ranks and came to within an arm's length of Captain Hadden. "Maureen Li." Murdoch had seen her last night in Fishguard, in the group with Portelance that had arrived on the second ferry from Portsmouth.

"You. Second row, first rank. Stand forward and state your name."

Murdoch moved to stand alongside Li. "Colin Murdoch."

Captain Hadden nodded once. "Li, Murdoch, square off to four meters, free-style, first knee to floor."

Murdoch arched one eyebrow, but Li had already taken her place four meters away, and Murdoch's mind laid out the other two corners and the lines of the square. He used imperfections in the flooring to keep track of the bounds. Li came to his shoulders; she was solid but not heavyset. She looked at him, and their eyes locked for an instant.

He brought his right forearm up in time to block her fist to his plexus. Bringing up his left arm trapped hers, but only for a moment. She spun, and he took the kick on the fleshy part of his hip, rather than the groin. He caught at her foot and jerked his arm up, but she touched the floor with one hand and was up again. Murdoch made a leap that carried him nearly to the ceiling; his boot descended at her. A slight twisting at the waist and he instead landed on the floor to one side of her and behind; his arms gripped her in a full nelson. She tried to slip free, then spin out, but could not. Murdoch switched to a half nelson (she almost got away), reached for her right calf, preparatory to immobilizing her fully. As his hand touched her boot, she kicked away, arched, twisted, and his hands held nothing. Instinctively he spun to the side, and her boot, rather than breaking his jaw, merely bruised him and rendered him unconscious.

They didn't know the rules; that was part of the training. When Murdoch regained consciousness, he had his theories. As he'd fallen, two cadets had stepped forward to help him. A third had tried to restrain both with a word of warning. There was a rumor that the three cadets in the room across from Murdoch's own, the one he'd been assigned with Li, had fornicated. And the rumor mongers had not appeared on the following day. Totally unrelated, there had been a fight between two male cadets over some insignificant incident. Murdoch's was convinced that any offense against social order or union or efficiency, large or small, was met with the ultimate punishment: expulsion, here; in space, death.

By the end of the first week, only two dozen cadets remained.

June 2063
Manchester, The Outstepper Forward

This chamber is one of the combination galley-and-recreation halls. The ceiling is high, brightly-lit; the walls are filled with soft, slowly moving colors. A bank of automats marks the boundary of the dining and gaming areas. It is Murdoch's custom to frequent the dining area near recreation deck six, but it is much more crowded than usual now, with the attraction of a view of Wolfe 359 and, if one's eyes are particularly sharp, the Outstepper Forward.

The gaming area here is less than half full, and the galley is totally empty save for Murdoch. Sound baffles catch most of the mob-noise from behind him. He sits at a small table away from both the entrances to the galley and the automats. He has finished his reconstituted meal, and sits now with his fingers interlaced, studying an order-screen on the table before him. Statistics and timetables slide past his eyes at a programmed rate. They are completing the approach to the first target. These notes of Murdoch's were memorized nearly two years ago, high-time, but he checks himself just the same. Yes . . . approach patterns, bombardments and tactical targets, weapons capabilities, all are as he remembers.

He looks up from his work as a half dozen arguing crewmen enter the hall. Murdoch ignores them as best he can and continues to study. A few seconds later he looks up again, concealing his annoyance, as the orders on his screen fade to invisibility.

"Could you stand a few meters away, please?" he says to the two crewmen standing across the table from him. "My screen is proximity-coded."

"Oh. Sure." The one who has spoken is short and wiry, and unshaven. His companion is tall and broad, and with a full beard. His eyes are set in a perpetual squint. A hull worker, perhaps. They pull themselves to the next table. "Far enough?"

"Yes. Thank you."

"Can I do something for you?" Murdoch asks neutrally.

"We can see you're busy there, but we just wanted to know—you're Murdoch, the death-man?"

Looking up, Murdoch notes that the other four crewmen are sitting near the exit. One of them looks at him at the mention of his station; then he speaks with the others in low tones.

"The weapons master," says Murdoch. "Yes."

"We thought if anyone would know what's going on, you would," says the crewman. Murdoch glances at the man's companion, who is evidently included in the "we." His expression is totally unreadable.

"What is your question?" asks Murdoch.

"This planet we're going to, the Forward. There's nobody there now, is there?"

"That is what the long-distance probes have told us."

"Then why are we going there?"

"That's kept information," states Murdoch.

The man's look is blank.

"One level below confidential," Murdoch explains. "It means that I am allowed to tell you if I feel it is necessary for the good of the ship or the success of the mission, and can support that opinion later, at a board of inquiry, if need be."

"Oh."

"So you can't tell us either." The big man's voice is loud, a deep basso.

Murdoch shifts his gaze to him. "No, I cannot. I'm sorry."

The big man shakes his head. "Well, damn it, someone should tell me. I may have had nothing after the war, but at least I knew where I was, and why." He looked at Murdoch. "Why's that confidential?" Murdoch does not correct him: the information is not confidential, merely kept. The hull worker stands up suddenly, one hand gripping the edge of the table to tether himself, and Murdoch thinks for a moment that he may, perhaps, attack, but he does not.

"Were you one of the ones working with the reclamation crews?" Murdoch shakes his head. "I was; I guess most of the crew was with them at one time or another. I handled a skycrane, the biggest model we used. One sweep of concrete rot"—he swept his hand through the air—"and five hours later, no matter what the size, down she comes. Any building, any size. Then the little buggies come in and strip the steel out. And now I spend my time outship, tending that same steel. You see what I mean?" Murdoch shakes his head slightly. "You're the death-man, maybe more important than the captain, more important than anyone but him for sure. But I built *Manchester*, Weapons Master, and I live in her, like you. I'm not stupid. I can't handle a zankowich, but you couldn't tackle a skycrane, either. How come I can't know?" He stares at Murdoch.

"I would tell you if I could," says Murdoch, though in reality he would not consider telling them. "But I cannot. I'm sorry." He clips the order-screen to his belt. "I have to go now." He pulls and pushes himself to the exit, where he stops. Two crewmen bar his path. He knows one of them by name, a hull worker named Bierman. "Excuse me," says Murdoch.

"No," says Bierman's companion, and Murdoch suddenly realizes that two more crewmen—not those he has spoken to, but two others—have fallen in behind him, and that he is surrounded. Bierman's boot comes out straight from the man's place by the wall, missing Murdoch's chest but striking him in the stomach, sending him spinning. A well-muscled arm catches him, stopping his rotation. The arm is around his throat and he cannot breathe.

"Stop it, you asses," comes the voice of the hull worker, and Murdoch feels a jarring impact and he is suddenly floating free. The man who had been choking him careens past, his mouth slack. "The rest of you move out of his way," says the hull worker. He turns to Murdoch. "Get up to officer country." Murdoch catches on to the back of a chair and throws himself through the cleared exit. A descent-shaft a few meters down the corridor takes him deeper into *Manchester*. It is only once he has returned to familiar decks that he notices the terrible pounding in his temples. He takes hold of a nylon line and stops to catch his breath.

Drives silent, Wing 23 glides in toward Wolf 359. The star swells in the opticons, a diffuse cloud of dully glowing gases. It drips lazy tendrils of prominences that lick at the approaching ships. Hull temperatures rise. Auxiliary pumps churn to life as additional coolants are forced through metal veins.

Murdoch is at his place in the weapons room. The

U-shaped instrumentation bank has opened for him, and he is within it, attending the zankowich. The compartment is barely large enough to accommodate himself and the webbed couch that smothers him completely. Leads and tubes enter his uniform at various points, and he is immobilized, his joints padded and secured. A gray, featureless helmet covers his head and shoulders completely. Two cables as thick as a man's forefinger lead from it to the close ceiling. He does not feel the pressure of his restraints. The air has an overwhelming electric tang that he does not smell. He is isolated.

Inside the helmet, inside his skull, he hears the voices of the command crew and sees the Outstepper Forward grow beneath him. The worldlet skirts close to the flames of its sun, obscured by sheets of plasma planets wide. Its surface is furnace-hot and liquid, where rock has run. Sublimated metals provide an atmosphere of sorts. It has been, until the coming of the starships, 359's only companion.

Murdoch blinks. The surface of the Forward dissolves like a fading dream. Computer-enhanced radar and gravitational images let him see that, inside, the Forward is compartmented through and through. Its density, a nixie voice informs him, is low: it is steel and dense plastics, but it is hollow as well. Murdoch's eyes trace with difficulty the maze of corridors, cross-ways and shafts that link chambers ranging in size from those not large enough to hold a man to several roomy enough for *Manchester*. A sculpted world. Quite possibly, even its present orbit is a creation of the Outsteppers. The computer informs him that the Forward is now thirty thousand kilometers distant.

And the captain's voice, behind his ear: *Weapons Master, prepare to fire.*

"Weapons master ready," Murdoch sub-vocalizes. Computer informs him the systems are under Murdoch's control, and that computer stands by to assist.

Seven ships circle and dance over the world-pebble. The recreation decks are all retracted, the cooled engines are cloaked now in steel skirts. The collection-maw has ceased to glow. Riding lights wink along identical two-thousand-meter hulls. The ships, with bursts from control jets, take up their stations in synchronous orbits. The planet stands ready, deserted as they had expected it to be, the power core that has supplanted the planet's core dark, and making no impression on the ships' energy sensors.

Casually, almost disdainfully, *Adelaide* drops an atomic charge onto a surface structure. The blast far outshines Wolf 359.

Weapons Master, commence firing.

The echo has not died in his inner ear before Murdoch clenches fists, closing contacts. His jaw moves imperceptibly, making minute corrections in attitude and range. The slave servo-mechanisms that control the weapons blisters comply.

His missile is away, and detonates six hundred meters over Lock Crater C (as it appears on his charts), boiling away the surface strata and revealing tougher alloys beneath. Detonations flung from *Vancouver* and *Mindanao* shatter the lock doors, and gases puff outward, pulling detritus with them. Another charge from *Mindanao.* At full magnification, Murdoch can barely glimpse twisted supports and warped decks through the clouds of vapor and particulate matter.

Somewhat less than a quarter of a minute (*12.76 seconds,* supplies computer) and Lock Crater C, a dozen kilometers in diameter, with the armor and machinery beneath it, has been obliterated as if it had never been.

Manchester shifts orbit slightly. The ship drops to within three hundred kilometers of the surface. Plains and twisted mountains glide rapidly beneath; fire gleams on the horizon, and clouds of debris rise up at

Murdoch from those places where *Manchester*'s sisters have already visited and touched with their poison.

The mass of architecture below the surface is too confusing for Murdoch. Helpfully, computer delineates target number 2 for him in a pale-orange outline.

Neither the long-range sensors nor *Manchester*'s own eyes have identified any structure that may definitely be said to contain an offensive weapon. Yet, there are a number of buildings and compartments clustered about Portal Central, the primary target. *Manchester*, followed in single file at one-thousand-kilometer intervals by four other starships, travels at high speed toward the plain under which the Portal is located. When computer cues him, Murdoch points at his delineated targets with all his fingers.

Lasers, so intense that computer must polarize the view to near blackness, lance out and down from *Manchester*'s belly and touch the low metal structures that break the surface of the plain and are sunk many meters into it. The target swiftly passes out of *Manchester*'s range, but the other ships follow and their lasers scour the area as well. Puddled steels mix freely with the liquefied plain, until all congeals into an unrecognizable mass.

Manchester withdraws the protective skirts from about her engines and uses hydrogen from her reserve tanks to boost out of her present orbit and into a higher one. Behind, Murdoch can see that the Outstepper Forward has been re-sculpted: mountains have been brushed smooth, craters filled, plains cracked open and warped.

Weapons Master stand by. Computer places *Manchester*'s weaponry on a lower-alert status.

Several hours pass, but for Murdoch, attending the zankowich, the computer-meld, it seems that there is no pause before *Vancouver* opens the doors of her main cargo lock and a large shuttle-craft wins free and drops groundward. It is winged, meant for transits of a substantial atmosphere, and it falls far too rapidly in the tenuous wisps that cloak the Forward. After its thirty-minute descent it impacts hard against the surface; metals and plastics shower outward, and it traces a kilometer-long skid in the solid rock. It has been a good landing, though; the shuttle is expendable and rests now in the smoking crater that lies above Portal Central.

At full magnification, with radiation and infrared and sunglare filtered by the omnipresent computer, Murdoch sees movement on the surface. Explosive latches blow the side of the shuttle away, exposing an enlarged cargo compartment. Tank-treaded robots nearly ten meters long, each massing several dozen metric tons, crawl out from the ship. Five of the robots are modified military vehicles equipped with laser-cannon and missile tubes. The sixth is an open cargo truck that follows the rest.

Vancouver's operators guide the team to a point deep inside the crater to which *Vancouver*'s computer, in turn, has guided the operators. Laser-cannon open up the rock, exposing an Outstepper-made shaft leading downward. The sixth robot's manlike cargo climbs down from the vehicle and slogs through molten rock to the shaft.

And down.

February 2051
Fishguard

"I can't see a damned thing," said Beaumont.

"If you'd keep your mouth shut, maybe we could see better," said Portelance.

The training frame had been erected sometime during the afternoon sleep period. Murdoch could barely pick out its size and configuration in the moonless night. It was nothing more than a series of tubular supports arranged in a complex pattern fifteen meters high and twenty meters square. Scattered widely were platforms large enough to accommodate a standing man. Each of the three cadets were clad in full space armor. Captain Hadden, they knew, would be back at the house, watching them and monitoring their radio communications.

The suit dragged at Murdoch. They had spent the last three days walking around in their armor and getting accustomed to its feel and the limitations it imposed on the wearer, but that had not prepared him for this. Murdoch was into the frame now, clambering more or less steadily upward. Portelance was a cumbersome figure five meters below and to the left, Beaumont was somewhere behind him, out of sight. Murdoch was quickly approaching the eastern limit of the frame—and he wondered where his rabbit would lead him from there. The fist-sized mechanical device crawled along the tubes ahead of him, guiding him through the exercise. The route was not random; Murdoch was certain it had been precisely plotted for a standard duration and difficulty factor . . . but he found it tortuous. The rabbit stopped when he was lagging about three meters behind it, almost as if to let him catch up, then it advanced straight up the next joint in the frame. Murdoch paused when he reached the spot. He had lost it.

One of the metal platforms was directly above him, three meters up, at the very top level of the training frame. Maybe the rabbit was on the platform . . . ? He gripped the tubing with gloved hands and pulled himself halfway up, to a crosspiece. Sitting on the bar, he leaned back dangerously and gripped the edge of the platform just as his center of gravity shifted. He nearly lost his grip. He inched his fingers forward on the platform, getting the best purchase he could, then untangled his legs from around the crosspiece and swung free. His fingers started to slip, and tightened spasmodically. He knew he could easily break his fall, but that would constitute a failure of the exercise. He worked at bettering his grip again, gathered his strength, and hauled himself up until he could lean his chest on the platform. The rabbit wasn't there. He scrambled on top of the platform.

Stars, sharp and bright, were overhead. He sniffed, but only stale suit air met his nostrils. Half a kilometer away he could see a few lights on in the house, and the moving lights of a heavy truck just beyond it, passing along the road from Fishguard. He looked down, and saw the other two men still following their own courses. Starlight glinted from the carapace of Beaumont's rabbit, but Murdoch's was still nowhere to be seen. Should he wait here in the hope that he would catch sight of his own guide again, or report to Captain Hadden?

A voice in his headphones spared him the decision. "Cadet Murdoch, training exercise completed. Proceed to ground level along indicated route."

"Murdoch acknowledging."

The rabbit poked over the edge of the platform. Murdoch swung his arms back once to limber them, then followed the machine down along a route childishly easy after the one he'd just completed. When his feet touched the flattened grasses, he was instructed by Captain Hadden to return to the house.

Murdoch unbuttoned his helmet and breathed a lungful of Welsh air, fresh and delicately scented after the blandness of his own recycled air supply. Two days of training remained. His chest expanded deeply, just for the sake of breathing, and the very slightest of smiles played across his usually stoic features. Murdoch had maintained a low profile during his entire stay, believing the best way to escape expulsion was to escape notice. He had, perhaps, overcompensated: his effected blandness had earned him a number of nicknames, all derogatory. He was not upset by them. The faint smile was there now, but it would be gone by the time he reached the house.

"Colin."

Murdoch turned—and allowed the grin to stay in place. "Hello, Maureen. There was more than one training area?"

"Outer hull maneuvers?"

He nodded. The trail was wide enough for them to walk side by side.

"It's almost over, our training," she said after a moment.

"Yes. Maureen. Is anyone opting for further training? Are you?"

"There are a few who are," she said. "Portelance is, for sure. I don't think I will. I'm not sure. Actual assignment to a ship requires such precision and responsibility . . . I'm not sure I have that—or want it." She looked down.

He nodded in what he hoped was an understanding way. "I feel very much the same. Up to now, this has been well within my limitations. But for something like active training, another ten months—it would be difficult. I don't know if I'm worth an effort like that."

She looked at him. "An odd turn of phrase. The Force?"

"It's not a motivation itself," he said. "Call it an exercise. It's evident I've completed that exercise—or I will have, tomorrow. I've been wondering what's next—further exercises, or the application of what I've learned?"

She stopped walking suddenly, still looking at him. "There's more to you than you let show." She paused. "Colin, why so into yourself? There certainly isn't any opportunity to socialize here—but still, you could do something to interact. I hear them talking about you, and it's painful to hear. They have named you—"

"I know. I've heard them."

"Then you know what I'm talking about," she said. "You've let yourself become an object of scorn or pity. That's not good."

"Is that a fault in myself, or in them?"

"I don't know. If only . . ."

He cut her off sharply: "And which is it for you? Scorn, Maureen, or pity?"

"Colin, I only wanted you to understand—"

"What'?" The syllable was a rifle shot. "Understand what?"

She was silent, shocked, and then he heard them. Footsteps, heavy, plodding, from behind them. Four figures, bulky-suited as he and Maureen trudged down the path toward them.

Murdoch saw that Portelance was heavily fatigued. The sweat glistened on his face, traced small streams on his neck seal. Still, he smiled, broadly, flashing white teeth. "Maureen? Did you make it? And quickly, too! See you tomorrow, fellows," he said to the other three cadets. Beaumont literally could not lift his feet, and dragged his boots through the dirt with soft sounds. "And Murdoch, as well," Portelance continued. "We don't see much of you."

"So I've been told." Murdoch nodded farewell to Portelance, then Maureen. With long strides, he passed the other cadets.

Murdoch had learned long ago to recognize her footsteps on loam, on grass, on the wooden floor of the dining hall, and on the stairs as she ascended, and on the floor outside as she approached. She hesitated for a fraction of a second on the threshold, then entered and walked quickly to the desk that was hers. Murdock lay perfectly still in his bed, eyes closed against the un-dimmed ceiling panels. He heard the old chair scrape back, and the miscellaneous sounds of a search for stylus and board, then writing.

He opened his eyes. Not turning his head, he looked at her. Her uniform, sweat-stained, followed the arch of her back as she bent to her work. One booted foot rested atop the other, and she was sitting slantwise in the chair. Shadows picked out the highlights of her cheekbones; light and dark, colors he had never found the precise terms for. A reaction started in him, and he turned to face the wall to conceal it.

The stylus clicked down against the desk top. "Damn it, Colin." He stiffened. "Do you have to be so self-righteous? No one thinks you're a suffering hero because you can't get along with the rest of us. I certainly don't." He did not turn. The chair scraped again, as the overheads dimmed. "You don't have to be impolite, on top of everything else." He hesitated, then grudgingly rolled over to face her.

"You don't speak to anyone," she said, "and then you undoubtedly wonder why no one walks to the very end of the dining hall for the privilege of sitting with you."

He wondered at her tone. Sarcasm, biting cynicism . . . hatred? "I've found, in the past—and if it's any of your concern," he said, "that I simply do not have much in common with most people. I could not possibly interest them, and I refuse to burden myself with people who could not possibly interest me."

He felt something change in the air, though the expression on her face was unwavering. "How do you know?" she asked quietly. "How could you possibly know how anyone else feels about you?"

"I know," said Murdoch. "I know precisely."

"No." She stripped quickly and slipped into the bed alongside his. "You don't know at all. Not one damned thing." Blackness shuttered them completely, as the schedule board briefly glowed with FULL REST, then also extinguished itself. "How could you know? You don't see; perhaps you're afraid to. You don't see me, not anyone."

"I see you," he said to darkness.

"But you don't. Or, at least, you haven't."

Something rose in his throat. Salton, the body shops and fun places. An endless succession, one to another. . . . *It's ended,* he thought. *No more of the things that come to nothing in the end.* And so he said, speaking of Porte-lance, "Would the corporal approve of the turn this conversation is developing?" It was, he knew, precisely what was called for him to say.

There was silence.

"Oh." This from her, very quietly. "Oh."

June 2063
Manchester, The Outstepper Forward

For Murdoch, the conference room has a familiar aspect. It is about five meters square, furnished only with a long table with chairs facing a wall of opticons. He has, of course, been here many times before. Weightless, he floats to a chair to the right of the captain and velcroes himself in place while representatives from navigation, maintenance and life support, engineering, communications, and personnel seat themselves around him. Invisible cameras stare blankly at them until *Manchester*'s captain, Hamlyn, presses a key on the small instrument board before him. The opticons before *Manchester*'s officers glow, carrying the images of the other six ships of Wing 23. Simultaneously, their own faces are duplicated in the conference rooms of the other ships.

Captain Newell of *Vancouver* begins: *"Vancouver's* Special Section successfully retrieved the Portal Central records housed in the human-occupied portion of the Foreward. Recovery was made by a humanoid telefactoring device that we destructed after a search of the human-inhabited district was made, revealing no survivors."

"Were there any signs of violence?" asks *Adelaide*'s Captain Howard.

"None apparent," answers Newell. "The entire Forward is deserted. The power core was shut down in orderly fashion. All devices of human origin we found were still operable: Portal Central's computer banks, for instance. But examination of Outstepper artifacts revealed them to be inoperative, though they appeared to be undamaged. Attempts to secure Outstepper artifacts for possible transport to *Vancouver* resulted in failure. All devices were secured to the superstructure of the Forward. When they were removed from their holdfasts, they quickly sublimated. We have analyzed the chemical composition of the destructed objects, but this study was largely worthless. It tells us nothing of the devices themselves."

Newell continues: "Records in Portal Central have been duplicated and transmitted to all ships of the wing. These records confirm some data we already possessed, and they have given us more. Briefly, there were 4,700,850 citizens of Earth off-planet, through the Portal, when the Portal War occurred. Records we have retrieved from the Forward tell us that 3,900 were there, either as staff or waiting for transfer to their destination-worlds, at the time of the War. These persons are unaccounted for. I have lists detailing the numbers of immigrants to each of our sixty-three colonial worlds."

Captain Hamlyn says, "After we arrived here, I opened this wing's orders. Following the completion of our duties here, we have the option of getting under way to one of four colonial worlds." Hamlyn presses a button. On one of the opticons in each of the seven ships, words appear:

CAULDRON	7.0	2,818
STAPLEDON	7.2	59,802
FLANDER'S PLANET	9.0	15,700
LADY	12.7	112,675

"The third column," explains Hamlyn, "represents the population of each world. These agree with your figures, Captain Newell?" Newell nods. "The second represents the worlds' present distance from us in light-years. For our transit-time, in rough figures, add one year to these figures. That's home-time, of course."

"Are there any priorities listed in our orders at this point, Captain," asks Murdoch, "as regards our next target?"

Hamlyn shakes his head. "None. There was, of course, no way Rescue Expedition Planning could have predicted the abandonment of the Outstepper Forward. Had the Forward been defended, it is perhaps doubtful we would have survived to select another target. There was a provision for utilization of the Forward's Portal to reestablish contact with our worlds, and to discover the world or worlds that launched the attack against Earth. With the power core shut down, this option is closed to us.

"As the situation now stands, we may select one of four worlds, and our selections must be based on deduction and extrapolation of what data we have on hand. We have all had access to both the data *Vancouver* rescued and the background data on these worlds from our own memory banks. We must make a decision."

"I say Lady," says *Oceania*'s weapons master. "Most populous, least agricultural, least self-sufficient. It seems we could aid the most people by going to Lady."

"The 'qualifications' you've given for Lady," objects *Berlin*'s Captain Alder, "seem to rule it out. At maximum acceleration to light-speed, it would take us fourteen years and three months to reach the planet, home-time. By then the inhabitants would either be self-sufficient or extinct. This all assumes that the planet wasn't attacked when Earth was. We still can't get any probabilities on that from the computers."

"A valid point," says Hamlyn. The heads in the op-ticons nod, even, after a brief pause, that of *Oceania*'s weapons master. Hamlyn continues, "I favor Flander's Planet. Low population, highly self-sufficient, and not a key trade world. Assuming the attackers had to limit the scope of their operations, Flander's Planet is not a strategic target, and may have been spared."

"What about Stapledon? That's the oldest world. It may have been high on this theoretical strike-list of the attackers, but it is also a well-established world, and a well-entrenched population." It is *Oceania*'s weapons master speaking again.

"And Stapledon," adds Colin Murdoch, "is only a few objective years' distance from Cauldron, the clos-est world. Three lights, or roughly four years' travel time. It seems logical to make for Cauldron, then Sta-pledon."

Hamlyn says, "But Cauldron totally lacks self-suf-ficiency. Beyond that, it was an exporter of nuclear ma-terials for Earth. A key strategic resource."

"That is based on three assumptions," says Murdoch, "none of which we have data to prove or disprove: first, that any worlds aside from Earth were attacked; second, that the attackers hold our own priorities as to what is and is not strategic; third, that Cauldron, or any of the other colonial worlds, was unable to destroy its Portal before it received much damage—and so could seal itself off from further attack." There is a smattering of assent from the other ships.

Hamlyn pauses, watching Murdoch briefly. Then he says: "Cauldron, then? Followed by Stapledon, with a decision as to the other two worlds to be made after the completion of the next phase of the mission." Assent is given. "If there is no other business, then?" His hand hovers over his cut-off switch.

"There is other business," says Offord, the captain of

Hyderābād. "I submit the following table to you." It appears, superseding the first:

	year	home time	high time
LAUNCH	2054	0	0
OUTSTEPPER FORWARD	2063	9	2.4
CAULDRON	2071	17	4.5
STAPLEDON	2080	26	6.6

"I fail to see the significance of these—" someone begins.

"It is quite simple," says Offord. "We left Earth in 2054, arriving at our present location in 2063, nine objective years having elapsed, while approximately two and four tenths years have elapsed for us. You will note that the second column of figures, our objective elapsed time, progresses much more quickly than our subjective elapsed time. You will also note, however, that time does indeed pass for us."

"I believe we were all aware of that before you brought it to our attention, Captain Offord," states Captain Newell drily. A lesser officer on another ship laughs briefly, but quickly stills himself.

"My point is this," she says, "if you will be so indulgent as to listen to me for a few brief minutes. Each of our ships carries a complement of over six hundred. Our living areas are expansive, but still overcrowded by any traditional, terrestrial standards. Incidents of violence have already been reported. More will undoubtedly occur. But I direct your attention to the last figure in the last column of the table: six and one-half years. I submit that maintaining loyalty and cohesion among the crew will be impossible for the entire duration of our voyage, and even among the officers."

"I can testify to the complete and utter loyalty of _Adelaide_'s entire complement," protests her captain.

Offord ignores this, saying, "I often have found my-self wondering if, over two decades after our depar-ture—or even more, should we continue after Sta-pledon—the razing of what cities were still extant on Earth after the War for the material to build our ships, and our own investments of life-times was worth—"

"You doubt our mission?" asks *Oceania*'s captain coldly.

"I doubt," corrects Offord in a similar tone, "the ability of any thinking person to refrain from having some doubts as to the advisability of continuing an operation which may develop into either a perpetual burying-crew on an interstellar scale, or a fruitless search for either an attacker we've not identified, or for survivors of hypothetical attacks."

"Therefore I decided to leave the country," someone begins, "Therefore I have come as one charged with a special duty . . ."

"Yes, I know all that," snaps Offord, her composure gone. "But all that aside, we must consider that the crew has not been trained as we were, and thus may not—" She catches herself. "They may not realize the value of the Rescue Expedition."

There is a moment's pause, then Hamlyn says, "I trust you have suggestions for maintaining stability for the complete duration of the mission."

Murdoch waits. Some details are lost in the opticon, but he knows that emotion is passing over Offord's face. But the captain only pauses a moment before say-ing, "I merely wished to bring the problem to the at-tention of all."

"And it is appreciated," says Hamlyn. "I will instruct *Manchester*'s own personnel section to investigate the matter, and I expect all ships will co-operate fully in this. Now, if there are no additional reports, we will ad-journ."

Hamlyn turns to Murdoch, but before he may speak,

the weapons master says, "Captain Offord is essentially correct. I go armed myself now," and he touches the top of his boot, where a short-bladed regular-issue knife is tucked.

"Yes, that incident a few days ago. But I find Offord's attitude more troubling."

"Oh?"

"You surely noticed. She practically suggested we abandon the mission."

"Had she suggested it," says Murdoch simply, "she would not have been the last."

Hamlyn's eyes narrow. *He cannot conceal emotion,* Murdoch thinks, and says, "With over four thousand people spread over seven ships, the matter is bound to come up. A minority, whether active or vocal, could do much damage."

"What, then, can be done to ensure the completion of the mission?"

"I am the weapons master, Captain, not a member of personnel."

Impatiently: "Your opinion, Colin."

"Ultimately? Nothing." He releases himself from his seat and goes to the exit. He turns back to his captain. "I find that disturbing. Measures must be taken. I have no suggestions." He leaves.

The seven ships of Wing 23 trace computer-directed orbits in to Wolf 359, where hydrogen is sucked in by collectors. They describe a parabola, then engines flare astern and they climb outward. Hours pass, and the ships are lost to the stars.

Behind, the Outstepper Forward, aided by nuclear charges placed all about its power core, by lasered faults in the crust, and by tactical warheads on the surface, breaks slowly and majestically apart into what will be, one day, a diffuse asteroid belt that will contain no hint of the original construct.

April 2051
Amsterdam, **Near Space**

SFS *Amsterdam* was not a large vessel, even for a trainer. She was barely a hundred meters from propulsion bells to command sphere; most of her mass was propellant, most of her bulk a complicated network of struts that somehow held it all together. She boosted now, at a full four Gs, out from the Force station at Trojan Point Three.

Murdoch did not notice the acceleration unless he concentrated on it, and then only as a sensation of vague discomfort. He floated—seemed to float—dreamlike, and in darkness.

Amsterdam was laid out before him as a multicolored schematic. Rods of orange light traced pulsing fuel lines; the fission reactor glowed in the proper golden hue; the electrical lines were white threads and laced the entire ship, the circuits, and relays small, bright stars. All, Murdoch saw, was well. Digital readouts in the blackness before him verified this in precise terms.

There were five forces in the command sphere, six aft. Those in the rearward section of the ship had been induced to a catatonic state and cared as much for the G-forces as did the six: these were locked into their zankowiches. In the command sphere, with Murdoch as systems engineer, were the captain, the pilot, the navigator, and the life-support engineer.

Amsterdam was hardly complex enough to require the skills of five cyborged officers; Captain Anson monitored all of his students, as well as the functions of the ship, without undo strain on either himself or his zankowich. Anson nodded to himself as his pilot cut the engines and acceleration abruptly ceased.

A voice, Anson's, whispered in Murdoch's inner ear, *Murdoch, lock down and come aft with me.* Murdoch started, he still found the sensation—like that of an intimate whisper, but cold and metallic—disquieting.

Locking down, he sub-vocalized, and an elaborate shrug activated the cued computer and its servo-mechanisms. The zankowich was a rough cylinder, half again the breadth and height of a man. It was studded with the coolant pipes for its cyogenic circuitry and inlaid with biomedical monitors and systems over-rides.

Within, the isolation helmet withdrew as the shock padding, shut through with servo-actuators, released Murdoch from the cocoon in which it had held him. He unstrapped the nylon bands that bound him in the cramped space and breathed deeply of the stale, acid air. A hatch under his feet, stenciled on the outside with his position, pulled away with a pneumatic hiss. Murdoch pushed himself out.

He breathed deeply again, and squinted in the sudden light. His vision cleared quickly, and he saw the zankowiches: the auxiliary unit was dark; three now stood open and the remaining two hummed and blinked quietly to themselves.

Anson was a small, quiet man who nevertheless possessed a definite air of command. He nodded to Murdoch. With them was McArdle, their life-support engineer. "Come aft," said Anson again.

Amsterdam was cramped—a voyage in her was like nothing more than spending several days in a ground-car. There was the resultant frustrating clumsiness and an urge to push the walls out to get some more room. McArdle, tall but slight, followed Anson into the narrow tunnel that led aft with ease. Murdoch was more clumsy. His hip banged the lip of the tunnel painfully; he clamped teeth together and was silent.

The aft chamber was seven meters long and three meters wide. Murdoch held himself in the center of the room by one hand on an overhead ring. Behind him, to either side of the mouth of the tunnel, were stores of food, water, medicines, enough for a one-month voyage. Lockers of parts, personal baggage, and space armor were on either wall, and encroached on the ceiling and floor as well. The rearward wall was completely taken up by six acceleration tubs, man-sized receptacles of gel that almost totally absorbed the shock of acceleration. The crewmen occupied the tubs. "Get out," ordered Anson. "Fifteen seconds to disengage yourselves."

Thick webs and tubular straps held the crewmen securely in place. When Anson called time, only one person was not floating free in the room. Murdoch watched the man tug and wrench at the final cable that held him. He looked up at Anson, breathing heavily. "Damned thing's stuck, Captain."

"So what are you going to do?" asked Anson quietly. "If we were losing pressure, you'd be unconscious already, so it's all academic, but what would you do?"

"These things are supposed to be foolproof," said the cadet. He tugged at the cable again.

"Damn it, you idiot." From somewhere on his uniform, Anson pulled a short-bladed knife. He kicked himself over to the cadet, and as Murdoch watched, fascinated, Anson sliced down, into and through the cable. "*That* is what you do." He slipped the knife into a boot sheath. It was the ornamental blade they all had been issued when they passed the battery of admissions tests that had preceded their active ship training. Murdoch had forgotten his.

"A knife," Anson was saying, "is the most universally applicable tool ever devised. You can cut with it, poke with it, beat with it, mash with it, dig with it, and pry with it. I see some of you have remembered that regulation uniform requires the presence of your knife. Yet not one of you suggested to Gilmour to cut himself out, nor did you try to assist him."

"With all respect," said Mason, another cadet, "six

weeks ago, helping someone without specific orders to do so was punishable by elimination from the training program."

"And that's why the rest of you didn't move?" asked Anson. There was general assent.

"We are," began the captain, "in a bubble of air and water surrounded by a quarter-inch-plate membrane which separates us from a fatal environment. We are not in Todos Santos, Alice Springs, or Fishguard. That was a game, played roughly, but a game. I cannot 'fail' any of you at this point. I am to train you in the operation of an Atlantic Union space vessel. Had I not used this same blade to bend the release pin on that clip a few minutes before we went under acceleration, I might well have dropped the pressure in the hull to add some realism to the drill." He looked at Gilmour. "You would have died." He turned to the others. "You men on watch return to the command sphere. The rest of you check our stores for damage and otherwise amuse yourselves. You go on watch in two hours."

Murdoch let McArdle and Anson leave before him. He paused for one instant on the threshold of the access tunnel. Cadets were already busy opening lockers and checking for fallen or broken articles. Maureen had her back to him, and was pulling space armor more securely onto hooks. Murdoch closed his hand on the lip of the tunnel and pulled himself through.

He pulled a checklist from its holdfast on his zankowich and started through the routine series of notations and adjustments that should be made. The cadets were to spend two weeks here, drifting outward from the Earth to the orbit of her moon, and then to land on that satellite.

The days passed quickly, absorbed by the routine of things, and by Anson's lectures and demonstrations, until only five days remained. More extensive checks of the ship's systems were made in preparation for the upcoming maneuvers.

Tensions among the ten crewmen and the captain, if they existed at all, were well hidden and never surfaced, except for the occasional snapped remark that was immediately apologized for and excused. Had it been otherwise, Murdoch realized at one point, Anson might well have terminated the mission: hostilities in a worldlet little bigger than a bus could prove fatal with alarming ease.

Maureen and Murdoch were awake at the same time for four hours each ship day, but he saw little of her. Those few times when a small duty or errand carried him aft or forward to where she worked or rested, he stayed but briefly and prevented his gaze from lingering on her. Their respective duties were such that he spoke less than two dozen words to her in ten days.

On the eleventh day, Anson and he were checking bundles of cables and molar bypasses set under the removable sections of plate that formed the bulkheads of the rest area.

"Murdoch, go forward and find out what the hell is going on." Anson pulled a meter from a bypass. "This line is getting a double load, could burn out." Murdoch nodded, pulled himself from the gap they'd made in the wall, and eased himself into the tunnel.

Maureen was systems engineer this watch. Zankowiched, she was not aware of Murdoch's arrival. He glanced quickly over the banks of monitors that covered the side of her cylinder. Sure eyes found the problem in seconds. He slapped a switch, sounding a buzzer alarm in the zankowich, and opening a comm-link.

"Yes?" came her voice from a grille near his left hand. She sounded tired.

"Wake up and check your circuits," he said. "You

have an overload coming through the number one hundred twelve trunk."

"Which—?" But he had cut the connection, disturbed.

Asleep? Negligence was one of the few court-martiable offenses. Did she care so little for her duties?

When he returned to Anson, he told him it had been nothing serious, and that the item had been corrected.

"It would've been serious," replied Anson. "Looked like an override on the bypass."

"Isn't that hold-down coming loose, sir?" asked Murdoch.

July 2071
Manchester, Cauldron

Electromagnetic screens are deployed, computers and men are linked in battle-alert status, but, as long-range sensors and unmanned probes have revealed, as visual contact now confirms, there is no need.

Murdoch watches with gray eyes the planet watching him with one blind eye of dull red mottled with yellow and white flecks that waver and flicker. Smaller eyes glow dully at various points. Rigid in the weapons zankowich, Murdoch peers and the computer brings this world closer for his examination. Ash covers much of the surface. An area in the northern hemisphere half the size of Australia has run like water and glows still. Radioactive fires (planetary bonfires) light the nightside. An electronic overlay shows him how the shores of the two continents have been altered by the melting of the polar caps. The water is steaming, blackened near the coasts by sludge, and is uniformly covered with the detritus of dead sea-life, undecayed in an atmosphere cleansed of bacteria by slaying gamma rays. Freak lightning plays in the stratosphere, giving the hell-world a halo. The only major city (the computer indicates its site for Murdoch) has been scooped out of the crust and molten material ladled into the resultant crater.

Cauldron, first colonized. Bought outright by the Force to supply its bases and ships with fuel, later subletted to commercial mining concerns, but still under the auspices of the Force. A military world. An unattractive world, the northern continent rife with earthquakes and geysers, the southern landmass slightly more hospitable. Nowhere, except at the poles, would the temperature fall below thirty degrees Celsius, and the norm was two and a half times that. The atmosphere's high carbon-dioxide content had made self-contained air supplies a necessity for the inhabitants.

There were no complex life-forms. Evolution had not progressed beyond unicellular life resembling diatoms, and one colonial creature like seaborne slime mold. A young world, which one day would be a terrestrial world. Rich in radioactive materials formed during the megayears of the planet's birth, largely undecayed. Now a world stripped entirely of its biosphere. . . .

Murdoch wonders aloud what the surface temperature may be and computer provides him with a four-figure reading.

The wing has been downgraded to a stand-by alert status. Murdoch is in his quarters, in the auxiliary monitoring center that adjoins his rooms. It is a simple affair: an intraship commlink with access to the intership systems; a set of alarms linked to the weapons room that will warn of intrusion or mechanical failure; a series of opticons keyed to various channels. On the widest of these, Murdoch has called up the view presented by one of *Manchester*'s orbiting cameras as it monitors the actions of *Vancouver*'s special section.

It is a man-form telefactoring device they are using: a metal-and-fiber-and-plastic construct two and two thirds meters tall and broad, limbed and tracked. Nearly featureless, with concealed and armored sensors, for any protrusions would be torn to fragments in seconds by the scalding, hundred-kilometer winds that buffet the machine, etching fresh patterns in its metal carapace. Velcroed in his comfortable formfit, Murdoch can almost feel the planet's volcanic breath. The view breaks up in a tumble of static, then returns. But this is an animated view, pieced together by *Vancouver*'s computers, and Murdoch sees the man-form extrude from plated feet to lock it to the ground as it waits for further instructions. Keyed to action, the telefactor soon strides forward again. Against the grayness of the native rock are white and cream flashes like patterns in black marble, where buildings have been melted into the surface. Radio-dating has established that Cauldron was attacked at approximately the same time Earth was, seventeen years ago. Many areas are still molten. Often Murdoch sees the crust break under the telefactor's feet or treads and suddenly it is wading or swimming through pools of liquefied stone. But the telefactor readily advances, proceeding toward the red point superimposed on the animated horizon, marking the source of the radio beacon. It is inaudible from orbit, weak and drowned by the radioactive hiss from the surface, and it is only by chance that a surveying robot comes within the beacon's short range and reports it to the mother ship. In minutes the goal is achieved: the beacon was once a sphere three meters in diameter. Now both its ablative asbestos coating and most of the concrete buffer have vanished, vaporized, and the inner containment shell is warped and discolored by heat. The telefactoring device produces several tools from its incorporated backpack supply and begins to work.

Murdoch notes the time. He estimates it will be several hours at least before the telefactor can crack the well-worn sphere. He rises from his chair and turns off the opticon.

Two security guards are waiting for him when he leaves his quarters. They, or others like them, have been his constant companions for over one subjective month now. One always travels ahead of Murdoch, the other lags behind, and both are armed with long knives and pellet projectors, and are fully trained in zero-G combat.

"Weapons Master?" asks one of them; his name is Whiting.

"The main cargo lock again," answers Murdoch.

The way is familiar to the guards. They travel a route well off the main corridors and arrive quickly. Murdoch's men wait with a dozen or more other guards in the foyer outside the lock's access. The first door slides open for Murdoch and he pulls himself down a short, brightly lit corridor to a second, heavier door. This leads directly to a pressure door that stands open. Murdoch pulls down a knife-switch and this door closes behind him. Computer instantly verifies that the cargo lock is under pressure, and the other door of the airlock opens.

Aside from the cargo lofts, this hangar is the largest compartment in *Manchester*. Above Murdoch, the control and observation decks jut out on a shelf of steel. To either side of him are corrugated sliding doors fifty meters wide and twenty high that can be pulled back to reveal *Manchester*'s primary landing and cargo shuttles. The rails they will ride into the void run straight out from their holding areas, across thousands of square meters of deck, to huge pressure doors that open to free space. To Murdoch's right and left are smaller pressure doors, three to each side, that lead to the major cargo lofts. Overhead are the cranes and winches that are used to transfer cargo when *Manchester* is under drive; crouched against the walls are the robotic and telefactored pods that assist in zero-G. The lighting is bright but free of glare, provided by light strips laid across all the walls and much of the floor and ceiling.

New equipment has been added to the compartment. Small generators are placed at even intervals around the floor, and thin gray strips interconnect them, forming a grid. Perhaps thirty men and women float or are tethered in this area; they travel from one point to another by means of a large net and an array of lines. About the floor are thousands of papers, artifacts, and charred bits of substances that Murdoch cannot readily identify. All have been sprayed with an adhesive iron-dust coating, all are attracted to the floor by the improvised electromagnetic grid.

Murdoch has not been in the room for more than a few seconds before Chief Technician Ivor Tupelov sees him waiting by the door and makes his way to him with a surprising rapidity.

"I have some news for you," Tupelov says. "This latest batch of materials from the surface has completed some of the fragments we'd begun reconstructing earlier. We've managed to piece together about ten percent of a plastic newssheet that carried some news of the day before the attack, including some Portal arrival listings."

"This from the same source?" Murdoch asks.

"Yes," says Tupelov. "It appears that only the populated areas and the mines were struck. Cauldron also had two small settlements, on the southern continent—a meteorological station, and an exploratory base in the interior. Records we've found indicate there were survivors at both these sites as recently as thirteen years ago." He gives Murdoch a quick smile. "The meteorological site has an incredible wealth of information. They were in radio contact with the main population center, where the Portal was located, at the time of the attack."

"And? Did they know who launched the attack?"

"No—and I'm certain if they had known, it would have been recorded somewhere. But the attack was analogous to that against the homeworld: short-range plagues launched simultaneously with robot warheads at more distant targets. The difference is this: the Force closed the Portal on Earth before the attackers could enter into the next phase of their attack, hydrogen warheads of stupendous megatonnage. Utter destruction. More of a purge than an attack. An attempt to wipe the planet's surface of any sign of habitation. Either that, or a gross miscalculation of Cauldron's defensive capabilities. An incredible overkill."

"The purge has not been entirely successful."

"What have we salvaged?" asks Tupelov. They have stopped, and Tupelov waves his hand across the floor of the cargo-lock. "Not even a half ton of records, tools, and other artifacts. It was a very thorough job."

"Any corpses?" Murdoch asks.

"No. With conditions as they are down there, it's doubtful we'd recognize any remains for what they are . . . not after a decade and a half of exposure to the elements."

"True. Now, what have you to show me?"

Tupelov grabs a section of netting and pulls himself to within a half meter of the floor, beckoning Murdoch to do likewise. Charred and wrinkled plastic sheets with gaps and tears are laid out below them. Each group of fragments thought to be of the same page are grouped and labeled as such, their faxed obverses laid out alongside them. "This is the planetary bulletin for the twenty-third of March 2052, corrected to Earth-standard; the day before the Portal War. Twenty-seven people are listed as having arrived through the Portal on this day, and thirty-two more were expected on the following day. I suppose it's academic whether they made it through before the attack, or were waiting to pass through from the Outstepper Forward."

Murdoch nods, studying the list of names.

"What we found was a small stack of bulletins like this. They were piled in random order, probably waiting for disposal, and the bottom sheets were hopelessly fused together. We have about a dozen editions that are good reading copies, though, all with lists of the day's arrivals. You're primarily interested in those, correct?"

"Yes," says Murdoch.

They begin to move to another area a short distance away. "Are you looking for survivors you might know personally?" Tupelov asks after some hesitation.

"In a way," says Murdoch. "There were, of course, numerous Force and political officials, scientists and technicians, off-planet at the time of the attack. If we can pinpoint the location of any significant number of these people at the time of the attack, or determine if they are missing or actually deceased, it may affect our mission program. Are these the papers you were referring to?"

"Yes. You can see they're in good condition."

Murdoch nods. Actually the only difference between these and the others he has looked at is that these are somewhat more complete, slightly less burned. They are still warped and the print is almost impossible to read. "May I handle them?"

"Oh, yes," says Tupelov. "They're quite sturdy."

Murdoch slides the toe of his boot into the mesh of the netting to secure himself, and begins turning pages. It is, he notes, largely figures and forecasts. There are ore tallies from each of the mine shafts, meteorological predictions and conditions for local areas and the planet as a whole, some small news and human-interest features which interest Murdoch not at all and, occupying a third of one column, the list of the day's arrivals from the Portal. Murdoch drops the paper onto the electromagnetic strips and peels away a second. He looks at Tupelov. "Thank you," Murdoch says. "I'll be here for a while."

There are actually fourteen of the papers, and half of a fifteenth, but not the half Murdoch is interested in. He passes a hand over his eyes to ward off the strain; when he can see clearly again, Tupelov is coming toward him. "Another arrivals list, Weapons Master. I think this is part of the last paper you looked—"

There is a commotion near the personnel lock. Three security guards take positions to either side and above the door. Captain Hamlyn enters, followed by two more guards.

Hamlyn is an older man, perhaps fifty years subjective, and zankowiching has made him soft and flaccid. Hamlyn's breathing is deeper than it should be when he reaches Murdoch's place.

"Chief Technician, you are doing an admirable job. I congratulate you," says Hamlyn to Tupelov.

"Thank you, Captain."

"If you please, though, I would like a word with the weapons master."

"Of course, Captain." Still half smiling at the compliment paid him, Tupelov again moves off.

"Yes, Captain?" asks Murdoch, when Tupelov has gone out of earshot.

"I'm not surprised to find you here," Hamlyn tells him. "You have either been here or in an observing area on all your free time, of late."

"As you say, Captain, it is my free time."

Hamlyn continues in a hushed voice that betrays a hint of anger. "You are exhibiting an unusual degree of interest in this phase of our mission." He waves a hand before Murdoch can speak. "As you broadly hinted, this is none of my business, and you are correct in that. When it affects your duties, however, it is very much my concern." Murdoch waits. Hamlyn continues: "I have access to your personal histories, of course, as I do the histories of everyone on this ship, and the others. It is my opinion that your arguments at meetings to decide policy are shaped by your personal concerns."

Murdoch's face darkens. "More specifically?"

"This is, for the moment, off the record," Hamlyn says. "I have not discussed this with anyone, and my inquiries into your history are covered by my personal seal.

"I believe you may be endangering our mission by making it into a personal quest. I know—"

"I know of whom you are speaking."

"Do you deny that your motion that we explore this planet was influenced by the fact that this individual booked passage here?"

"That was not the deciding factor, no."

"But it was a factor," Hamlyn presses.

"I assure you, Captain," says Murdoch after a short time, "that personal events did not form substantial factors that influenced my opinions. I still feel that my opinion would have been the same."

Captain Hamlyn nods. "I have never doubted your loyalty, only your judgment. If you say your opinion was unbiased, I would be inclined to believe you. But this—" He indicates the papers at Murdoch's feet.

"I never claimed to lack personal interests in the matter, Captain. I merely said they had not affected my judgment."

Hamlyn nods again. "A good distinction; you are correct. I myself had relatives on the other side of the Portal when it was destroyed, but this wing won't be visiting their world. Tell me, have you pinpointed the woman's location?"

Murdoch hesitates a moment before saying, "No, I haven't. She stayed here only briefly, then moved on."

"A pity," says Hamlyn. "You have learned of the finding of the radiosonde?"

"Yes."

"No leads there, I'm afraid. The telefactoring device opened it and found it was a time capsule: a list of the names of the original explorers, some antiques, little else. Worthless to your purposes."

"Data for our banks, just the same," says Murdoch.

"Yes, always data." Hamlyn surprises Murdoch by grasping his shoulder. "You are a fine officer, Murdoch." He turns and starts toward the personnel lock.

Before he can reach it, security guards virtually boil out of the exit; twenty or more are inside before the door is sealed behind them. Murdoch sees that there are now guards on the observation deck as well.

"What is it, Captain?" Murdoch asks, reaching the door.

The security officer answers. "There's been a general disturbance. Some of the crew are armed; we're defending this and other vital areas. I've lost five men already, in fifteen minutes."

Murdoch looks to his captain, who speaks a word that comes unfamiliar to his lips: "Mutiny."

September 2051
Aztlan (Force Headquarters), Earth's Moon

There were research stations on the Earth's Moon, and observatories, and a few factories and magnetic launch-tubes, but only in Aztlan were there pyramids: twenty of them, one for each of the ancient day-signs. Sixteen were arranged in a great circle laid out over several square kilometers of the Sinus Aestuum; the four administrative pyramids formed a hub from which half-buried transport-tubes radiated, like the spokes of a great stone wheel laid down in the dust.

Native rock—basalt, primarily—had been lasered free from the mountains of the Lunar Highlands, and had been stacked to form large, thick-walled tetrahedrons. Those same lasers had fused the rocks together to form an airtight seal, then the structures had been finished inside with cheap, locally manufactured synthetics. It was an economical method of construction, and the rock was sturdy and guarded against most radiations.

The interior of Aztl (a name which means water) was brightly lit. This pyramid was nearly all one chamber, and Colin Murdoch could see across the half kilometer of its base and up across inward-slanting walls to the roof, two hundred meters overhead. High waves that would have been powerful and even dangerous on Earth were splashing and playful as they raced to within meters of Murdoch's feet, and retreated from the crushed pumice beach. Swimmers skimmed over swells and divers executed impossible dives as they lazily descended from diving platforms six and seven times the height of a man.

"It's nearly time to leave," said Colin.

"Not yet," Maureen said, leaning across to kiss him.

"Soon," he said, and they embraced for moments that lingered. Gently he sat back from her and crouched to rise, holding out his hand to her. "Now. We can't be late."

"No," she said, with a touch of anger or frustration, "we mustn't keep the Mad Priest waiting."

His expression was pained. "You shouldn't call him that."

She saluted him, then laughed at his look. "As you wish, my Captain."

He smiled also, if briefly. They dressed and boarded the tube to Coatl. This close to the ceremonies, there were few aboard the train, but Maureen took a seat well to the rear of the car, under a garish, block-lettered poster done over in twelve hues and three dimensions. TO THE STARS . . . NOW, it said. And:

Join the men and women in the fast-growing ranks of the Portal Exploration Corps. Fifty worlds and more are but a single footstep away. Be at the forefront of the greatest wave of exploration and discovery in the history of the Human Race.

And after this was the bulk of the display, a combination of animated and actual photographic views of as many wonders of as many worlds as could be crammed into a 1-by-1½-meter space.

And in smaller print at the bottom:

PORTAL AUTHORITY
Administrative Offices
Omaha, Atlantic Union 0113

As advanced classmen, Maureen and Colin had been allowed rooms only a short distance from Coatl's tube-station. Their compartments were cramped and austere, but also temporary. Three rooms were enough, with the knowledge that Earth was a week away.

She was waiting for him when he emerged from the bedroom resplendent, as she was, in the sienna-and-cream dress of the Force. His classman's pips shone with fresh polish on his high, stiff collar, and his boots reflected and distorted the ceiling panels' light. His training knife was tucked into the flap of the left boot. His eyes, bright, glittered with an anticipation that made Maureen warm to see. "You are proud," she said.

"Yes." And he smiled.

The tubes took them to Cuauhtli, which means eagle.

And an eagle raged at them from over the high, broad doors that led from the tube-station and which were the main entrance to these offices of the Force. Ten-meter wings cloaked and guarded an arch of Lunar gold, and, in six languages and a binary code, a

legend was inscribed over the arch, on a ribbon held in
the mouth of the eagle, "Multi-National Trans-Orbital
Force," and directly beneath it, "To Preserve the Peace
of All Mankind."

The significance of the motto and of the eagle were
half-forgotten carry-overs from an era that began the
Age of Space.

Maureen looked at him. "What did you say?"

He quoted the motto. "It's really true, isn't it?"

"Enforced with orbiting warheads, to be sure, but a
serviceable peace."

He glanced quickly at her, but she was smiling. They
entered into Cuauhtli.

A great hall, with seating for two thousand persons,
made up the bulk of the pyramid; it occupied all its
lower levels. It was broad-columned, the roof arched,
in a display of extravagance that would have been impossible for the first Lunarians to imagine. Yet all the
materials were of the Moon, and cheaply obtained.

Though they were among the last to arrive, the hall
was only a third full. This was a function for the grad-
uating classmen alone. The forward part of the hall
was a sea of uniforms. The stage was curtained in the
official colors, and the eagle watched over them here as
well. On the stage were a large podium and raised dais
with a half dozen chairs. The flags of the Atlantic
Union, WSSR, and Japanese Empire were draped in
the background.

Colin and Maureen took their seats.

The figure that Chief Commandant Joe Hood Priest
cut was an imposing one, in a heroic tradition. He was
in his early forties. His face was lined, but not severely.
His form was tall, straight-muscled, energetic but controlled. He was followed by some of his chiefs of staff
and Murdoch's class representative. Arms crossed, he
looked out over them, and lights bounced from the
multiple sunbursts at his shoulder and danced into
Murdoch's eyes.

This was the man who had vaporized Yining and Lop Nor and so ended the Formation Wars before they had begun.

The Mad Priest.

He said: "I will not take much of your time. I will not waste the little I will take from you. You have completed, to the satisfaction of your board of tutors, all the requirements set for you in all your studies and training. What you do with this knowledge and these skills is your decision, and you all have six months from this day to make that decision. The Force remains the one alternative of the adventurer, the explorer, and the protector. Remember, the stars will always be there."

"Talking about the Portals," someone whispered behind Murdoch.

"If you decide in our favor," the commandant continued, "you will spend a minimum of ten years with the Force. And the majority of those that complete that term of duty will spend the rest of their lives with us.

"Citizens, I expect we will meet again. For the peace of all Mankind!"

He saluted them, then he left. The rest, the speeches from various officers and tutors, the awarding of the ensigns' suns and the gilt-edged certificates, was an anticlimax.

"I feel as if I'm leading you," said Maureen outside. "Wake up."

He smiled. He had been doing that quite often, of late.

"And dispose of that idiot grin somewhere. You don't look natural unless you're grim," she told him.

"Sorry."

"Don't be." She kissed him. "Need I call you 'sir' now?"

"Only in public."

They picked up their baggage at Coatl, long-tubed to

the lift-pads at Copernicus, and were among the first to
leave the Moon behind and to be swallowed by terrestrial clouds.

She, buffeted by winds that seemed thick and foul,
sweating under a too-warm sun and surrounded by
thousands of people she had never seen before, looked
at him, and outside the landing fields to the strange
towers of Sacramento, and said, "Must you smile *constantly?*"

Which only made his smile broader, of course.

October 2075
Manchester, Deep Space

The instrumentation winks at him, not disturbing
the utter silence of the weapons room. Murdoch
reaches out and runs his outstretched fingers over still
dial-faces. His checks are over, but he hesitates to
leave. His two escorts, Reynolds and MacDonald, will
be waiting outside. But still he lingers.

Abruptly, in one continuous motion, he spins on his
heel, drops the checklist into the destruct-bin, stows the
marker, and opens the egress.

The first item he notices: The door opens heavily,
sticking as it traverses its arc.

The second item: MacDonald, slumped against the
wall of the corridor, his chest a confusing mass of flesh
and bone, and the smear on the wall behind him, the
puddle beneath him.

Murdoch tries to fall back into the weapons room as
a shot is fired at him from a position down the corridor
to his left, and he tries to twist away to avoid the bullet.

The third item: Reynolds, his head gone, is behind
the door to the weapons room. His limbs are folded as
if to compact him for closet-storage. With this comes to
Murdoch the realization that he will die and that the
door to the weapons room stands open. As his booted

foot kicks out, a ligament shoots fire from his knee to his groin, then the door slams shut and seals itself.

Murdoch rolls onto his stomach and gains his feet, only to have them swept out from under him. It is only now that he realizes he has been shot, that there is a man in crewman's clothing perhaps ten meters up the corridor, that he is surrounded and, as he reaches for his sidearm, that he will never take the weapon from its holster.

Thunder breaks the air, and steel whines as projectiles ricochet from wall to floor to wall to ceiling in a dangerous gavotte. Then the man before him falls with the coming of a numbness in Murdoch's hand, and he vaguely realizes that he holds his weapon and has indeed fired it. Then there is more thunder, heralding the coming of night.

The first thing he notices: *I am alive.*

Three medicos, white-clad with red crosses on their backs, eat standing across the room. Dimly he sees two other men in officers' garb, but his vision is unfocused and shot with colors and lights, and so he cannot make out their section insignia. Murdoch attempts to speak, but he cannot do more than move his tongue and work his jaw slightly. An attempt to move his limbs produces no response at all.

He is conscious of a great numbness in his right leg, and it is as if a weight had been placed uniformly across his body, bringing a constant, dulling ache and making it difficult to breathe. He takes a deep breath of air, but no air enters his lungs. Before his vision clouds over entirely, he is aware of the ringing of an alarm beside his head, and he wishes desperately for someone to come to turn it off.

"—us quite a scare, Weapons Master." The voice is a whisper, and none of the words seem to fit together into the proper patterns. "If you can hear me, nod your head." Murdoch does so, and now it feels as if the bones in his neck had cracked. He winces. "You have some pain? That'll pass. You'll be all right in a few days. Until then, I'll notify the Captain you won't be available for duty."

Rest, thinks Murdoch. He is tired, as if he had been hauling some great load all day. A few days' rest. . . . His eyes widen.

"Ruddy, come here! Give me an injector of tranquilizer!" calls a voice.

Murdoch struggles against the hand, the single hand that holds him down, but it is as if the medico were an immovable giant of stone.

"He's saying something," someone points out from a distance.

"He's having some sort of convulsion," someone else says.

"Here's the injector."

Then, blessedly, someone—and Murdoch is certain that it is, inexplicably, Maureen—cries out, "Wait!" and there is silence for a time. Murdoch quiets, and after a moment he feels the pressure of the hand on his chest disappear.

"Murdoch?" asks the medico, injection pad ready.

"No injection," says Murdoch. He moistens his lips.

"Colin?" And now Murdoch sees a blond head come into his field of vision, and he sees that it is Theresa Burdick. She turns to the medico and says, "He's quiet now."

A pause. "So he is." The hand reaches out of his tunneled field of vision, and when it returns the injection pad is gone. "We'll leave him alone with these monitors, and let him rest." The doctor seems slightly disappointed that he has lost the opportunity to dope a high-ranking officer. "If you'll follow us out, Engineer?"

"No," says Murdoch. His voice is now easily heard, though perhaps slightly hoarse. "Burdick stays."

"Doctor?" asks Burdick.

"As you wish," the doctor says, and his tones are clipped. "It doesn't matter at all." He and his people leave.

"Thanks," Murdoch says.

"You should get some rest," she tells him. "You were shot in the leg."

Murdoch is not surprised. "What time is it?"

"Oh-four-forty-five."

"I have to make my watch soon."

"You can't. You're too weak."

And Murdoch is weak. The conversation is draining him of vitality. Doggedly he shakes his head and says, "I must make the watch." He closes his eyes briefly, then opens them. "Sit me up and get me something to drink," he says. She complies, pressing a button that raises the back of his couch to the perpendicular; she leaves for a moment, then returns with a glass of dark liquid. He reaches out for it, but she brushes his hand away easily and feeds it to him. It is warm and thick and flows easily down his throat, clearing his head and warming his limbs and guts. He recognizes it for a concoction of *Manchester*'s hydroponics section, a fruity liquor called starwine. Halfway into his second glass he chokes. She takes the glass away, wipes his lips and chin, and waits until his coughing subsides.

"Enough?" she asks.

He nods. "Thanks. MacDonald and Reynolds are dead."

"Yes," she says. "You were fortunate. Five crewmen tried to ambush you, but your guards got three of them. You killed a fourth; did you know that?"

"I thought I'd hit him. A lucky shot. The fifth?"

"We never found him. I and some others from Engineering were coming down the corridor with our escorts when we heard the shots. We scared him off."

"I think he was the one who shot me."

Burdick nods.

This is the first time Theresa has been admitted to Murdoch's quarters. As an officer of high rank, Murdoch has been allowed five rooms. There is his work area, with desk and data-link, immediately inside the entrance, then the large sitting room with its thick-piled rug and incorporated furniture. As one enters this, to the left is an instrument-filled room; to the right the bedroom; adjoining this the bath. His bed is one she had not imagined would be possible amid the austerity of *Manchester:* a form-fitting couch that can, when preprogrammed instructions are called up from its simple computer, assume any of seven different positions. Now it has formed a reclining chair for Murdoch, and Theresa sits in the conventional seat next to him. There is here also his chest of drawers, his closet, a second opticon, and on the wall a large framed photograph, a portrait of a woman of Oriental cast. The background, she recalls, is a strange one, a scene of evergreen trees against the backdrop of immense, frosted mountains; the sky is a clear and utterly cloudless blue.

After a time she asks, "Are you feeling better?"

"Yes." He adds, "Thank you." She smiles.

She—somehow this is not to Murdoch's surprise—kisses him. He is submissive. There is a time, Murdoch reflects—with a suddenness that he must stand away from, and be startled at, and not examine too closely—for an end to all things.

At 0600 he is again in the weapons room.

October 2052
Prince George

The city's only concession to the twenty-first century was a single transport-tube from the Vancouver-Seattle

Urban Tract. The five-car train was nearly empty on the afternoon Colin and Maureen rode it into the Prince George Station. It slid to a stop between tall plexiglass wind-buffers, the rush of displaced air soughing off to nothingness. No city sounds penetrated the double walls of their car, and the stillness was nearly as complete when they stepped from carpeted steel onto (unbelievably) echoing hardwood. A young couple and an older woman exited behind them and walked straight across the platform to a wood-and-brick building.

"We can get a cab to the hotel," she said. "We'll only have to stay there until tomorrow."

"What's tomorrow?"

"The house, you imbecile." And she laughed at him. "Our house." She kissed him suddenly. He began to notice that most of what she did was done suddenly. "Could you have waited until tomorrow?" she asked him.

Her lips met his. The front seam of her suit fell apart. "No," he said through flesh.

Their house was only a kilometer from the Laos' house, and it was built much the same as theirs. But for Colin, who had been living independently since the age of fourteen, it was neither the feeling of freedom, after two years of Force training, or the strangeness of his environment, but other things. Their lovemaking had seemed fiercer and at once gentler both last night and this morning; and he found the domestic aspect of the situation curiously romantic and gratifying. He winced again at the clatter of dishes from the direction of the kitchen, but did not leap from his seat in panic, as he had earlier in the day.

From his seat near the parlor window, Murdoch could see children playing outside in the deep snow.

"Want to go out?" he heard Maureen's voice from behind him. She was dressed in scuffed and worn blue slacks of some coarse material and a patterned shirt predominantly red in color. Looking outside, he half wondered if it was some sort of uniform; so many people wore it.

"Out there?" he asked. "It looks like it would be hard to walk."

"It is. That's one thing that makes it fun."

"Oh," he said.

She tripped him and pushed his face in the snow when he kicked some of it at her.

Collapsed, breathless, in a snowbank that was warm but exceedingly wet, they gazed at clouds coursing overhead. "I called Force headquarters in Salton today," said Colin after minutes.

"Oh? What for?"

"Tell them our location, for one."

"No one ever does that," she said.

He shrugged, pushing snow. "Regulations. And I talked to the aide to the Commandant."

"One of them," she corrected. "I'm surprised you got that far into the bureaucracy."

"He assured me that we could probably get assigned to the same ship, when our leaves are up. Interesting that not many people ask," he added, half to himself. There was silence, and he looked at her. "Is anything wrong?"

"I'm just not absolutely sure I'll be taking Commandant Priest's gracious offer of a life in zero-G, where the calcium runs out of my bones like water, and where I'm speared by x roentgens of cosmic rays each second."

He looked at her, mouth open, not caring that it was.

"Don't move too fast, Colin. Don't spoil anything by outrunning me," she said quietly.

"But—what else, besides the Force?"

Maureen looked at him for a moment, then sat up. He did also, and studied the back of her head because her face was turned from him. "You're a task-oriented person, Colin, among many marvelous things, and it's damned possible I'll spend more time with you than either of us can know right now." And she stressed the word "either" to be sure he understood. "You joined the Force, I guess, because it appealed to you all by itself. But I'm more selfish than that. When I joined, it was because I wanted, someday, to see the stars from the outside of the sky. I'm beginning to suspect that the Force won't ever be able to give me that. If it can't, and if I still want the outside of the sky, then maybe I'll opt for a few months with the Portal Authority. And none of this ten-year tour crap."

"No!" He was on his feet now. "The hydrogen ramjet is being finished now; not more than a few more years—"

"Oh, Colin, shut up. I don't want to talk or think about it now. You brought it up; I told you. Now shut up." She rose beside him. "Let's go back to the house and I'll show you something new."

And she made him smile, but when it was over and the water was running in their bathroom, and their warm bed was rapidly cooling, he heard some huge event echoing up and down the corridors of his mind, and there was a taste of ashes where their mouths had touched.

March 2080
Manchester, Stapledon

Manchester and her five wing-mates, decelerating still, send flares across Stapledon's skies. *Vancouver* is not with them. Struck dead on—against all probability—by a meteoroid too large to deflect, her wreckage has passed through and beyond this space months ago.

Klaxons sound, as the fusion torches are extinguished and sensors may again function. It is an alarm that has been heard only in practice drills, and one Murdoch has never truly expected to hear . . . not after the *Marie Celeste* atmosphere of the Outstepper Forward. The alarm is high and keening, interrupted at irregular intervals by low bass notes. It is a singular and easily recognizable alarm. Murdoch spills out of bed, totally heedless of Burdick, pulling on suit and boots, slamming out of his cabin, flying down the corridor to the weapons room (the white scar of a near-miss mars the black door yet), bruising his shoulder painfully on the doorframe as he enters, lunging across the room in zero-G to the weapons zankowich. He melds with it quickly, for the alarm warns *Manchester*'s officers and crew of an alien ship contact.

Full battle-ready status is achieved in seconds, computerized defenses have been ready since the alarm first sounded. Murdoch's gut tumbles into his throat as he catches sight of them, at the very limits of his vision. Dozens, each fully as large as *Manchester.* . . .

Forty-two ships, supplies computer. Each *2700 meters in length overall, 540 meters through greatest cross-section, displacing 3.2 by 10 to the—*

"Inter-ship channel," Murdoch orders computer, and computer complies without question.

"This is Murdoch of *Manchester.* Stand down from attack status." He repeats the order twice more. He has no authority to give such an order, but it may give him the time to verify his theory. . . .

"Communications," he begins, "this is the—"

Communications to all ships' officers. Stand down from red alert. Weapons officers stand down. Coded message received from Rescue Expedition Ship Brooklyn, *wishing us welcome to Stapledon. Stand down from the alert.*

Murdoch unclenches his fists from the nuclear warheads and the zankowich releases him.

The shuttle falls away from *Manchester*'s gaping lock. Its main engines flare, and the ship spirals downward.

Stapledon is proximate to Earth in all respects. There had been few obstacles for the first Portal colonists to overcome, and so they have multiplied. With the addition of the personnel from the Rescue ships, Stapledon's population now stands at well over three quarters of a million persons.

Fifty of *Manchester*'s officers form the initial landing party. Modern ground-cars that have been supplied by the orbiting starships meet them at the landing field servicing Stapledon West, the planet's largest city and its capital. Murdoch is ushered into the second of twelve cars, with two personnel officers, and they are away.

The city of fifty thousand is laid out in a grid pattern. This part of the city is primarily residential, as most of the city seems to be. Many of the houses are of native woods, and these are varied in style and size. Others are the pre-fabricated plastic structures of the type *Manchester* stores in her holds.

"You seem to have done very nicely for yourselves," one of the personnel officers says to their driver.

"Did the Outsteppers get to you?" asks Murdoch.

"No," answers their driver. His name is John. "We didn't even know there had been a war until the first Rescue ships came. Our Portal just stopped working one day . . . disappeared. No one's been out to see it in years."

"I see," says Murdoch. This is vital data. All Colonial worlds have not been attacked. What were the determining factors that spared Stapledon? There is too much to know, too many questions to ask.

"Here we are, gentlemen."

It is an unprepossessing building, a low structure of wood and glass and, here and there, of steel. Their car comes to a stop on the concrete-surfaced square before the building. *Manchester*'s men assemble. A flag snaps overhead in a sudden, brisk wind: the black ring of the Portal on a field of vivid orange, the flag of Stapledon.

A half dozen men in simple black uniforms come out
to meet the Force party and lead them inside through
double steel doors.

This carpeted lobby is dark, after the light outside,
and darkly furnished; the chairs are upholstered in a
black material that may be leather. The uniformed
men separate the officers into several smaller groups.

Their guide is speaking now. Murdoch gives him his
attention.

". . . At your captain's request, you will all be given
a tour of Stapledon West, and an introduction to the
planet and what we've been doing the past forty years."
The guide smiled automatically. "Those are Stapledon
years. That's nearly twenty-nine Earth years, or about
seven years ship-time for you fellows. We've a lot of
catching up to do.

"Some of you are to meet with our Council now." He
reads from a list: Colin Murdoch, Ivor Tupelov, Lois
Garvin, Keith Dunford. If you people will follow me,
I'll show you to the Council chambers." Murdoch
leaves with his three shipmates through a door that
opens on stairs leading upward. Halls and another
flight of stairs lead to ornate doors. Their guide opens
them for the officers, but he does not himself enter.

The light of Stapledon's sun flashes off a polished
wooden table. Half a dozen Stapledonians are within,
and all rise for *Manchester*'s officers. "We are glad to
have you," says one. He extends his hand first to Murdoch, then to the others. He is an older man, and bald-
ing. His outdated suit is loose across the shoulders. "I
am Richard Colvin, chief councilman of Stapledon." He
smiles. "And that's the first bit of information we have
for you."

"You've received our report and ship's log, Councilman?" asks Lois Garvin. Both she and Keith Dunford
are from Communications' records section.

"Yes, and though I personally have not read it all—it

is quite lengthy, even in summary—I think I can appreciate some of the trials you people have gone through. *Vancouver*—what was her crew?"

Vancouver is rarely discussed. "Twelve hundred eight," says Murdoch, but the chief councilman has not noticed the terseness in his voice.

"A pity. A pity. Still, the living must continue. Before we get right down to matters here, are there any important questions you want to ask at the start? And, please, sit down." They take seats across from the councilmen.

Manchester's officers look to Murdoch, perhaps hoping he will allow them a question. But he says, "Only two of immediate importance: How is it that you were not attacked, and why are there elements of *seven* Rescue wings here?"

The last question carries a tinge of intentioned hostility. The chief councilman's eyes widen fractionally, but he says without losing stride, "Cory, perhaps you will answer Officer Murdoch's first question."

Cory is a matriarchal woman of indeterminate age. She passes her hand before her eyes in what may be an indication of nervousness. "Until we received word from you on the Cauldron attack," she says quietly, "we knew of no war."

"No other worlds were attacked?" asks Tupelov incredulously.

"No."

Murdoch glances down the table at his fellows. He turns his pained gaze to Richard Colvin. "How is this possible? Then . . . you do not know who the attackers were?"

"No," says Colvin, "we do not." He clears his throat. "We simply do not know anything about your war, beyond what we have been told by the Rescue ships. We never knew they were coming. How could we? We've heard all their reports. They did assist some worlds, and without the Rescue Expedition, those worlds may have died. Some did: New Akron, Sirois, Rama-Tut, their populations died without Portaled supplies. The Peking/Mao dual system was nearly wiped out. Perhaps a quarter of the worlds could not survive. Another quarter, our own planet among them, would have survived easily without assistance. The majority of the Colonies lay somewhere in the middle."

Murdoch is wholly silent.

"As for your second question," Colvin goes on, "one ship was left orbiting each inhabited world that the various wings found, and the supplies on those ships will ensure that those populations will survive until we can put together some sort of network for supply and communications, using modified starships. Some of the ships in orbit here are undergoing modifications to increase their speed and cargo capacity, and we will export what we can. We are trying to increase our productivity. We are doing all we can."

"But not all wings are here," says Dunford.

"No, of course not. Stapledon was targeted for five of the wings here. One wing learned of our plan when it arrived at One Step, where our ships had already been. Another encountered elements of another wing at Peking/Mao. We can only hope that the other ships can either find us or work out a similar system of aid centered on another planet. You know that there was some target overlap among the wings; yours is the last due here. I don't think it's likely we'll get any more ships here for a good many years, if ever."

"But many of the wings must have further targets," Murdoch says slowly. "Our own wing does."

Colvin shrugs and looks both hurt and pitying. "If you continue—that is of course your decision, and we won't try to influence it. One ship, *Jersey City* of wing—"

"Sixteen," supplies one of the councilmen.

"Thank you. That ship opted to continue. We don't have any idea where it is now."

"There is no provision for option in the Rescue Manual," says Murdoch.

Colvin again shrugs. "As I say, the decision to continue is yours."

"If we have no inkling of who the enemy is," begins Lois Garvin, "perhaps it is best that we participate in your program. . . ." And Murdoch can think of no words to refute her.

The meetings have been adjourned until the afternoon of the following day; Murdoch and his fellows ride across town to the apartment complex where they have been quartered. The area bustles with activity, Murdoch sees as they come to a stop. Several hundred more from *Manchester* and the other ships have been shuttled down in the last few hours, and acquaintances that had languished during the voyage are being renewed. Planet-fall is being celebrated.

Murdoch leaves the car, automatically acknowledging the farewells of Tupelov and Garvin. He makes his way through the small, tightly packed crowd to the building's entrance.

The press of people is unrelieved here. Murdoch plows to the elevators with brusque movements and curt apologies. He touches a button and waits for the elevator car.

"Listen to me!" Murdoch hears someone cry, softly and urgently.

He turns. "Are you speaking to me?"

This man is not of the starships. His clothes are worn—not yet ragged, though they soon will be. His face is old, wizened, reddened by exposure and excitement. His hands are arthritic claws that clutch at Murdoch's uniform. There is a reek on his breath. Alcohol, Murdoch realizes.

"You can hear me, can't you?" asks the man. He is not old, he merely *seems* old. He cannot be more than forty. "I'm dead, Dead James, but you can hear me, can't you?"

"I—" Murdoch begins, then he feels the elevator doors open behind him. He steps back into the car. The man does not move to follow, as if the threshold of the car formed a tangible partition.

"Dead James knows!" Murdoch presses the button for his floor. "I was in the cauldron, the cauldron of hell! Dead James knows who started the hell-fires burning!" The doors close. The car rises smoothly.

The apartment is small, but well planned, giving an illusion of greater size. Murdoch looks into the kitchen and bath, but Burdick is not in the apartment. He kicks off his boots and stretches out on the unmade bed.

Almost immediately the comm-link—the *phone*—rings. He fumbles after it. "Murdoch."

"Weapons Master, there is to be a discussion and vote for officers at the central stadium of Stapledon West at twenty-two hundred hours, local time. The subject is the decision to continue the mission. Plurality rule. Vote via commlink if you cannot attend."

"By whose order?" Murdoch asks, before the operator breaks the connection.

"Captain Hamlyn of *Manchester,* and the captains of Wing Twenty-three."

The connection is broken.

They have wasted little time, thinks Murdoch, and tries to shut his ears to the sounds of revelry below, that he may rest.

A kiss touches him awake. His eyes snap open as he struggles out of nightmare to light. He focuses on Theresa's face looking down on him.

"Colin, what's wrong?" She sits on the bed next to him, runs one finger across his forehead. Gently, gently.

"Nothing. A dream, that's all." He shakes his head to dislodge the sleep from him. "A very bad one." She asks him about it, but he shakes his head again. "You look as if something is bothering you, too," he says.

"I have news."

"It can't be good, judging by your face," says Murdoch.

"I can't judge. This woman you told me about, Maureen Li . . ."

Murdoch's heart beats once, impossibly loud, a vibration that fills the universe. "She is here?" he asks.

Burdick says: "Yes."

The route to the place where Maureen now lives, Theresa tells him, is a rather long one, and her unfamiliarity with the roads and with the vehicle the Stapledonians have lent her make it longer. After fifteen minutes of driving through darkened streets, Murdoch says, "I believe I only mentioned her to you once, Theresa."

She nods. "It seemed important, so I remembered. She was listed in the census banks at the Council Building." She laughs briefly, and not altogether sincerely. "At first I told the helpmate at the office that I was looking for an immigrant of the past ten years . . . he just looked at me. Silly."

"Thank you," Murdoch says to her.

The curbs of the road glow with electrical implants that guide their car out of Stapledon West and into the outlying districts. The only sounds are the hum of the car's tires on the smooth road and, once, the call of an owl whose ancestors had been imported from Earth decades before. Native trees, like club-moss, grow side by side with willow and oak. The machine-fabricated structures of the inner city are not in evidence in these suburban areas. The houses are larger, with great expanses of open land between them, and they are set well back from the main roads. After perhaps forty minutes, their car slows and Burdick turns the machine into a drive leading to a house that is, if anything, even grander and more expensive than the others Murdoch has seen. The car pulls to a stop.

"This is where she lives," says Theresa. "I'll wait. Are you planning to attend the meeting?"

Murdoch shakes his head slowly. "I can't see any point. The decision has already been made."

"Then don't hurry."

Murdoch nods, then he leaves the car to stand on a brick porch before a white-painted wooden door. He hesitates a moment, searching for an annunciator, then he knocks on the door. The wood scrapes his knuckles.

As he waits, knocking once more, the car hums away. He turns, but Burdick has only pulled farther down the drive. There the automobile waits, riding lights glowing faintly in the strong light of Stapledon's moon.

And, when Murdoch has nearly prepared himself to turn and walk from the door, to go to the car, to leave, the door opens. "Yes?" she says. "May I—"

Gray streaks her hair, and her eyes and the corners of her mouth are etched with fine lines, like shatter-marks in porcelain. The warm honey of her skin is now faded, as if some chemical bath had robbed it of its original luster. She is dressed in a simply cut dress that reaches nearly the floor.

Her eyes are the same.

"Hello," Murdoch says, realizing that he is smiling at the incredible humor of the—

"*Colin?*"

Suddenly (she does things suddenly) his arms are filled with her.

"Colin," she says. "My God, when the first ships arrived, I thought perhaps it would be just like you to . . . but then another wing arrived, and another, and I thought how stupid it would be to expect you on any one of them, and I've hardly kept track of the last few arrivals, and—my God—you're *here.*"

"Yes," he says. "Yes."

"Oh, damn, come in!"

The furnishings could have been that of any upper-class family on Earth—his parents' home in Salton, for example. Light-panels laid out in intricate geometric patterns provide illumination; the carpet underfoot is deep and warm with an inner heat, the walls are decorated with photo-landscapes of Earth and other worlds, and with computer-generated abstracts. But it is Maureen: the walk that reminds him of her former walk, the way of carrying herself that has remained the same, though now her body has been subtly altered by the passage of time. The sudden distortion of her—but no, that is the wrong term. He has not thought of an alternate when they have left the entrance hall and stand in the large parlor. A fireplace burns in one wall, and the night thrusts against a wide window to Murdoch's right.

"You *are* here," she says.

"Yes," Murdoch says. "You've said that."

"I know, but you must realize what a shock—how old I must look to you! The Fitzgerald-Lorenz time contraction, of course. How long has it been for you? Five years? Ten?"

"Very nearly seven."

"Then you're only twenty-eight. And I'm forty-five, old enough to be your mother."

"You're still a beautiful woman, Maureen." This is the first time he has said her name in nearly two decades, objective-time. It has a strange taste, a strangely familiar sound for her. "I think you might have some years on you yet," he says, and laughs, as does she.

"Sit down," she offers. "Tell me—everything."

He shakes his head, smiling still. He has not stopped smiling since she opened the door. "You first."

"Guest's privilege. And it won't take me as long to recount my twenty years as your—seven?" He nods.

With the main lights extinguished, with the firelight

recasting the planes of her face, it might have been possible to see her as she had been. With effort, Murdoch refrains from making the attempt to do so.

"What can I tell you, Colin? I got here, they needed technically trained people for a while . . . then the Portal went, practically as I was stepping out of it. Or six hours later, if you want the unadulterated truth. I went crazy the first few months—I guess most people did. Then I faced up to the fact that this was the end of the line, that it was a world, and that it was mine. I got settled in. It didn't take very long." She nods at a look on his face he hadn't known was there. "Yes, I married, within a year. He's dead now, but he left a lot behind him. He was a councilman for a while. I have two children, grown. That's all."

"You came here via Cauldron," he says. "Why?"

Her look is downcast, and he wishes the question had gone unasked; he knows the answer. "I wasn't sure if you would follow. I didn't want that."

Before the silence can develop, he asks, "What do you do now?"

She shrugs. "I taught a school for technicians a few years back, but some of my students are doing that now. I come in when they need me." She rises from her seat by the fire and sits next to him on the sofa. She radiates the fire's warmth. "And now it's your turn."

He twists to look out the window behind them. His eyes wander along the drive, the horizon. "Things pretty much fell apart after the war," he says. "You must have heard the story from the ships before us."

"Yes, but the worlds you've seen?"

"Cauldron," he says, "and the Outstepper Forward. Only two." At her prompting, he tells her of them, never once turning from the night-cloaked scene outside (and her reflection in the window), though he speaks for nearly an hour.

"You've seen a lot," she says, "more than I will ever see." She sighs deeply. "I didn't think it would work out this way. It was *I* who—"

He shakes his head. "No, I made the mistake. Seven years of my life spent in high-time, and now I've learned there's no hope for the completion of the mission."

She looks at him. "What do you mean?"

"The enemy. We expected—we *knew*—we would find them." He clenches his fist. "We destroyed the Outstepper Forward, but we didn't find them there. We found Cauldron burning, but we didn't find them there. We've traveled twenty light-years to get here, and no one here knows there was a war. All wasted. . . . Each of our ships was named for the city that was leveled to build it. They're like scalps. And now we have nothing."

"Dead James . . ."

His face registers shock. "What?"

"Dead James," she repeats. "Our local character. The man from Cauldron." Her face has a sad look. "A pitiful man."

"What about him? I think I've seen him."

"Where?"

"Where I'm staying, in the city." He describes him, and their encounter. "I thought he was a drunk. . . ."

"Not a drunk," she says, "a madman. He came here from Cauldron about a year before the war. I knew him; my husband worked with him up to the time of the war. When the Outsteppers shut the Portals down, that was when he started calling himself Dead James. After a few months he stopped babbling in public. He calmed down—at least I didn't hear anything more about him until the first Rescue ships came. Then he started again. He met the crews, as they came down . . . and he came to you, too."

"Why?" Colin asks.

"He knows—he *says* he knows—how the war started. I don't know how much of it is true."

"Tell me," Colin says intensely.

"He was a minor official on Cauldron. He says that about two years before the war—2050, it must have been, or maybe '51—"

"Go *on*."

She looks at him, startled, and is confronted by his eyes. She continues, "Pedler . . . his name was James Pedler. About 2050 he discovered that nuclear weapons were being sent to Cauldron through the Portal, disguised as supplies for our men there. Pedler took the matter to the governor of Cauldron.

"The governor was of course with the Force. He knew all about what was going on, of course, and drafted Pedler into his service to keep him quiet.

"It was an elaborate plan. The Outsteppers would never allow weapons to pass through a Portal—interplanetary warfare would be bad for their business. The warheads had to be disguised, overtly to get them past human port inspectors, but also with devices and instruments to get them past the Outsteppers' monitors. James Pedler was a genius in electronics. He founded the electronics school here his third month on the planet. He made improvements on the camouflaging devices, under his governor's orders. The weapons were coming from Earth, under Force seal, and they were to be sent from Cauldron—armed—to a third world."

"But *why?*"

Maureen shakes her head. "It sounds insane—it is insane. But listen: I remember Priest. Earth spent herself to the limit buying planets before the boom crested. Every museum emptied, animal species exported wholesale, in exchange for trade goods and concessions on worlds we could colonize. We had about fifty planets by the time of the war. Priest hated that . . .

that and the fact that the Force was of second priority next to the Portals.

"So he destroyed them. Or so Dead James says. He comes here, sometimes, for food or medicine—sometimes just to talk, I think. People say he lives up in the mountains, but I don't think that's true.

"There were a few worlds at our technological level which we traded with, and that also roughly paralleled us in development. The ones that were like us, the ones we could trade with. . . . Would a plant-being be interested in Egyptian sculpture?

"Most of those worlds would have done. Priest had the warheads sent to Alpha Crucis."

"How do you know this?" Murdoch demands.

"How else could it have happened? Dead James had to know where the warheads were going, so he could get them past their own safeguards. The plan was to start a war through the Portals. That would force them to be shut down. But Priest couldn't start the war himself, not overtly." She shrugged. "He miscalculated. The Alpha Crucians must have spotted the warheads before they exploded, and stopped them. . . . They destroyed Cauldron, then went for Earth. Priest underestimated their speed, their striking power, something went wrong. He must have planned all along to bomb Omaha in 'self-defense'; let through one missile from the other side and shut the Portal down then. But they got more than one missile through. And viral agents. Gases."

She looks at Colin Murdoch. "I believe it. I think everyone who's heard the story does. It's something the destroyer of Sinkiang would do, don't you think? The Force over the entire universe . . . or what's left of it."

"No," Murdoch says slowly, shaking his head. "No." He stands, then he walks to the center of the room. "But, yes, the Alpha Crucians duplicated our war technology very closely. If only things hadn't been so upset after the war, if the Portal records at Omaha had somehow survived, we could have learned they were the ones using the Portal when the war started. . . ."

"Colin, didn't you hear me? They didn't start the war; Priest engineered it, the Mad Priest again! The war is twenty-five years dead, and if anyone on Earth ever found him out, so is he."

He glances at his watch. "The meeting's started," he mutters.

"Don't you think the other ships know this by now? It must be common knowledge. They're rebuilding what's left. . . ."

"I have to go," Murdoch says.

"Your duty calls—again." There is a bitterness in her voice that is infinite. Murdoch does not hear it.

"I have to go," he repeats. Automatically she rises to walk him to the door. At the threshold he kisses her on the cheek.

"I will see you again," he says, and runs to the still waiting car. Maureen glimpses the woman driving as the car pulls away.

"No," she says quietly, as she closes the door.

March 2052
Omaha and Earth's Moon

The Portal Authority Building had doubled and redoubled its size since last Murdoch was here. The debarkation slip had grown to encompass passenger waiting-areas and complex arrangements for the pumping of liquids and the transference of electricity across infinity. The naked concrete was now hidden beneath artistic tile facades.

Murdoch and Li stood on a railed balcony overlooking the complex. A line of colonists shuffled toward the blackness of the Portal. Uniformed guards encouraged those who hesitated. Soon all were gone and the floor was momentarily clear.

"Have you finally decided where you're going?" he asked. "It's strange that I don't know."

She nodded absently. She was staring at the Portal.

"How long do we have?" asked Colin.

"Only fifteen minutes or so," she said. It was obvious that this was the first she'd heard him since she'd entered the building, and had been captured by the moment and the magic of the event. His hand traveled across the steel railing to enclose hers. "Don't make it more difficult for yourself," she said. "No one will think you're noble."

He sighed, released her. "Was that necessary?"

"Yes," she said, turning to look at him, "I think maybe it was. I've enjoyed being with you these past few months, but I have other things to do. I'm sure you wouldn't leave the Force for me. You haven't."

"It wouldn't matter. And it's not the same."

"It never is."

Silence.

She looked at him. There were five minutes left, and her group was beginning to file out from the door under the balcony, joining the guards and their guide to the Outstepper Forward. "I do love you, Colin, you must believe that. But I don't think I should have to give anything up for you. That wouldn't be right, would it?"

"No," he said, not sure that he felt that way at all. "It wouldn't be right.

She smiled. She kissed him, and squeezed his hand. "It's time for me to go."

"Good-bye," he said. "Look me up when you get back." It was precisely what he was supposed to say.

"I will," Maureen said.

She turned from the rail and went down the stairs to the debarkation slip. He saw her walk across the floor to join her group, and saw the baggage cart run through the Portal. She turned on the threshold and waved, and he waved also. Then she merged with infinity, even as he lunged against the rail, strained forward, and shouted, "Wait! You never told me—"

But she was gone, and the slip was empty except for the guards, who looked at him curiously.

He stared at the surface of the Portal for moments, unbelieving. She had not told him her destination.

He rode the shuttle up from Kansas City to one of the orbital stations, and transferred to one of the spidery Lunar buggies. Within hours it brought him to the Force installation nestled in Copernicus. He followed the half dozen passengers into the receiving area, and into clamor.

Once past the sound-proofing partitions separating the handling areas from the lobbies and offices, alarms could be heard ringing loudly in the air. Red lamps flashed, and the public-address system repeated taped announcements at frequent intervals. He listened to them all, clutching his duffel with an overwhelming sense of uselessness until he heard, "All Force personnel out of Aztlan report to the tube-station immediately." And then the most-often-heard announcement: "This is a Class-One emergency. Repeat: Class One."

The last time there had been a Class One had been— He almost stopped in his headlong rush to the tube-station. There had never been a Class One emergency before.

He guessed that most of the Force personnel from Aztlan had already been shipped out: there were only a few dozen men and women at the station. "Murdoch," someone called to him, and he joined Portelance near the edge of the boarding platform.

"What's happened?" asked Murdoch. "Has one of the pyramids blown?"

"No," said Portelance, "nothing like that. I've heard a lot of bits, but nothing that makes much sense. Something about an attack through the Portal, wide-spread and with very heavy civilian casualties."

"The Portal? From where?"

"I don't know. The attack's stopped now, of course. The Commandant ordered a nuclear warhead into Omaha."

"My God," said Murdoch. "My God."

Later
Colin Murdoch

My ship is the *Manchester*. She is severely undercrewed, and until modifications can be made in her systems to streamline operations, she will not be at full battle effectiveness. We have transferred the reaction mass from the wing's other ships; our engines are warming, and the final preparations are being made for the collection run around Stapledon's sun.

The command center is about me. I am tied to the Captain's zankowich, and the weapons master's as well by means of newly installed relays running up from the weapons room. The combined displays are at times confusing, but the situation shall last only until a new captain can be selected from among the higher-ranking officers. I suspect that Theresa, highest ranking of *Manchester*'s old crew here now, next to myself, may be the best choice. There are officers from other ships who have elected to go with us, who may be better suited. There is time to make a decision.

I speak the order to prepare to leave orbit, and my words are transmitted to my officers. (I hear them echo upon me as the weapons system transmits them back to me.)

The computer displays *Manchester* for me, and she glows a steady green, indicating that all systems are fit.

"Navigation?" I sub-vocalize, locked in the zankowich.

To leave orbit in two minutes, thirty-eight seconds—mark—Captain.

"Engineering?"

On the mark, Captain.

I wait. We all wait. Four hundred of us, all that could be drummed up from the entire wing.

Captain?

"Communications," I acknowledge.

A message from Captain Hamlyn, sir, and the Stapledonian Council. They wish us all speed.

Hypocrites. It took veiled threats of taking her by force before they allowed us her. We were fortunate for Offord's support, and that of the others.

"Acknowledge the message."

There is a second, Captain, a personal one from a Citizen Maureen Dwyer. Shall I—

"Acknowledge that also."

Shall I record it for your pleasure later, or do you wish it now?

"That won't be necessary. Advise Stapledon that we are closing communications."

Fifteen seconds, warns Navigation.

Earth lies fourteen light-years distant, the satisfactory culmination of the Rescue Expedition at journey's end. Two years' travel-time.

And I will be the weapons master.